THE QUESTION OF THE WEDDING PEARLS

GRAVESYDE PRIORY MYSTERY, #4

PATRICIA RICE

PLEASE JOIN MY READER LIST

Please consider joining my newsletter for exclusive content and news of upcoming releases. Be the first to know about special sales, freebies, stories from my writer life, and other fun information. You'll even receive a thank-you gift. Join me on my writing adventures!

To Join, Please Visit —
https://www.subscribepage.com/ricehr

AUTHOR'S NOTE

For those who enjoy following the growing family relationships, I have included a brief history of Wycliffe Manor, and additionally, there is a partial of the earl's family tree on my website, https://patriciarice.com/wycliffe-family-tree-2/

For those of you who have difficulty remembering names (as I do), a character list follows, along with a brief history of Wycliffe Manor.

These books can stand on their own, but it's a little more fun to start at the beginning to see how the family comes together and grows and watch the village and manor come to life again.

For the grammarians among you, I have chosen to modernize the spelling of "blond/blonde" because I can. Unfortunately, I cannot single-handedly eliminate the idiocy of lie/lay. I must hand that to future generations. . .

CHARACTERS

FAMILY and FRIENDS

George Reid, Fourth Earl of Wycliffe—deceased; left Gravesyde Priory to all his family

Captain Alistair Huntley—US Army engineer; Wycliffe's great-grandson

Clarissa (Clare) Knightley—spinster; Wycliffe's great-granddaughter

Oliver Knightley Owen—Clare's seven-year-old nephew

Daniel Walker—Hunt's friend, steward

Arnaud Lavigne— Hunt's artist cousin, eldest son of Comte Lavigne

Henri Lavigne— Arnaud's younger brother, tavern owner

Meera Abrams Walker—physician/apothecary; Clare's best friend

Honorable John (Jack) de Sackville—retired soldier, son of Baron de Sackville

Lady Elspeth (Elsa) Villiers—Wycliffe's great-granddaughter

Earl Villiers—Elsa's half-brother

Elena Villiers Turner—Elsa's widowed mother

Benedict Bosworth Jr.—banker; Wycliffe's illegitimate grandson

Paul Daniel Upton— new curate

Henrietta (Nettie) Upton—curate's stepmother; manor housekeeper; Wycliffe's great-niece

Patience Upton—Nettie's daughter and curate's stepsister; gardener

Baron de Sackville—Jack's father; bibliophile

Lavender Marlowe—illegitimate granddaughter of Lady Lavinia

Lady Lavinia Marlowe—dowager baroness, Wycliffe's daughter

Elaine, Lady Spalding— dowager marchioness; Wycliffe's granddaughter; Hunt's aunt

Marquess of Spalding—stepson of Lady Spalding

Dorothea (Dottie) Reid Talbot—granddaughter of Wycliffe's brother David

Davy Talbot—Dottie's 8-year old brother

Frances Reid Huntley—Hunt's mother; Lady Spalding's sister

OTHERS

Terrence Birdwhistle—tutor

Sir Oswald Champlain —knight; seafarer

Lady Penelope Champlain— new wife of Sir Oswald

Comte Avignon—Mrs. Turner's escort; Dottie's former suitor

Nadia and Leon—Champlain servants

Victor Turbin—Jack's French valet

Marie Turbin—Victor's wife and Elsa's maid

Jones—Villiers' secretary

Roberts—Villiers' valet

Ernest—Spalding's valet

Norsworthy—Spalding's secretary

George—Avignon's valet
Jean-Jacques Barbeau—dead messenger
Adele and Jules Lavigne—Henri and Arnaud's aunt and uncle
Sofia Lavigne—daughter of Adele and Jules
Garret Browning III—solicitor from Stratford

THE HISTORY OF WYCLIFFE MANOR

Wycliffe Manor is the ancestral home of the Earls of Wycliffe, built on the remains of Gravesyde Priory, for which the village is named. In the way of medieval fiefdoms, the earls resisted district boundary changes, so the estate, in 1815, is an exclave of Shropshire, although south of Birmingham and surrounded by Worcestershire, creating legal havoc when it comes to crime.

George Reid, the fourth Earl of Wycliffe, lost his only son, and with no male heir apparent, arranged to distribute his wealth and all other estates to his female relations upon his death in 1781. His son's widow, Lady Gabrielle Reid, had a life interest in Wycliffe Manor and lived there until she died in 1801.

The fun begins when the trustees of the last earl's estate attempt to dispose of the manor after the viscountess's death. Since the earl left his worldly goods to ALL his relations, the manor now belongs in equal parts to every Reid descendant, including that of his siblings and a growing family he never knew.

Except this is the turn of the nineteenth century, and the male trustees are reluctant to turn over a substantial estate to females, bless their feathery little heads. The lawyers insist on a male to accept the inheritance and the responsibility, and the only one they can find is an American Army officer, Captain Alastair Reid Huntley. Family legend says he is a descendant of Lady Reid's affair with a French count, but the marriage lines and birth are appropriately recorded.

By the time these legalities were decided, however, Captain Huntley was busy fighting the British, and it took two more years of war and recuperation from serious injuries before he agrees to sail to England.

Amidst all the legal squabbling, the manor was abandoned to a pair of elderly caretakers for nearly fifteen years. The earl left a legacy for maintaining the manor, so important repairs were made, but bats will play when the master's away.

And so our story begins in 1815, in *The Secrets of Wycliffe Manor*, with the arrival of Captain Huntley. As the heirs gradually return to their ancestral home, they discover unresolved mysteries and stir up new ones. Fortunately, the Reid family enjoys a good puzzle.

ONE

CLARE: MONDAY MORNING

JUNE 19, 1815

"SLEEP, WAKE, EAT, GO TO BED AGAIN. . . IS THIS WHAT MY LIFE *has become?*" Dorothea Talbot dramatically read the passage from the late Lady Reid's diary as if it were Shakespeare. "It sounds as if she's prepared to do something dreadful."

The slender heiress should have been dancing through London's glittering ballrooms, not immersed in the tribulations of a lady from a prior century in a decrepit manor in rural Gravesyde Priory.

Copying her ink-splattered, cross-hatched manuscript onto a fresh page, Clare—Clarissa Knightley, soon to be Huntley—didn't glance up at her drama-prone young cousin. The passage from the diary described her own boring life before she'd cast it off and taken up residence at Wycliffe Manor. After living through multiple deaths in a state of constant chaos these past months, Clare wondered if boredom might not be preferable.

Like Clare, Dorothea possessed most of the Reid family features: blond hair, widow's peak, blue eyes, dimples, oddly attached earlobes, and backward thumb. The earls of Wycliffe had left their mark on their younger generations. But what ought to be the deciding factor, Clare had recently concluded, was *eccentricity*. She had thought it only her nephew and herself, but after finally meeting the rest of her family. . . They were simply not normal.

To prove her point, Dorothea continued, "I believe we have a ghost."

"Fine, as long as I don't have to invite it to the wedding, you might direct it to the east wing. The late viscountess will enjoy the company." Clare continued copying pages. After bats, pistols, and murderers, ghosts didn't score high on her scale of fear.

Dottie didn't leave but asked warily, "You know about the spirits?"

With a sigh, Clare removed her spectacles and set down her pen. It was obvious her heiress cousin wouldn't leave until she had whatever she'd come in here for. "The lady's *perfume* haunts us. It is in everything. May I help you?" She gestured at the diary the girl held.

"I think The Lady is fretting. I do not generally have this strong an impression from those who have passed. I'm not certain what she expects." Vaguely defiant, Dottie showed no sign of embarrassment at this admission to humbug.

Clare had dismissed the aloof heiress as a little too high in the instep for the mostly impoverished relations in the manor. But Dottie's eight-year-old brother had accompanied her to the manor, and she had offered to help pay for the tutor, so Clare felt obliged to pay attention.

"How does one know that a ghost frets?" she asked, reasonably enough.

"It is just. . ." Dottie waved her hand helplessly. "A sensation that she paces, I think. If you are laughing at me, I will go away. I just thought it would be remiss not to mention it. Her anxiousness may mean an unwelcome

2

intruder among our guests. Or staff—I believe we've recently hired more?"

Ah, the arrival of her unwanted former suitor as one of the wedding guests no doubt agitated *Dottie*, but if the chit wanted to blame the late viscountess. . . Clare really needed to find out more about the debonair Comte Avignon—later. "I have more than enough to do worrying about people I can see. I will leave you in charge of the unseen. If you discover the lady's problem, we will do our utmost to help."

Clare had yet to encounter ghosts, but that didn't mean they didn't happen. And if anyone could figure out how to return as a ghost, it would be a Reid, although the poor, unsuspecting viscountess had simply married into their insane family. That was probably enough to make one mad enough to return and haunt the next generation or three.

It wasn't until Dottie bobbed a curtsy and departed that Clare wondered why her cousin had chosen to read that particular passage aloud. It did sound as if the viscountess had been in serious doldrums. She should have asked the date. They'd never learned exactly how Lady Reid had died, but she'd only been in her fifties, much too young to depart this mortal coil.

Given her own catastrophic life, Clare understood why her novel writing inclined toward the Gothic. Saving the heroine from villainy gave her a control she did not otherwise possess. But she wasn't about to investigate a possible ancient crime on the eve of her nuptials. She had quite enough on her plate juggling the ever-growing household and arriving guests, and hoping to finish copying her new manuscript before the dual ceremonies. The final wedding banns for her cousin would also be read this Sunday.

Less than a week to go. . . She blushed just thinking about Hunt's increasingly ardent attentions. Bookish, plain, bespectacled, she'd never considered herself an object of desire, but her American fiancé apparently saw more in her than she did.

She knew she was marrying an intelligent man, so she hoped that was Hunt's wisdom and not his blind eye showing him what wasn't there.

First, she needed to send off this manuscript. The small income she received from her writing paid for her seven-year-old nephew's tutor, in a roundabout sort of way. She didn't dare tell anyone except her best friend and Hunt that she was a novelist writing under a male pseudonym. Her father's rural, very conservative family would call her scandalous and try to remove Oliver from her care, as they had once before. So she had to pretend Oliver's education was paid for by her grandmother's trust, which barely paid living expenses. Like all their current residents, she'd found a haven from poverty in Wycliffe Manor.

Wishing Dottie hadn't left the office door open. Clare returned to her copy work, ignoring the men tramping in and out through the courtyard door.

A rising argument from the direction of the library, regrettably, could not be ignored. The last earl had left an immense library, knocking down walls and expanding the original space to include all the tomes he'd accumulated over his lifetime, plus all those from his ancestors. The earls bought books the same way they collected jewels.

Fortunately, or unfortunately, depending on one's viewpoint, the fourth earl of Wycliffe had been the last earl. After the death of his only son, he'd broken the entail, sold all his estates except the Reid ancestral pile, and consolidated all the libraries here, to the delight and consternation of many.

She locked away her pages and set out to calm troubled waters.

"My father was not mad," Lady Lavinia was shouting as Clare arrived in the library doorway. Wearing her hair in a towering gray pompadour fashionable in her youth, the mole on her thin lips quivering, Clare's great-aunt glared her contempt. "Wycliffe simply did not wish any jackanapes to come along and help themselves to the family treasures."

Undeterred, the scholarly, white-haired Lord de Sackville sat with one long leg crossed over his knee, inspecting a list on his writing desk and jotting notes. "Hiding a fortune in gems is mad. If he wished the family to have the family jewels, he should have added them to the estate inventory and stored them in a vault, as any sane man would."

The baron waved away the lady's splutters. "One must be mad to be a Reid, sorry, my lady. My son is marrying a Reid heiress who prefers to work in a kitchen, so I'm not blind. Reids do not think as others do. If anyone knew that, the earl must have. He granted all his immediate heirs fortunes before he died, then left Wycliffe Manor to any and all family, knowing no one would live in this ancient isolation unless they were in dire need of funds. Genius is almost always mad, and I believe the earl was a genius. He has provided for future generations, well aware that his immediate heirs were unlikely to have anything left for their offspring."

"Well, I never." Lady Lavinia threw down copies of the late earl's eccentric map and rose to her narrow feet. She wore the full skirts of another era, and her high heels were visible. "My sons were *never* deprived of anything they needed."

"Your sons died unfortunately early, my lady." Clare took the dowager's thin arm. "And the earl knew that Reid men are too adventurous and don't live long lives. And women and children suffer for their losses. He was a compassionate, understanding man."

And a lunatic, but she didn't need to say that.

"Hmpf." Lady Lavinia shook her off. "If you'd marry well, as one must, you needn't worry about finding what wasn't meant to be found. I will admit, your Captain Huntley is a fine figure of a man, but looks don't put food on the table." She sailed off in the direction of the long gallery, where her illegitimate granddaughter held sway. There was another argument in the works.

"I take it she cannot work out the puzzle," Clare said dryly, glancing at the pages her aunt had scattered on the library table.

"The codes you've found in the earl's family paintings are devilish," the baron admitted. "I thought if I could put the codes in order, we might find any maps faster. I do not wish to sell books that might hide further clues."

They'd broken the codes concealed on two paintings from the gallery, using them to locate maps inside two old tomes. The earl had included a letter with one saying it was actually the fifth map. Neither of the drawings they'd uncovered had been much more than a square with odd niches and an X outside the lines, not particularly useful on their own.

"One must assume the other maps are pieces of paper like the two we've found. It is easy to shuffle through pages to discover if anything is hidden. I'd rather translate the codes and find the books that way, not that I'm any good at it," Clare said.

"That's what I attempted to do," the baron admitted.

"And Lady Lavinia thought to join you?" Odd. Her great-aunt generally preferred sitting in her upstairs salon, poking needles into cloth. . .

Like her granddaughter. Clare dithered in the doorway, wondering if she should follow the lady. Lavender was only seventeen, the result of a liaison between Lady Lavinia's young son and a maid. Lady Lavinia had sent Lavender to boarding school but never accepted her in any other manner.

"The baroness is looking for trouble," the baron agreed. "You should allow her to meddle more in the weddings, perhaps."

"Elsa has a menu prepared for the breakfast. Henri is cleaning up the tavern in preparation for entertaining the village. I cannot imagine what she might do to aid in the cause." *Sleep, wake, eat, go to bed again.* . . Clare heard the late viscountess's plaintive cry.

Acknowledging the importance of keeping the aunts from disturbing Jack's bibliophile father, Clare sailed off to engage in peacemaking. They needed the baron to finish preparing for the book auction meant to help pay the mortgage.

Lady Lavinia needed occupation. Lavender would fling her grandmother out of the sewing room the way the baroness had flung Lavender's mother out of the house. The scene promised to be immense.

Why, oh why, did Clare have to be the adult in the household?

TWO

HUNT: MONDAY MORNING

"We none of us have what might be called a solid income." Captain Alistair Huntley, commonly known as Hunt, kicked through years of wood debris and weeds. "I am terrified of marrying Clare, then discovering we can't keep the manor. I have nowhere else to take her."

"Elsa will put you up on her Newchurch estate," Jack, the former Lt. John de Sackville casually offered. The son of a baron, he had a loose idea of what constituted supporting a family. "For now, I am grateful to have a roof over my head and food in my belly. . . and amazingly excellent food at that."

As former soldiers, Hunt and Jack had deep respect for their current ramshackle situation. That did not mean genteel ladies appreciated poverty. And Wycliffe Manor, to put it gently, consumed every farthing in their limited pockets and demanded more.

Paul Upton, the son of a curate and only recently ordained, had lived in poverty all his life. With a frown, he gazed down the muddy wooded path they traversed. "I would like to be my own man, reliant on my own abilities, but admittedly, carpentry pays a great deal better than the church. If this path ends at the brook, I can build a bridge, but even making the chapel's field accessible does not mean I can rent it out. The path does not seem well-used."

In front of them, Arnaud Lavigne shrugged. "No one knows of it but me. It's not as if there are any young men left to farm these fields with a war going on."

Taller than Hunt, his half-cousin had lost a great deal of weight in a French prison and later, living the life of a hermit after he'd fled Napoleon's censorship police. An overly-principled French count, and a brilliant artist, Arnaud spoke seldom and lived for his art. They'd only dragged him away from his easel on this sunny June day because the women had turned his studio gallery into a madhouse with final preparations for the weddings and the onslaught of guests that had just begun.

Six more days. . . Two weddings on the same day may have been a little much to undertake, but neither Hunt nor Jack was willing to wait longer. And then Jack's father wanted to hold a book auction directly after the weddings, so he might return to his own home. The immense manor was chaos even without all the new, untrained, hires.

"Try being an artist and earning a living," Arnaud continued. "Especially here, in rural nowhere."

That may have been more than Arnaud had said in the past week. Hunt had to listen. "So you're looking for the earl's jewels in hopes we can set you up with a studio in London?" He couldn't hide his amusement. The earl's jewels were a myth as far as he was concerned.

"I want a finder's fee if I find them." Arnaud strode ahead, stomping overgrowth with his battered boots.

Arnaud had been the one to discover the code in the earl's paintings that had led to odd maps and hidden letters about jewels. Since he'd lived here longer, he'd had more time to explore than the rest of them. He was the one who had told Paul about this nearly invisible path leading from the manor to the field the late earl had donated to the church.

From the looks of it, only Arnaud had used this muddy track recently. Given the London highway direction, perhaps their banker might have used it occasionally, if he arrived on horseback, but it wasn't wide enough for a carriage.

The lane did, however, seem to be a more direct path to the chapel than the winding carriage drive.

Hunt glanced over his shoulder. The upper stories of Wycliffe Manor's faux towers were all that were visible above the overgrown canopy of trees. Anyone riding this path would be invisible until they reached the house. "We may need to put up a gate on this lane for security. The brook, river, and cliffs create barriers to the rest of the grounds. The drive gives us a good view of anyone approaching. I've always considered the manor secure, but this. . . is concealed enough to be a smugglers' path."

"Poachers, maybe," Jack objected. "We are too far from the sea for smugglers."

"You want to explain away that cellar full of brandy that we inherited?" Hunt asked cynically, before continuing, "This comes out in a field and not the road?"

"There's a low place in the brook, an overgrown hedgerow, and a deteriorating stile before we reach the road. Paul can fix that." Striding ahead, Arnaud kicked aside a fallen branch—and halted abruptly.

They were all on foot. Jack caught up first, cursed, then kneeled in the muddy leaves.

Hunt and Paul stopped beside Arnaud. The late morning sun broke through the thick canopy of beech leaves and pines to illuminate a man sprawling on his back in the mud. Not far away, his horse nibbled weeds.

"Faint pulse," Jack called. "He's alive."

Hunt bit back expletives to kneel on the man's—the boy's?—other side. "I don't recognize him. Did he fall off his horse?"

Paul pointed up. "That branch hangs low. I could probably ride under it, but a tall man. . ."

"Would have to be riding hard not to see it. I've ducked below it. I suppose at night. . ." Arnaud reluctantly bent over the stranger. . . and froze.

"You recognize him?" Hunt had only met his half-cousin a few months back, but he was learning the artist's many moods. This was one of wariness.

"I could be wrong. It's been years since I've been to my estate. But that flat, long nose is distinctive and resembles that of Barbeau, a lawyer my family used upon occasion. This man is too young to be him, but he had several sons, all with the same unfortunate beak. I don't know what would bring one here." He kneeled down to lift the lad in his big arms.

Despite his bad knee, Hunt returned to his feet before his cousin, taking the placid horse from the clergyman's inexperienced hold. "We'd better keep this one alive," he said wearily, patting the mare to steady her while Arnaud settled the unconscious stranger over the saddle. "The women are likely to have hysterics if we have one more burial. Aren't all Frenchmen gathering to fight Wellington?"

The news from the continent arrived slowly and not particularly accurately, but it seemed certain that now Napoleon was back on the throne, there would be war. Again.

"If this is just an accident, there shouldn't be a problem. Elsa and Clare have sensible heads on their shoulders," Jack said. "But why the devil was *anyone* on this path that even we didn't know about?"

Hunt glanced at his cousin. Arnaud knew the hidden route. But his artistic cousin's expression had closed up, a certain sign that he was retreating to ugly memories.

"Why was any Frenchman here at all?" Arnaud asked gruffly.

Less than a week until Hunt could finally call Clare his, and they had another damned mystery on their hands. He winced as the boy groaned. Maybe he could talk his betrothed into leaving these shores and going back to America with him. England didn't appear to be as safe as one would think.

"Let us try to keep this from the women until we know more," he suggested, knowing he only protected them until gossip ran loose.

THREE

ELSA: MONDAY MORNING

"*Him*, I find in your new chambers, where he does not belong!" Their newly hired French valet shook his small, old-age freckled fist at a taller, younger valet with a head full of blond hair.

Lady Elspeth Villiers had thought retreating to a kitchen more peaceful than dealing with her querulous noble family. Foolish of her. Now she had all her family's *servants* under her feet.

The target of the little Frenchman's rage was her half-brother's valet, Roberts. She supposed the young man had been in their bridal suite, spying on her fiancé at her brother's behest. She'd deal with his prying lordship later. Flinging her heavy skillet on the stove, she glared at the pair invading her domain. "Roberts is Villiers' man. Take your quarrel up with him."

"I was merely seeking Mr. de Sackville," Roberts said stiffly.

She'd not met Roberts before. Her noble brother must have retired his elderly servant and replaced him with this handsome jackanapes, who was a little too full of himself and hadn't learned to stay out of her way.

Jack—Mr. de Sackville's—new valet was also new. A fussy, irritating little man, Victor had been all they could find willing to live a far remove from civilization. An added benefit though, Victor had brought his wife, Marie, who had agreed to be Elsa's maid. They'd come from the agency with impeccable references, although most of the couple's former employers appeared to be deceased. The pair weren't young, but they were immensely competent.

With two weddings in less than a week and guests arriving daily, Elsa desperately needed the experienced hand of a trained lady's maid, and Marie was good. She didn't want to lose her.

"Roberts sticks his nose everywhere," a third valet, George, complained as he trotted down the stairs carrying used linens. Of medium height, build, and age, George looked the part of invisible valet, except for his pockmarked skin and the red rash on his jaw.

Reminded that her mother had brought her lover and their servants to add to the bedlam, Elsa flung onions in the hot skillet, then grabbed her cleaver to chop more. She had an assistant, but she found wielding the cleaver resulted in intelligent men backing away.

George didn't seem to be particularly intelligent. Valet for the no-doubt fraudulent French count her mother had persuaded to accompany her, he helped himself to a leftover breakfast roll. "I found Roberts wandering downstairs last night."

Elsa disliked the buffoon, perhaps because she disliked his employer. She hadn't expected her mother to attend her wedding. She definitely hadn't expected her to bring Comte Avignon, an escort Elsa had never met, along with an entourage of servants the moldering manor could scarcely house with any degree of comfort. The attic servants' quarters hadn't been used in decades, and now their limited staff was divided between opening the vast attic and cleaning guest rooms.

She had formed no solid opinion of the stout Avignon, but if George's annoying habit of not understanding his own stupidity was any indication, the count was a dolt.

"If you saw Roberts downstairs after everyone retired, that means you were downstairs as well," she pointed out in irritation. "Why is everyone bothering me?"

"Monsieur desires to know when the buffet is ready." George wasn't any more French than Elsa, but his scowl was fierce.

Roberts and Victor intelligently stalked out when she waved the cleaver. George merely tore apart the roll to cram it between his skinny lips.

Before Elsa could chop off his fingers, Nettie Upton trotted down the stairs. A newly-discovered family member and their marvelous new housekeeper, Nettie was also a former curate's wife, with experience in ordering people about—and pacifying outrage. She swatted George with a cleaning rag and silently pointed at the stairs.

The fool departed under her withering glare.

Upstairs/downstairs hierarchy did not exist at Wycliffe Manor, where heiresses cooked and family members held the highest staff positions.

"Lackwit," Elsa muttered, flinging chopped onions into the skillet.

"No more so than the coachmen Paul found in his church-yard claiming they were looking for family graves." Paul was Mrs. Upton's son and the village's new curate, the reason the weddings could finally be performed.

The graveyard was at the manor, not the church. Elsa rolled her eyes. "Surely treasure hunters don't believe the earl buried jewels in a grave?"

The mystery of the missing family jewels had captured

everyone's imagination, most likely because they were bored far from the city's entertainments.

"Or your lordly brother is spying. His secretary was in the gallery at dawn. And I just caught your new maid in the unopened *west* wing, where she had utterly no reason to be." Nettie sat down at the trestle table where Elsa's mostly new and inexperienced kitchen staff worked at their various tasks, absorbing the tittle-tattle and sensibly staying out of her way.

Elsa found a boiled turnip and whacked it into mash. This had been her fear all along—that Villiers would attempt to stop her marriage. Her half-brother was only trying to protect her, she understood. But he still thought her a terrified adolescent, incapable of fighting off villainous money grubbers. He didn't recognize that she'd learned a thing or two since her one failed London Season.

She'd loved Jack since childhood. Now that he finally felt confident that he could take care of a wife and was ready to marry her. . . She wouldn't let her meddling brother intervene.

Villiers' secretary was no doubt conversing with Lord de Sackville over the settlements, wreaking havoc with their marriage plans. Her new maid's wandering was the least of her problems. "Marie was probably searching for linens or a better chair. She has elevated notions of our consequence."

"That's the odd thing." Nettie polished a spoon that didn't meet her standards. "I could swear I've seen her before. She seems more familiar with the manor than I am, yet I have lived here before, albeit twenty-five years ago."

Elsa glanced over her shoulder at all the listening ears. Most of her staff were not local. She declined to add to the speculation.

But if her new maid had lived here when Nettie had, she, too, knew of the missing jewels.

She'd have to check Marie's references more thoroughly.

FOUR

HUNT: MONDAY NOON

AFTER LEAVING THEIR INJURED VISITOR IN THE INFIRMARY IN THE manor's back hall, Hunt ran upstairs to scrub off the worst of his filth. Trained as a U. S. Army engineer, he'd never expected to become lord of a manor and had yet to learn how to stay neatly attired. With a houseful of company, he had to pretend to be decent for Clare's sake. A genteel lady who still suffered from the horror of seeing her sister die in an Egyptian riot, his fiancée would imagine the worst of an unconscious stranger practically on their doorsteps. He'd at least look civilized before breaking the news.

In quiet resignation, James, a former batman, took Hunt's mud-splattered coat, holding it with distaste on one finger. Hunt had a hard time calling the peg-legged ex-soldier a valet, but James was learning his ways. "It is a very good thing that you still have your uniforms, sir. One hopes the household will be repaired before everything you own is in the dustbin."

"You're starting to sound like Quincy, James. Is that to teach me to speak properly too?" Hunt stripped off his shirt. Quincy was their ex-prizefighter butler. Hunt had no idea how the man had learned educated speech.

"I would not presume." James caught the linen before it hit the carpet. "Mr. Walker brought up a letter for you. He thought you might wish to see it immediately."

His best friend since childhood, Walker knew Hunt better than anyone. If he personally delivered a letter, Hunt had better read it. He hoped this was good news for a change. He didn't have much to offer Clare as a wedding gift, but he could at least try to give her peace.

He located the fragile folded paper on the washstand, and recognizing the handwriting, ripped off the seal. He scanned it eagerly with his one eye, then grabbed a monocle to peruse the hen scratching again.

Unheeding of his filthy uniform trousers, he collapsed on the nearest chair. Combining elation with despair would do that to a man. He shouldn't have asked about his father's ring.

"Sir?" James asked worriedly.

"Where's Clare?" He couldn't even think until his ever sensible bride-to-be read this. Cursing and cheering at the same time would simply scare poor James. Clare would understand.

Or should he hide the letter, pretend it came too late? That's what he wanted to do, he realized. It was wrong. He knew it was wrong. It was no way to start a lifetime's journey of wedded bliss. But the interminable wait to have Clare in his bed was down to less than a week. . . He went about half-cocked all day as it was. He'd have to take off the roof to keep occupied.

But if they waited. . . He might give Clare a better ring than he'd been able to afford.

With a groan, he hurriedly washed and threw on the clean shirt and waistcoat James handed him. The stiff neckcloth was more than he could tolerate, however. Donning his morning coat, he crammed the letter into the pocket, but brushed away the neckcloth. "I'm just grabbing a bit of luncheon before returning to work on the plumbing. Let's not waste the laundry."

He clattered down the marble stairs with the letter burning a hole over his heart. Clare wasn't in the small dining parlor where a buffet was laid out. She wasn't in her office or the library.

Loud voices carried from the long gallery at the front of the manor. Hunt assumed the original Wycliffe who'd sacked the priory had preserved the two-story Gothic cathedral façade so he might build his new manor with an impressive portrait gallery and ballroom for his ladies. By the sixteenth century, fortresses must have gone out of favor.

To provide income for the locals as well as the manor, the creative Reids had turned the two-story gallery into a button manufactory and seamstress/tailor business. Arnaud had set up a studio near the cathedral windows. All far more useful than a ballroom, in Hunt's opinion.

Reaching the gallery, he focused on Clare—slender, blond, patiently listening—before he realized she was involved in an imbroglio involving her young cousin, Lavender, and her elderly Aunt Lavinia. As a descendant of a long line of aristocrats, Clare spoke as if to the manor born and generally did not need to raise her voice. Except her relations were also descendants of the earl—and more arrogant.

"This is *my* home, my friends, my family. You are not allowed to come in here and usurp them," young Lavender shouted. Once given permission to sew anything she liked, the lovely blond adolescent had bubbled into a cheerful soul. Shouting was not normal. "Go back to one of your very many estates that you will not allow me to enter!"

Hunt winced at the direct blow. The little seamstress was an *illegitimate* Reid.

"Your *mother* was not welcome," the slender old lady overrode her. "She was a trollop who got your father killed. I sent you to school so you'd learn to be the proper lady he'd be proud of!"

Hunt suspected this fight had been a long time coming. He didn't want any part of it. He glanced pleadingly at Clare, who seemed unprepared to separate the combatants.

"Ladies, this is no way to settle your differences." Apparently understanding his unspoken plea, Clare inserted herself into the argument more forcefully. "I think we should call a family council after luncheon. Lady Lavinia, if you will return to your parlor, I'll have your meal served there. Lavender, you are providing a very poor example for your workers. Go outside and cool off a bit. Your puppy needs his walk."

Reminded of her pet, Lavender swooped down to pick up the dog mop—the reason she'd left the school Lady Lavinia had installed her in. Having said her piece, the elderly lady stalked out, head high, her stride more militant than usual.

With a sigh, Clare took Hunt's arm and let him lead her away. "That storm has been brewing for a while. I feel as if I'm a mother to a household of adolescents, and that includes the aunts. What happened to your neckcloth?"

Just hearing her voice calmed his inner turmoil. Clare might be spooked at gunfire, but she had sufficient experience with upset apple carts to keep a cool head.

Ignoring the comment on his improper attire, not knowing how to say what needed to be said, Hunt merely handed her his letter. He was an engineer, not a diplomat. He didn't know how to explain bombshells. They just exploded. If he survived this one, he'd tell her about the stranger they'd carried into the infirmary.

She cast him a surprised glance and unfolded the cross-hatched page under his new gas lamp. The instant she read the signature, she removed her spectacles from her pocket and donned them. "Your mother? She has replied to your news of the wedding already?"

"No, there's not been time. Our letters most likely crossed." His family lived outside Philadelphia. Ships were fast these days, but they'd only decided to wed a month or so ago.

She scanned the letter quickly, then more slowly, her eyes going rounder behind her lenses. "She's coming *here*? She's crossing an ocean to see the home she never knew?"

The earl had disowned the adulterous viscountess and her second child, Hunt's mother. Once she'd grown to adulthood and married, Frances Huntley had sailed off for America, never having seen Wycliffe Manor.

"I think the news of her mother's journals set her off. That, and I may have mentioned you. After I nearly died, she hasn't stopped worrying about me." Hunt had always gone his own way, off to school and the Army without giving his family much thought—until a British bombshell had taken his eye and nearly his life.

He was thirty now, about to start a family of his own, and he wanted. . . He wasn't entirely certain what he wanted. Clare could probably explain it to him, if he asked.

She blushed at the knowledge she was about to meet his family, then apparently did a mental calculation. "She says she's sailing soon after she posts this letter! She could be here any day. That was almost a month ago!"

"A passenger ship will be slower than a mail ship, but yes, surely in a week or two." He waited for her to grasp his dilemma.

It didn't take long. She clutched the letter to her breast and studied him, wide-eyed. "We must postpone the wedding until she arrives! She ought to see her only son wed after coming all this way."

Exactly what he feared. "But the house will be filling up with bidders for the book auction," he warned. "Are you certain?"

Before she could respond, Jack strode down the hall,

21

looking furious and anguished at the same time. Hunt's heart fell to his feet.

"The patient has died," the blunt ex-soldier announced, regardless of the effect on delicate females.

Clare, predictably, screamed, "*What?*"

Perhaps he should have mentioned the accident first.

FIVE

CLARE: MONDAY NOON

CLARE'S BEST FRIEND, MEERA WALKER, LEFT THE INFIRMARY, drying her hands and shaking her head. Meera's Hindu mother and Jewish father had both been apothecaries. Their daughter had followed in their footsteps, until their premature deaths. Alone and bereft, she'd followed Clare to this Gothic horror of a manor and found love.

Walker, her new husband, emerged from the infirmary to rub Meera's shoulders. Hunt's best friend and a descendant of African slaves, he had a head full of book learning he employed for the manor's benefit. Not an exceptionally tall man, he still towered over his wife.

"I couldn't save him," Meera whispered mournfully.

"No one could have saved him," Walker corrected, hugging her.

Clare buried her face against Hunt's broad chest in sorrow. He had said the patient was a stranger. That didn't mean they shouldn't feel grief. They'd seen too many deaths in the past weeks.

Hunt's open shirt gave her too much access to the enticing musk of his chest. His comforting arms surrounded her, but her mind wouldn't rest. She had so many questions. . . "Do we know who he is?"

Lounging against the wall, Hunt's younger French cousin wore a troubled mien. Henri looked much like Hunt—tall and muscular, dark-haired, with square chiseled features, but he was younger, more slender, and usually had more charm. He answered grimly, "Nothing on him but a pocket watch and a coin purse. If it weren't for those, I'd think a cutpurse had attacked him. If he was coming here, why wasn't he on the drive?"

They'd seen a few too many deaths since arriving in Gravesyde Priory, making the village's name portentous. Clare leaned into Hunt for a moment longer, then straightened her weak spine. They needed more information. "Did he say anything?"

Meera shook her head. "He muttered about weddings and pearls or earls or whatever else might rhyme. A blow to the head can scramble one's wits. And the fall from his horse. . ." She shook her head. "It was only a miracle he lived long enough to speak. He snapped his neck."

Weddings and pearls? Was he a guest? Must Clare look to see if she recognized him? She didn't know any young men.

Hunt released her to pace. "I'd like to know how the devil he managed to fall from his horse. I've run into tree branches. Hurts, but unless one was galloping in the woods, which does not bode at all well. . . I want to take another look at where this happened, but let's go over his horse first."

Henri pried himself off the wall at Hunt's gesture toward the stable.

Her beloved had his priorities, and they weren't hers. Clare had to deal with the people left behind, but in this case, she had no information. "I don't know what to do. Do I send everyone in to see if anyone recognizes him?" Which meant she must do so. . .

"He wore a gentleman's clothes." Meera puckered her

brow in thought. "Perhaps not terribly wealthy, but well made. I don't know enough of fashion to say they are fashionable. Arnaud said he may have recognized his features, which might make him French. Start there?"

Relieved to have direction that didn't involve studying a corpse, Clare nodded. "I'll talk to Arnaud. Sit down and rest. There is nothing you can do now." Meera was carrying a child almost larger than she was. By her own medical orders, she had to keep her feet up.

Meera hesitated. "I wonder. . . Would it be possible to see the branch he hit?"

Walker groaned and steered his wife toward their chambers. "I will have it cut down and brought to you, but please, do not make more of this than a very sad accident."

It was already far more than that. A mysterious stranger and an inexplicable accident on a lane no one traveled, carrying no letter of recommendation or introduction. . . Clare hurried off to find Hunt's artistic cousin.

Dottie pounced on her before she passed the breakfast parlor. "The viscountess is *prodigiously* agitated. I don't know what to do."

That made the two of them. A houseful of cantankerous relations, a mysterious death, and an agitated ghost—really, she ought to run far, far away. Whatever had she got herself into?

Give the heiress a task. . . "Set out the journals. See if your ghost opens any of them." Which was a perfectly ridiculous thing to say, but Clare knew how to be creative.

In the gallery, Arnaud claimed not to recognize the man, just his familiarity. He promised to sketch his likeness, then write the Barbeau family he knew in France to inquire about any missing sons. They both knew the slim likelihood of the missive reaching a country on the brink of war.

"Perhaps Lord Villiers could send the message in a diplomatic pouch," she suggested.

After Arnaud set off to the infirmary with his sketching materials, Clare hurried upstairs to the suite the aunts shared. Once belonging to the earl, these were the most luxurious chambers in the old part of the manor. In deference to their elders, Clare and Elsa had chosen the suites they would share with their new husbands in the far wings that had been abandoned for decades. Their limited staff had been hastily refurbishing them.

Clare needed to tell the elderly ladies about the dead stranger before gossip had more murder and mayhem laid on their doorstep.

Her *real* concern was how to tell Hunt's aunt, Lady Spalding, about the arrival of Hunt's mother, the sister she hadn't seen in over thirty years. After reading the late viscountess's journals, Clare was certain there had been animosity between the siblings. Their mother had fled the abusive viscount and returned home to France when Lady Spalding was only a child. Hunt's mother had been born of an illicit liaison between the viscountess and the late Comte Lavigne, Arnaud and Henri's grandfather, during that visit. The scandal had ruined them. Clare could hope forgiveness came with age, but she wasn't counting on it.

Deciding it was Hunt's task to inform his aunt, Clare merely gave the ladies the news about the unhappy accident. They were more interested in their luncheon.

Leaving them, Clare hurried up to the attic floor to see how the schoolroom fared. She needed a little innocence to restore her faith in the world.

She found the boys on the floor, newssheets scattered about, and rows of tin soldiers lined up across a map that looked vaguely like a flattened globe drawing of Europe. She didn't have a significant education, but she'd been enamored of her father's globe and recognized France. So much for innocence.

"Napoleon is on the march," her nephew Oliver informed her.

She glanced at Mr. Birdwhistle, their handsome, young tutor, but he crossed his arms and let the boys speak. Probably a good policy.

"Yes, I believe he is defying the sanctions put on him, so now he must defend the throne he claims." She didn't particularly understand any of it, except that after being sent home once, English soldiers were again gathering in Brussels. The men discussed it, but as long as Hunt and Jack didn't feel called upon to join Wellington—and Hunt, being American, couldn't—she'd seen no need to keep up.

"Napoleon's army is more experienced," Davy said solemnly. Dottie's little brother didn't speak often. Clare had wondered about his intelligence, but it seemed he was simply another odd Reid.

"Will he defend his borders or attack our troops?" Oliver pushed his soldiers forward. "He always attacks."

"Yes, very well, that sounds most unpleasant. Have you had luncheon?" She'd merely wanted to remind Oliver of her presence. It felt odd to have someone else looking after him after all these years as his main caretaker. She loved Oliver as only a mother could. She thought maybe she might be decent at raising her own children.

She simply wasn't prepared to deal with everyone else's children—and childish adults. Except for that one disastrous trip to Egypt, she'd always led a solitary life.

"Lady Elsa takes good care of us," Mr. Birdwhistle said, when the boys didn't reply. "Later today, we mean to make her a wedding gift in thanks."

"She will enjoy that. Lady Elsa always gives more than she receives, so that will be lovely. I shall leave you to your lessons then." She swept out and down to her own room to freshen up.

The room she'd taken at the back of the manor would not be hers much longer. She and Hunt had chosen the large suite in the west wing to share after they wed. Maids, their lone footman, and Ned, their jack-of-all-trades, had been moving in furniture, preparing fresh linen, and cleaning the cobwebbed draperies and dusty carpets all week. Hunt's one-legged valet had directed much of the action. She really needed to hire her own maid, but Elsa's maid, Marie, had been an unexpected blessing.

"Carriages coming up the drive, miss," Quincy informed her as she descended in hopes some of the buffet might be left.

Aiiieee—more guests?

She had no idea what kind of warning system Quincy had established so he was always prepared for visitors. The drive was nearly a mile long and not visible until it reached the top of the hill.

"They must have come from Birmingham to arrive at midday." The distance to London was longer and had no inns within easy driving distance. "More of Elsa's family," she concluded, since she had almost no immediate family and Elsa's estate was in that direction. "Send someone to let her know."

Heaven only knew where they'd house them. They'd installed Elsa's mother in the last of the newly refurbished suites. At her compulsive cleaning best, Mrs. Upton had attempted to correct fifteen years of neglect. She had seen that the ancient furnishings were polished and the deteriorating carpets cleaned throughout the main manor. She had barely started on the wings.

New guests would have to go in the small, windowless rooms in the front hall or deal with half-furnished chambers.

Clare hastily nibbled cheese and an apple, confident Elsa was already preparing trays for their guests. If Elsa ever chose to leave the manor. . . Clare had threatened to leave with her. They'd never find a better, more efficient cook, but better yet, Elsa had a sensible head on her shoulders that Clare relied on.

Hunt was still gone on whatever mission he thought necessary to deal with the accident victim. Clare gratefully greeted Elsa as she ran into the breakfast parlor, hastily tucking her disarranged hair into pins.

"It is bad enough that *Mother* arrived early," she complained. "Whyever is anyone else? Mother never leaves London until everyone else is gone."

"Her only daughter is to be married! She wants to provide you with motherly advice," Clare teased. She'd learned enough about Mrs. Turner these past two days since her arrival to know this was unlikely.

They waited in the Elizabethan great room. With ancient oak paneling darkened by age and smoke, any light eclipsed by the forest outside the mullioned Gothic windows, the gloomy room required oil lamps in daytime.

A maid ran about, lighting sconces. A commotion of traffic and voices in the vestibule entrance warned their guests had disembarked. Their servants, trunks, and carriages would continue on to the side portico and stables.

Elsa sighed and studied her clasped hands. "I cannot imagine who else might arrive from home. Mother was quite disappointed when she failed to catch me covered in cake batter."

"Oh, your mother is not disappointed. She is having a jolly time complaining about all the inadequacies in the manor. We are scarcely modern and can't offer the comforts of your estate." Clare nibbled a biscuit from the tea tray and waited for their butler to introduce the arrivals.

Elsa snorted at this admission and helped herself to a biscuit too.

"Lord Spalding and Mr. Benedict Bosworth, Jr., my ladies," Quincy intoned in his polished baritone. Their butler had not been properly trained to his exalted position, but he was learning quickly. Clare had hired him for his size. She'd wanted a door guardian. He'd become that and more.

"*Spalding*?" Elsa whispered in surprise as the guests entered.

Bosworth? Well, they had invited the banker, after all. As the natural son of the late viscount, he was a Reid, despite his refusal to admit the connection. Clare remained standing as they entered.

Lady Spalding's stepson was *not* a Reid. A slender man in his forties, the marquess was less intimidating than Elsa's formidable brother, Earl Villiers. Clare wished Hunt and Jack were here.

"I'm afraid Captain Huntley and Lt. de Sackville aren't here to greet you, my lord, sir." Clare bobbed a curtsy for the gentlemen. "We have tea if you wish to refresh yourselves while waiting for your luggage. Or Quincy may show you to your rooms."

No one traveled this deep into the countryside without expecting to stay the night.

"Is Lord Villiers here? We'll speak with him while the servants are unloading." Lord Spalding impatiently tapped his tall hat on his thigh.

So much for pleasantries. Whyever were they seeking Elsa's brother?

Before she could send for a servant, Hunt entered in the company of the Comte Avignon. Still wearing his riding boots, Hunt appeared annoyed. The stout count, on the other hand, looked impressive in his dandified London tailoring and gold buttons. Had he been expecting the arrival of the powerful marquess? It wasn't as if Spalding was actually related to anyone in the manor. He just helped Hunt from time to time at his stepmother's request.

The men all knew each other and didn't require introduction. Thinking it better to leave them to entertain themselves, Clare left with Elsa to find Lord Villiers—until Arnaud arrived with his sketchpad. The company swiveled in his direction. Hunt's cousin had that kind of presence.

Having escaped France a few years ago with little more than the clothes on his back, Arnaud was large, aristocratically imposing, and shabby. Clare suspected the artist had been shabby even before he fled Napoleon's wrath.

"Avignon." Arnaud stopped in shock. "What the devil are you doing here?"

Ouch, she'd forgotten. Arnaud had been in Birmingham yesterday when Elsa's mother had arrived with her escort. The artist did not often mix with company.

Arnaud knew the French count? Clare supposed that made sense, since Arnaud was also from a noble family.

"Same as you, *mon ami*," Avignon replied. "France is not what she once was. I had thought you dead!"

"Sorry to disappoint." Intent on his purpose, Arnaud handed his sketch of the accident victim to Hunt. "Is the likeness strong enough?"

The men politely admired the work, until Avignon took the sketch and exclaimed, "Jean-Jacques! Is he here? What a happy coincidence!"

Clare covered her mouth and let Hunt explain that the occasion was not so happy after all.

SIX

HUNT: MONDAY NOON

HUNT DID NOT NEED A HOUSEFUL OF LOFTY BRITISH ARISTOCRATS added to the bubbling broth of weddings and a mysterious accident. Why the hell had Bosworth brought in Lord Spalding? Had they known a man was about to die on the property —again? That was ridiculous. The banker had been trying to throw them out since he realized they meant to stay. This was bound to be another ploy.

A gathering of an earl, a marquess, a French count, and the banker who owned their mortgage did not bode well. And now he was indulging in Clare's imaginative thinking—had the mystery man some information they awaited and been murdered for it? Hunt longed to join the servants unloading at the side door. He'd pry far more out of them than the nobles.

While Arnaud took Avignon to pay his respects to the man he claimed to know, Hunt saw their latest guests off to their rooms. He was having second and third thoughts about Wycliffe Manor and its mad heirs. Once they were wed, could he convince Clare to run away to Philadelphia with him? He knew the answer to that. Having lost most of her immediate family, she was enjoying meeting her extended one, even if half were quite mad.

As soon as Arnaud returned, Hunt dragged him and Henri into his study and locked the door. "Explain."

Arnaud crossed his massive arms and leaned against the hidden panel to the library. "Our dead man is apparently Jean-Jacques Barbeau, one of the sons of my lawyer, hence his familiarity. Avignon claims to know the family but hasn't seen them in years."

"Rather convenient to meet again this way," Hunt said dryly, while his mind worked on why a French lawyer would send his son to the outposts of enemy territory. To find Arnaud? Avignon? "Why would he come here? Neither of you seemed to be expecting his arrival. And what of his last words? Pearls? Weddings?"

Arnaud grimaced. "Once upon a long time ago, my grand-parents had pearls. They're long gone. I don't like that he's a lawyer's son, though. Some legal matter back home?"

Henri lounged in a leather chair and propped his boots on the desk. Hunt was aware his French cousins had been through hell these past years, but no one in the manor had survived decades of war without scars. He waited.

Henri shrugged. "I was *un enfant* when I was sent here to school. I know less than nothing. I do not even know Avignon." He jerked his head in his older brother's direction. "Comte Lavigne here is the one who lingered in Napoleon's world and mingled with the warring parties."

Arnaud snorted. "Before Napoleon's defeat, it was difficult to tell one party from the other. There is nothing noble about greed. And when all are hungry, it is dog eat dog, as the English say."

Hunt ran his hand over his scarred temple and grimaced. "I understand all that. Let's start with basics. How well do you know Avignon? Is he really a French noble? Can we believe him?"

Both of his cousins laughed.

Again, Arnaud was forced to explain. "Who knows what is nobility? Feudal titles were abolished during the revolution. After that, the nobility was killed, as our parents were. And then Napoleon realized he needed the support of landowners and began reinstating titles related to land. I understand he is now dispensing them like candy to anyone of wealth and power. Anyone can say they are the third cousin of Avignon and the only family member left to inherit the title. Without land, or even royal records, the title is meaningless. So, what is to believe?"

"The Bourbon king has been on the throne these last years. Could he not have had the land and titles reinstated?" Hunt had simply accepted that all the lands associated with his French grandparents had been lost with their deaths during the revolution. But, of course, the land was still there. It was the titles—to land and nobility—that were uncertain.

"What good are fields without peasants to work them and wealth to rebuild? Our homes are in ruins, the lands untilled, the vines dead. Anything resembling our former wealth is lost. Unpaid labor was the source of our riches, so the peasants were right to rebel." Henri shrugged.

"All right, let's return to Avignon. Arnaud, you know him. Who is he? How does he know your lawyer's son?" Hunt wanted his facts straight before examining deeper.

Hunt stretched his legs toward the unlit grate and examined the loose sole on his boot. He understood poverty. He'd been reluctant to marry given his inability to follow his chosen career with only one eye. If anything or anyone threatened the manor. . . They jeopardized Clare. He couldn't have that.

"It is more a matter of how Avignon knows us," Arnaud responded. "He is some years older. His family and ours were from the same area, as was Barbeau. Our families are acquainted. Since the Avignon family owned land, it is not unlikely that they had titles, but the family I remember were never wealthy. Henri and I left the area before the war, when we were schoolboys. It is not as if we'd have had aught to do with a grown man."

"But you recognized *him*, not the other way around," Hunt insisted.

"That was much later, in Paris. I was one of many to him. People who refused to fight under Napoleon, men escaping conscription, journalists and artists fleeing censorship and the wrath of Napoleon's police. . . all trying to escape for whatever reason. We paid him to find us ships out of France. I gave one of his men the last of my paintings since I had not a sou to my name. I was too wounded at the time to do more." Arnaud sounded sour.

From what very little Hunt had been able to pry out of his cousin, Arnaud's paintings defied France's edicts and showed war and hunger as the horror they were. He'd landed in Napoleon's prison for his opinions.

"There you have the nobility of France," Henri crowed. "Long live the king!"

"Who courageously fled the throne before losing his head like the last one," Hunt said dryly. "It is probably best that you did not return to reclaim your lands since the Bourbons cannot stand up to Napoleon. Has Avignon explained how he knows our deceased visitor?"

The Frenchman had exclaimed in French upon learning of the death of his acquaintance. Hunt had understood only the imprecations before the comte had calmed down and asked to pay his respects.

"When we took him to the infirmary, he merely called him a colleague. I gather Avignon has a wide circle of so-called colleagues, many of them among the émigrés, I should imagine." Arnaud straightened. "There are a few people I know in London. I will make inquiries."

"I think we should enlist Jack." Henri shoved out of his

chair. "If Avignon has attached himself to Elsa's mother, it is best to know his intentions. As I understand it, left to her own devices, Mrs. Turner does not have the best taste in men."

"I suppose it doesn't hurt to make inquiries—I'll talk to Villiers. If he knows of his stepmother's attachment, he may have looked into Avignon already. Although Villiers may be delighted to have Mrs. Turner removed from his responsibility." Hunt despised titles and avoided them. Family responsibility, though, he understood.

He continued, "I had the men test Barbeau's horse with a rider of similar height. They say he ought only to have lost his hat. This death is looking less accidental every minute. I suppose I had better talk to Meera."

Intending to speak to Meera first—who was far easier to converse with than the toplofty earl—Hunt ran into Clare before he could do either. A wisp of blond hair dangled at her ear, ink stained her fingers, and she seemed harried.

"You realize you must speak to your aunt about your mother's arrival, don't you? And then we must tell everyone else that our wedding must be postponed." She sounded as aggrieved as he felt.

One more slice from his tough hide—Hunt didn't *want* to postpone, not when she stood there like Adam's temptation, and his defenses were battered from all directions.

"I'd rather take apart the plumbing. The cistern appears to be leaking." Taking comfort where he could, he wrapped his arm around her slender shoulders and steered her toward the infirmary. "Might I interest you in our mystery instead of domestic issues?"

"As well as, not *instead* of," she corrected, not objecting to his familiarity but his priorities. "If we say nothing about your mother, it is the same as running away and hiding. We'd probably starve on our own if we did."

"Engineers and writers are valuable," he argued. "We might not live in this splendor. . ." He gestured at the windowless walls adorned in ugly, dark paintings of dead pheasants and hunting dogs, and she laughed. "But we would not starve."

"Admit it, living as hermits would not be half so entertaining. You are an officer. You enjoy responsibility. And I love having family again, even if they are the most exasperating people alive."

They had reached the infirmary, and Hunt surrendered the fight, since he'd got what he wanted—the mystery and not the aunts.

Meera and Walker were already examining the tree branch that Hunt had his men cut off. No sense in risking more heads, or hats, of people insisting on riding down footpaths.

"The branch is only a little over two inches in diameter," Walker declared. "I am amazed it did not break if he galloped into it hard enough to knock himself flying."

"Do we know for certain this is the branch he hit?" Clare asked, studying the thin limb.

"It is the one he was lying beneath, and there are no other low limbs there." Hunt tried snapping the branch but it was sturdy. His gut ground. This mystery had all the making of another murder. . .

And a murder when he housed wealthy men who wielded power in the government spelled worse trouble than usual. His war wounds ached instinctively.

"He did not hit the branch," Meera said quietly. "There is no bruising on his brow, only on the back of his head."

Hunt hated this, but he trusted the little apothecary. He could not ignore facts.

"I cannot see how it was done," Walker admitted. "He had to have fallen to break his neck. Did someone sit on a tree branch and knock him off?"

"Not easily. None of the trees in that vicinity had strong branches." Hunt tried to picture the scene but couldn't.

"Have Jack and Henri finished taking apart the horse's saddle yet?"

"You hauled Henri in before he was done, and Jack's dancing attendance on his bride's family." Walker grimaced. "Almost makes me glad to be alone in the world."

Since he'd just been complaining about his own growing family, Hunt could not argue the point.

"I suspect Jack is also trying to protect his father," Clare added. "Lord de Sackville may be a mild-mannered bookworm, but he does not tolerate fools lightly. If Bosworth is arguing over the library sale again, he might flee home to his own library and never be seen again."

"The baron is an intelligent man. We should all go with him." Hunt took Clare's arm. "Now we must learn more about this Barbeau fellow and why he might be riding here."

"After we tell your aunt about your mother." She steered him firmly toward the stairs.

SEVEN

CLARE: MONDAY EVENING

By day's end, Clare confessed to exhaustion. After dinner, she collapsed on the sofa in the parlor with her tea while the men lingered at the table. "I fear it was a great mistake sending wedding announcements. Although, admittedly, Hunt's mother would have come anyway."

After personally apprising the aunts of the wedding postponement, Hunt had informed the rest of the family at dinner about the impending arrival of their unexpected American guest.

Elsa patted her hand. "You can still go on with the ceremony. No one said you must wait. We can't expect wedding guests to mingle with the auction bidders arriving next week."

And not knowing when Mrs. Huntley might arrive, they couldn't postpone the book auction. The manor needed the money too badly.

Patience Upton, their housekeeper's daughter and another eccentric Reid, one who preferred to be a gardener, sat uncomfortably in a wing chair. Tall and shy, she had only recently come to the manor and was still learning how to fit in. "I am sure once the third banns are read, Paul will happily perform a quiet service, then repeat a public one later."

"Is that not a form of lie?" Dottie asked, just entering. She might play least-in-sight, but the young débutante was not in the least shy. She usually took her dinner with the aunts upstairs. They must have explained the postponement to her. "You could not keep your marriage a secret if you share a suite. Do I understand correctly. . . *Comte Avignon* knows our accident victim?"

Clare was determined to believe the young man's death was accidental, but past events had given her a suspicious mind. "He was courting you, wasn't he? What do you know of him?"

Dottie poured her own tea and settled into a wing chair. "My *parents* were courting him, I do believe. It is said he has estates in France and an excellent income."

"One may *say* anything," Clare said dryly. "He is rather older than you, although perhaps not quite the age of Elsa's mother?" She lifted her eyebrows at Elsa.

"Mother is closer to fifty than forty." Their lady cook wrinkled her nose. "But I suppose if one ignores how much older Avignon is than Dottie, there should be no objection in the reverse—unless he is looking for children. But that is the reason Mother is trying to pass me off as an ingenue—to pretend she is less than forty."

"She is welcome to him," Dottie said dismissively. "He is a perfect gentleman. I imagine he is simply looking for entry into society. I am not interested in society."

Clare wanted to ask why not, but she was still fretting over the arrival of Hunt's mother and how the haughty dowagers would treat her. "At the moment, I'm simply amazed that the aunts aren't ordering their trunks packed and carriages brought around."

The late earl's family considered Hunt's mother to be a bastard, even though the viscountess had been legally married to Lord Reid at the time of her second daughter's birth. Frances Huntley might be legitimate in the eyes of the law, but she was not a Reid.

Which meant Hunt wasn't either, for which Clare was grateful. "They seem to be taking the news of the impending arrival of Hunt's mother's with equanimity."

Elsa laughed, diverted from Avignon. "You do not understand the world these ladies occupy. They delight in battle and are fully prepared to crucify poor Mrs. Huntley. They are imagining her as a weathered farmer in homespun and callused hands, speaking like a seaman's daughter. It is a pity the withdrawing room isn't serviceable. They need intimate opulence to wield their lethal tongues."

This shabby parlor had once been grand, meant for impressing visitors. The smaller withdrawing room for family. . . if it had ever been opulent, no one could tell. The caretakers had left it in a shambles of tattered furnishings ready for the rubbish.

"I will warn the aunts to be on their best behavior or I will send them home," Clare said grimly. "If I order the staff to quit waiting on them, they will leave of their own accord. I will not accept inhospitality."

"This is their home as much as it is ours. They will bring in their own servants," Elsa corrected with a laugh. "They have not spent decades maneuvering to the heights of the aristocracy without weapons. You are an infantryman in comparison."

"Then we need to command the aunts' loyalty," Patience suggested. "If they are loyal to the captain, then they must defend his mother to all society."

"Oh, yes, and let us find the jewels and solve the unaccidental accident while we're at it," Dottie said cynically. "The *grandes dames* were the ones who dragged me here and threw me at Lady Reid's journals. Do not think they are here simply to attend the weddings."

Clare pinched the bridge of her nose where her spectacles usually rested. "Perhaps I should go exploring and find a hermit's cave."

"No, you just need to rest." Elsa stood up as the backward clock in the hall struck midnight. Or noon, although it couldn't be more than nine. "I need to set the bread dough out. You should kiss Oliver good-night and go to bed. No mysteries. No ancient aunts. In the morning, it will all make sense."

"I will go up with you to see Davy." Dottie set aside her teacup.

Seeing an opportunity to learn more about her younger cousin, Clare finished her tea. Never comfortable in the parlor, Patience willingly departed for her own quarters downstairs, with her housekeeper mother.

As they scattered in the main corridor, batwings rustled in the dark shadows of the high ceiling. Clare had quit dodging the rodents months ago, as Hunt had quit shooting them. She glanced toward the vestibule—Quincy had left the door open again, in vague hope the bats would depart, and they could shut them out forever.

Pretending she hadn't heard the flutter of wings, Clare accompanied Dottie up the marble stairs. "Do your parents not have plans for educating your brother? He seems a well-behaved boy."

Dottie laughed curtly. "He nearly set fire to the stable experimenting with broken glass. His last tutor could never find him long enough to teach him anything. I am amazed that Mr. Birdwhistle hasn't been neglecting your nephew while he searches for Davy. My father has despaired of him and threatens to send him to a boarding school for wayward boys."

"Ah, your father does not understand that Reid boys are. . . different. And if your mother only had sisters, she probably doesn't either." Clare climbed the attic stairs,

42

listening for noises from the schoolroom. All seemed quiet. "I hired Mr. Birdwhistle because he assured me he knew how to work with boys who do not conform to the normal."

"I have only met Mr. Birdwhistle briefly, but he struck me as vaguely familiar. Do you know his family?"

"I know nothing of his family. I only looked into his references, which are impeccable. And Oliver has blossomed since his arrival." Since Clare had never been introduced to society, she knew few people beyond her own limited acquaintances. "Have you had any luck communicating with your ghost?"

"The pages in the journals turn occasionally, but I have found nothing useful in their contents. With so many guests, I cannot scatter books about the great room as I would like."

"What about the withdrawing room? I know it's cluttered, so floor space isn't open, but perhaps you might re-arrange a bit?"

Dottie almost smiled. "I have been wondering about that room. Perhaps I might find some interesting pieces in there. Thank you." Dottie admired antiques.

Thank all the heavens, Clare had found an occupation for the bored society chit. There were days she felt like head-mistress at a boarding school for wayward children.

When they reached the schoolroom, the soldiers and maps were still on the floor, but the boys were in bed, listening to their tutor read. Mr. Birdwhistle shoved at his spectacles before standing to greet them.

"The Odyssey?" Clare asked dryly. "Are you translating as you read?"

"It is a classic adventure tale. They will need to know it, so it might as well be entertainment." Young, handsome in a pleasant sort of way, the tutor smiled politely but did not offer more.

"The strange man was talking to the hedge," Oliver informed her as Clare leaned over to kiss his head. He wouldn't allow more affection than that.

43

"The strange man? One of our guests?" she asked, ruffling his blond hair.

"Maybe." Information imparted, he snuggled into his pillow.

She glanced inquiringly at Mr. Birdwhistle as Dottie awkwardly repeated Clare's actions with her brother, who squirmed uncomfortably.

The tutor shrugged. "I did not see it. They were in the window seat of the tower room, sketching. Now that there are more guests, shall I keep the boys upstairs?"

Oliver had claimed the bedroom tower connecting the old manor to the west wing when they'd first arrived. He'd since moved up to the schoolroom, but no one had yet taken his old room. Clare would have to study the view from those windows. "We may need the tower for new arrivals. I'll ask Mrs. Upton to have the rest of Oliver's trunks sent up here. But I see no need to keep the boys confined."

She hoped there was no need. Surely there was a good explanation for the death of a man only the Comte Avignon knew. It wasn't as if the comte had even been invited.

EIGHT

HUNT: TUESDAY MORNING

HUNT STALKED DOWN THE RUTTED MANOR DRIVE, unappreciative of the overgrown trees and shrubbery in full June bloom. "Avignon claims he knows little of Barbeau's family or how to reach them. The usual: France is in turmoil, I cannot expect letters to arrive swiftly. . ."

Which meant they'd be burying another stranger in the old priory cemetery.

"At least the count agreed to write to the dead man's last known abode. Arnaud was even uncertain of that." Jack studied the beaten dirt and broken weeds as they departed the gravel drive and approached the area where the man's body had been found. "The superstitious might ask if the monks aren't having their revenge."

Hunt suspected Clare's inventive mind was creating even wilder tales, but that was her secret to keep. He stopped to study the place where they'd found the mysterious rider. "I'd rather believe Meera is over-anxious, and the man was simply a bad horseman who lost control."

"A bad horseman who rode all the way to the middle of rural nowhere, not knowing anyone? Suicidal and he thought a place called Gravesyde Priory ought to suit?" Jack scanned the ground, but it hadn't rained in days. "Someone is using this path upon occasion, but like the walkway to the village, it's not meant for unskilled riders. People around here don't own horses. They walk."

Hunt studied the path's direction and glanced back at the house. As he'd noted earlier, the overgrown trees prevented a view of anything but the towers. "Anyone using it would be invisible from the manor, as well as from Quincy's watchers."

Jack whistled. "Hidden access? I wonder how many people know of it?"

"I'm guessing Bosworth does." Their banker was the viscount's son from the wrong side of the blanket. His adoptive father's bank had acquired the mortgage from the late viscount. He'd grown up in the district, as none of the manor's current inhabitants had.

Hunt leaned against a stately beech and examined the neglected hillside. There might once have been a manicured lawn providing a view, and trees lining the curving drive, but the property had been allowed to revert to nature. Most of the trees were twenty or thirty years old—not a mighty oak forest but wild-sown weeds.

"Not too many visitors arrive on horseback. Your homeless soldiers may be using it for some reason. Goes the wrong direction for the village though." Hunt studied the branches overhanging the path, forming an arch. Any narrower, and the path would not be passable by horse. A tricky spot for a galloping rider.

"Given the state of the weeds, the path hasn't been used recently. It comes from the direction of Stratford, so probably our banker's erratic visits?" Jack kicked through the longer grasses beside the path.

"That's my thinking. The right direction and Bosworth knows the grounds. Think he sent this Barbeau fellow? He's not mentioned it." Hunt frowned at what appeared to be a string blowing in the breeze from a limb over his head. "Take a look up there. My good eye sees distance reasonably well and that doesn't look like a vine."

Jack studied the branch indicated, then turned and studied the leafier tree with lower branches across from it. Jumping up, he grabbed a limb on the smaller tree, lifted himself until he could swing a leg over, and pulled himself astride.

"Peacock," Hunt said dryly. "I could have gone back for a horse."

Ignoring him, Jack rummaged among the branches. "There's another bit on this side. Not thick enough for rope." He pulled a knife from his boot, reached in, and cut off a length. He dropped to the ground again.

"Can we just pretend we found nothing?" Hunt's gut churned again as Jack handed him the length of twine. He'd almost convinced himself this death had been an accident.

"Who wants murder on the eve of their marriage?" Jack agreed, without agreeing. "This could have been hanging here for years."

"Exactly." Hunt studied the fresh cut Jack had made and the frayed end. "Except this would have turned black and rotted after the spring rain."

Jack eyed the two trees and the height at which the twine had been tied. "Intended to garrote anyone riding up the path?"

"If Arnaud and Bosworth are the only ones using it. . . ? And Barbeau was unfortunate enough to ride through first?" *Murder, again.* Hunt gritted his teeth and did a hasty inventory of all the people at the manor these days. He didn't even know where to begin among the guests. The attics were bursting at the seams with servants he'd never even seen.

"Or Bosworth told Barbeau to use this path instead of the drive, for reasons unknown?" Taking the string back, Jack stretched it across the width of the narrow path, studied the length of the unreachable piece Hunt had first spotted, and grimaced. "They had to have a horse to tie that bit over there. Or one of the ladders from the orchard."

Hunt studied the overgrown path leading back to the drive. "As noted, the path is invisible from the road or house. Carry a ladder from the orchard at night, no one would see."

Jack balled up the string and shoved it into his pocket. "We will not tell the women."

"We have a killer in the household," Hunt said grimly. "How can we *not* tell them? Although they're quite likely to abandon us and head for their homes if we do."

"Or grab their kitchen knives and pen sharpeners and stalk the halls. But this is not the act of someone who acts impetuously. This was planned, presumably for our stranger, unless someone is out to kill Bosworth, which is an excellent possibility. I can't see why they'd kill a penniless artist like Arnaud. Any way you look at it, someone knew a rider would come this way and didn't want them to arrive. It could be anyone in the village or manor."

"That does not make me feel better." Hunt studied the path. "Let's see if anyone else uses the footpath. We can ask around, pretend we're considering clearing it."

"Devious, I like it. I'll ask the men in the stables. They're mostly Elsa's men, except for the ex-solders."

"Villiers and Avignon brought their own coachmen and outriders. So did Spalding, but he arrived after the fact. I'll ask about strangers lurking." Hunt began the trudge up the hill.

"Don't tell Villiers. He'll demand Elsa leave. What if someone expected one of our guests to take the path and unfortunately caught a stranger instead?"

Hunt had already reached an unpleasant conclusion about that. "A stranger would not know that footpath. Most people barely notice our public drive with a sign beside it. Our mystery visitor and his killer knew their way in."

NINE

CARE: TUESDAY MORNING

"REALLY, ELSA, YOU CANNOT MARRY IN ANYTHING SO provincial! Let me send for my modiste. She knows the latest —" Mrs. Turner's complaint was drowned out by exclamations.

"A London modiste!" Lavender cried, adjusting a pin in the hem of Elsa's wedding gown. "I would so love to talk with her."

Clare watched in admiration as Elsa spun around in her silver blue sarcenet, admiring herself in the looking glass. The cut took full advantage of their cook's voluptuous curves.

"I chose this gown, Mother, and I will wear it," Elsa insisted. "You are insulting Lavender's hard work. This is perfect for me. No one could do better."

Clare happened to agree, but she'd never been an arbiter of fashion. "We do not have a budget for fripperies, Mrs. Turner. If you could have your modiste send her older fashion books to Lavender, she is very good at adapting to suit the individual. It is not as if we will be attending balls or operas."

Mrs. Turner waved a dismissive hand. "Now that Villiers has removed her funds from that dreadful Cit's bank, Elsa will come into an extensive inheritance when she weds. She can afford the most fashionable modistes."

Clare knew that had been Villiers' wedding gift. Elsa had been terrified that the funds her grandmother had left were lost when the small bank they'd been invested in had nearly gone under. Somehow, Elsa's powerful half-brother had rescued the balance and safely redistributed it. Sometimes the manor inhabitants forgot that their pragmatic cook was the daughter of an earl and a wealthy woman.

While Lavender corrected the hem, Mrs. Turner rattled on, oblivious to the effect of her prattle. "I'm sure Jack will allow my daughter all the fripperies she likes. It is best to persuade new husbands of your heart's desire, before they turn into curmudgeons."

In the mirror, Clare could see Elsa's eyes roll.

"Jack has arranged the settlements so the executors must recognize my requests. Villiers will no doubt argue the point, but Jack is not a man to change his mind."

"Foolish of him, but very wise of you." Tall and stately, Lady Lavinia sailed into the gallery in her old-fashioned, long-waisted full gown and nodded approvingly at Elsa's high-waisted draperies. "Wisps of nothing is what they wear now. That bit looks much like my niece's bridal gown, and she's all the fashion."

Clare watched in astonishment as Lavender beamed at her grandmother's approval. They'd been at loggerheads since the lady's arrival. What had happened? She was grateful, whatever it was. Lavender needed a mother, and Clare didn't feel competent. And Lady Lavinia needed an occupation besides antagonizing others. It would be nice to have a houseful of adults instead of combative toddlers.

Having been put in her place, Elsa's mother set out down another path. "You will need a trousseau of course. I'll write and have my modiste prepared with the proper fabrics so once they have your measure, she can rush right through it. They had a fabulous green silk. . ."

"We are *not* going to London, Mother." Elsa entered the makeshift dressing room their new curate/carpenter had constructed. "Jack can't leave his horses. My kitchen and *my* horses are here. Whyever would I want to visit the filthy city? In summer, yet. I cannot think of anything more unpleasant."

Well, dead bodies in the crypt. . . Clare bit her tongue.

Lavender's triumph turned to a glare as her grandmother frowned at the fabrics Henri had brought from Birmingham. Until he'd opened a tavern in the village, Hunt's younger French cousin had earned his living as a peddler and trader. Clare understood that he picked up whatever he could find cheaply, as long as it was sturdy. They did not need different dinner gowns every evening for family. They needed practical gowns to see them through their tasks. As the pampered daughter of an extremely wealthy earl, Lady Lavinia did not grasp that.

And Elsa's mother now looked decidedly unhappy that her daughter ignored her advice. Clare rather wondered at the state of the lady's finances. Had she hoped to bill Elsa for her own wardrobe now that her daughter had access to her funds?

Time to mind her own business. "Jack will be struck speechless when he sees you in that gown. I do not expect either of you to linger long at the wedding breakfast. I believe Patience and Henri are planning a musical entertainment and dancing to keep everyone in the village. If only we had a pumpkin to turn into a coach. . ."

Elsa stuck her head from between the curtains. "Villiers says we might use his carriage. We shall depart in style."

"Most excellent! You should arrive in style, as well. You cannot walk down in your new slippers and gown! I'm thinking a wedding a week, with parties and new gowns, would be a lovely idea. Shall we see if Patience or Dottie have any interesting gentlemen in mind?" Clare departed on a gale of laughter. Those two were meant to be spinsters.

As had Clare, she reminded herself. The manor had a way of attracting the right sort of man.

Sometimes, she amended, as she watched the Comte Avignon slip into the library. Another treasure-seeker, no doubt. A short, stout man, starting to bald in back, he dressed more fashionably than any of the Reids.

Well aware the library was seldom empty, Clare followed the French count. Jack's father guarded the books the way a dragon does its hoard. She often found the boys and their tutor in there. Today, Dorothea, the society heiress, and Arnaud had joined them.

They all appeared suspiciously studious when she entered. Clare thought that had more to do with the stranger than her. Usually, when they gathered in here, their arguments over the codes in the paintings and the enigmatic maps were vociferous.

Not acknowledging Dorothea, the girl he'd once courted, Avignon seemed unaware that he'd disturbed anyone. He perused the shelves of ancient fiction, removing volumes and idly flipping their pages. Voltaire, in the original French, might be the most recent edition, and that had been published over forty years ago. The viscountess had not been a reader, and she hadn't the funds to indulge in luxuries.

"You are interested in books, monsieur?" Clare asked, picking up one she'd been reading. She'd love to buy new books, but their budget wasn't any better than that of the late Lady Reid.

"I am interested in everything, my lady. It is how one gets ahead in the world. I have been told the earl left one of the largest libraries in the kingdom, and I am curious. So many in my country have burned." He sounded sincere.

"The duke of Castlefield has the largest these days," Lord de Sackville corrected. "But this one is older. Wycliffes have been collecting since before the first printing press. There is an illuminated manuscript of museum quality that I've had the captain lock away for safety."

"Extraordinary. My family were simple people who worked too hard to have time for reading. The Wycliffes were fortunate men." Avignon removed another book from the shelf and flipped through the pages.

"At the moment, Lord de Sackville is our only librarian. If you wish to borrow a volume, let him know. I believe some are too rare to be removed," Clare warned, knowing they'd already set aside a number of books to be auctioned in hopes of paying off the bank.

"No, I'm not much of a reader," Avignon admitted apologetically. "I was just idling time by indulging my curiosity. I was told there is a billiard room? It was once a favorite sport of mine."

He simply sounded like any man deprived of his home and country and looking for the comfort of the familiar. Clare almost sympathized. "In the west wing, but we have not attempted to restore those rooms. Ask the captain for a key."

She settled into a chair with her book. She didn't know why she was wary of the perfectly proper stranger. As Dorothea had said, her former suitor was polite and all a gentleman should be. In his elegant clothes and neatly barbered hair, he was far more polished than Hunt.

Once he was gone, Clare raised her eyebrows expectantly. "What have you discovered?"

"Nothing yet." Dorothea pushed a list of codes across the table for her to look at. "But judging by the two solved puzzles, it appears they may be in alphabetical order. If that means there is a map for each code, this could take us the rest of our lives."

Arnaud had uncovered the codes hidden in paintings. Jack had discovered that the first two letters in each code stood for one of the earl's siblings and the type of gem he'd given them. They'd found the first map after realizing C stood for Clare's grandmother Clarice and the S stood for her sapphire. The code on the painting for Elsa's grandmother had started with E and R, for Lady Eleanor and her ruby.

They'd eventually worked out a pattern for the numbers following the letters and found they referred to shelf and book order. But that had only worked with those two codes, none of the others.

Clare glanced at the list and wrinkled her nose. "Or numerical order," she added. "Two codes are not enough to go on."

They all groaned and flung their workpapers on the table.

TEN

HUNT: TUESDAY MORNING

CONCERNED ABOUT THE TWINE THEY'D DISCOVERED, HIS YOUNGER cousin and their housekeeper's daughter waited for Hunt in his well-worn study. He knew he ought to open the more spacious study in the west wing, but he felt more in the center of action in the gloomy fortress part of the old manor.

He'd told Henri about the twine across the path at just the right height to send a rider flying. Hunt found it interesting that Henri had thought it necessary to tell Patience, their gardener and orchardist.

"Avignon's valet has been asking questions about the dead man," Henri reported. "Patience, tell Hunt what you heard."

Ah, there was the connection. A gardener was in a better position to hear servants talk.

"Not much." She wrung her hands nervously. "I think it's only because he's such a strange little man for a valet that we listen. George asked if anyone knew Mr. Barbeau or had spoken to him, as if he might be investigating the death and the accident might be suspicious?"

It was definitely suspicious, but Hunt was more interested

in the interrogator. "Did this George person claim to know Barbeau?"

"Said he'd met him in London. He didn't seem very sad about his demise." Patience might be shy, but she wasn't ignorant. "He asked if Barbeau carried any papers on him."

A gentleman's valet had known the son of a French lawyer? Unlikely, unless Barbeau had visited with the Comte Avignon. Perhaps the count was investigating the death?

Hunt had wondered about papers. They had thoroughly searched Barbeau's saddle and clothing and not found any. A visitor should have arrived with letters of introduction. But how would a thief know his victim had fallen unless he waited in the shrubbery? They'd not found any evidence that anyone had hidden there. They didn't even know if Barbeau was the intended victim. Both Bosworth and Arnaud were known to take that path, and if it led to the church's field, then Paul Upton might also use it, although Paul didn't own a horse.

"I think it might be better if I do not question Avignon's valet," Hunt conceded. "Let us pretend we know nothing and just keep an eye on the gentleman. He might simply be prone to gossip and suspicion."

Patience looked relieved. "I'll tell Mother to listen, when she can. She sees the maid and valets often." She bobbed a curtsy and ran out, back to her orchard and garden.

Henri's gaze followed her, but he resisted leaving and dropped into one of Hunt's chairs. "Villiers' coachman was in the tavern last night, making inquiries, although of a more general sort, saying he'd heard about a body and asking the story."

"Given your clientele, I'm sure he heard some hair-raising tales, none of them with a kernel of truth," Hunt said dryly. "Both Villiers and Spalding have been avoiding me. I'll have to lay a trap. I just hate to irritate a marquess and an earl. They're our best allies."

"Villiers and Jack talk horses. Maybe Jack could ask a few questions?"

Hunt shook his head. "They're at odds over the settlements. Jack won't want to annoy Elsa's brother more. I should talk them into hiring us our very own Bow Street Runner."

Henri laughed. "A city man might be a little out of his element here—although it might not hurt to make inquiries in London. We don't know where Barbeau lived, but if he's an émigré. . ."

"I don't know anyone in London. I'll have the solicitors make inquiries. I hate this. I'd like to find any killers before my mother shows up!" Hunt stood. "I'll have to be the one to talk with Villiers and Spalding. We need to repair that damned billiard table."

Understanding Hunt wanted a nonconfrontational setting for a meeting, Henri shrugged. "Perhaps they might enjoy fishing. There are rods and reels in the west wing. Arnaud and I have enjoyed many a fish dinner."

After fleeing France, Arnaud had hidden in the empty manor, and Henri had used it as a home base in his peddler days. They weren't Reids but nephews of the late viscountess. After her death they had no right to visit, but they'd had to feed themselves somehow. Regularly stealing from the caretaker's larder would have attracted unwelcome attention.

"Good thought. I'll see if I can track our two nobles down. All work and no play and all that. . ." Hunt strode out.

Wanting to speak to the lords alone, Hunt didn't make a public display of his fishing trip but sent up a polite scrawl asking if either had any interest in joining him. He hadn't become an officer by waiting for matters to resolve themselves.

Through their servants, Villiers accepted and arranged to meet after lunch. Hunt thought this a highly civilized method of communication and wondered if he could train the household to send him notes instead of barging in on him and making demands.

The Marquess of Spalding was the loftier, older man, stepson of Hunt's aunt and not related to the Reids. He declined the invitation. Hunt was rather relieved to speak with Elsa's more amenable half-brother. The big question became how much could he ask an earl? It wasn't quite the same as discussing military tactics with a general.

Apparently, he didn't have to worry. Villiers came down in his tweed and leather country gear—which no doubt cost a year of Hunt's former wages—and bringing no servant. He took the fishing pole offered. "Hunting should be good in the autumn," he said noncommittally as they traversed the corridor to the garden door, past watching servants.

"I'll need to practice shooting with one eye or I'm likely to take out trees instead of deer." Hunt was learning to live with his difficulty. It was better than being dead or blind.

"Sorry, I'd forgotten the injury. It is not particularly noticeable." Villiers strode through the courtyard as if he had more purpose than indulging in idle pastime.

"Clare claims the scar is dramatic and adds character." Hunt didn't have to look at his phiz and didn't care, but being unable to walk without falling over his feet not only grated on his pride, but was a source of concern for protecting his own.

"Miss Knightley seems to be a sensible woman." Once they reached the wooded, rocky terrain leading to the river, Villiers changed his tone. "Glad you arranged this, Captain. We need to talk."

Not entirely certain he wanted to know about what, Hunt led the way. Even though gray threaded his dark hair, Elsa's half-brother could be no more than forty and had no difficulty keeping up with Hunt's cautious stride on the rough terrain.

"Let me hear what you have to say first," Hunt suggested

as they reached the riverbank. "Let's see if we're of one mind."

"I doubt it." Villiers baited his hook and cast his line toward a shady bank. "Unless you've dealt with French spies."

Spies? "Admittedly, that was not the immediate direction of my thoughts." Hunt moved further down the bank to throw out his line. "*English* spies now. . ."

Villiers grunted. "We've not time for you lot these days. We disbanded most of the army when Napoleon was captured. We barely had word of his escape. The French, however, are a hotbed of intrigue. Always have been."

"Well, my cousins aren't among them." Hunt stated flatly. "If that's your concern, let me lay it to rest."

Although Arnaud was the only one of the household who had known of that path. . .

"I wouldn't have allowed Elsa to remain here had I thought there was any chance of that. I am grateful that my sister is more level-headed than her mother and does not require much of my time, but I look to her welfare. Your cousins are exactly as they seem. Your other relations may not be." Villiers expertly trolled his bait along the edge.

"What other relations? The doddering aunts? They're mostly Clare's family, not mine, despite anything the lawyers claim." As a result of the liaison between the French viscountess and Arnaud's grandfather, his mother's family was decidedly French but hardly accessible in times of war.

"Understood. But we have records that say Lady Reid entertained visitors from France while she was alive." Villiers yanked out his line and cast it into a calmer pool.

"I have not read her journals, but the ladies have. They've made no comment about visitors. In fact, I understood she was lonely." Hunt hoped this was leading to Barbeau. He didn't want more than one mystery on his hands.

"Entertaining the enemy was a traitorous offense. She

would not have provided written evidence. Lady Reid was an intelligent woman. You do not really believe your most excellent brandy has been stored in your cellar since the earl's time?"

Hunt winced. He'd assumed his French grandmother had done a little illegal trading and might have earned a small profit dealing with smugglers, but that was too long ago for him to care much. The British habit of taxing foreign goods was not exactly popular where he came from.

"Back to my *relations*. Who are they and of what have they been accused? You do not think we're still smuggling brandy?" Hunt didn't want to strain his good eye reading the blamed French diaries if he could learn more by listening.

"The viscountess, Gabrielle *Champlain* Reid, came from a once prosperous, large, Catholic family. The Champlains are neighbors of the Lavignes, hence, the liaison, but mostly, the Champlains were seafarers and navy men. Adventurers."

"I have a notion you are not telling me this to introduce me to my ancestry. My mother could have done so had I been interested."

"When your mother was growing up in London, she would have been too young to understand the visits from her French cousins—or remember their servants and friends. During that era, we had only recently ended hostilities with the rebellious Americans. We hated the French court, as usual, and many Englishmen supported their overthrow."

Hunt rolled his eyes at the history lesson. "This was over thirty years ago! Surely any people involved are long retired, at the very least."

Villiers shrugged. "You are here. Your cousins are here. Your families did not vanish. Having been taken by surprise by the American revolt, the British government feared it happening here, so we began developing dossiers on our more active emigres like your family. Avignon is in our files. Barbeau is not. He came directly from France."

"You spied on my grandmother?" Hunt asked in irritation.

The earl shrugged. "I didn't. That was well before my time. Spalding has his ear to the ground more than I do. You need to speak with him to see what set him off. But he investigated your grandmother's family before he allowed his stepmother to visit."

"The Champlains? Do I have more family in England?" Hunt tugged his line, feeling resistance. He trolled carefully. "Did he find something of interest to draw him here? He has not mentioned it to me. His visit is a surprise."

"You'll have to ask him. But he showed me a report on this Barbeau that precedes the boy's death. Before riding here, Monsieur Barbeau attracted interest by visiting with solicitors and acquaintances who have long ties to the Champlain family and dossiers a foot thick."

"The government is spying on émigrés?" Hunt supposed that shouldn't surprise him.

"As needed," Villiers admitted. "We cannot know why Barbeau was coming to the manor. He may only have been meeting one of your guests, but since he is the son of a lawyer in the French village in which Lady Reid and the Lavignes once lived, it is more likely that it had to do with their families. As far as we are aware, the Champlains and Lavignes have been inactive since the Bourbons returned to the throne. The Champlains, in particular, have always played both sides in order to keep their lands and their positions. I doubt that either are of concern to the British government any longer, but they may be to you. Barbeau's death worries me. I wish to persuade Elsa and Jack to return to her estate, where they'll be safe from whomever is responsible for the lad's demise."

Hunt had not told his lofty guests that the death was no accident, but they'd obviously been doing their own investigating—hence coachmen in the tavern and prying valets.

Losing Elsa would devastate Clare. Might she want to

follow her cousin to a more comfortable home in the north? Hunt's gut clenched, but he had to think logically. Was the woman he loved safe here?

He began reeling in his catch. "You cannot persuade those two to do anything they do not want. Jack finally has lands of his own here. You might build them a house on it and let him remove Elsa there if a child is in consideration. Until then, they have other interests, and your tale will not influence them. Jack will want to fight."

"Yes, I'm aware of de Sackville's pugnacious tendencies," the earl said dryly. "Elsa can be persuaded if she thinks she must protect someone. For now, I suppose the best we can do is watch and wait."

"Are we to watch for French strangers? Because Elsa and Jack have just hired a pair of French servants sent by a London agency, and her mother, as you are aware, dragged Avignon out here. Foreigners tend to stand out. We have no others beyond me and my cousins." Hunt hated to suspect people because they weren't English. It seemed ridiculous. *He* wasn't English.

"We've sent for information on the servants," Villiers acknowledged. "Avignon is known to us. Lady Reid's London relations are essentially English these days. They've been here for decades, raised children. I cannot imagine what their sudden interest in Wycliffe Manor might be, but the fact that Barbeau made inquiries of them raises questions."

It did, indeed. "I don't suppose you can give me access to those dossiers?"

"No, but Jones will tell you what he knows. I brought him along for that purpose. He was an aide-de-camp for several generals during the last war and has access to information to which I am not privy."

"I cannot imagine how my cousins and I might be involved. We have no funds, and we've given up any claim to our grandfather's lands in France."

"Money," Villiers said succinctly. "Napoleon needs money. Everyone needs it. If Wycliffe left jewels, someone wants them."

Hunt grimaced. The manor's wealth was in its land and people, not invisible jewels.

He reeled in his catch. Once they'd admired the flounder, he'd decided on his answer. "If thieves can find the jewels where we cannot, they are welcome to a portion. If rumors are true, they're worth enough to fund a nation."

"Not if they go to supply Napoleon's forces."

ELEVEN

CLARE: TUESDAY EVENING

EVEN THOUGH HE AND VILLIERS HAD SUCCESSFULLY RETURNED with enough fish for a first course, Hunt brooded thunderously all afternoon. Clare wondered how the disparate pair found enough to talk about to stay out so long.

The limited kitchen staff delegated the fish cleaning to the ex-soldiers who performed whatever odd jobs were available in exchange for room and board. A manor housing dozens of people needed a great deal more staff than their budget allowed.

But her concern was Hunt. After dinner, she tracked him down in his study. "We are to go for a walk in the moonlight." She held out her hand to him.

He regarded it with suspicion. "It's a cloudy evening."

She raised her eyebrows. He wasn't a stupid man. He got up—which he should have done when she entered, but they were well past the niceties these days. One of the many things she loved about him—he didn't argue with her whims. He took her hand and let her lead him down the hall, past the clock striking three and through the front vestibule, onto what passed for their lawn. The evergreens blocked any sight of moon or clouds, but the occasional bat still flitted about the eaves.

Clare took Hunt's arm and led him away from the house and any listening ears. "You will now tell me what Villiers said to send you into the boughs. If we are to unite our lives for a lifetime, it behooves us to learn to work together, rather than independently. I do believe that is what marriage is about."

"I rather thought marriage was about sharing a bed," he retorted.

"I rather thought that's what you thought," she replied with aridity. "I mean to disabuse you of that quaint masculine notion."

He swung her into his arms, against his chest, and pressed kisses to her hair, which thrilled her far more than she would admit. When his lips trailed down her cheek, she pushed a hand between them. "Not until you tell me what is wrong."

He crushed her close and rested his chin on her head. "I know there was a reason I chose an unromantic, bookish female. I just cannot quite remember it."

She ran fingers beneath his open waistcoat and teased at his thin linen. "Because I was the only woman available, and you could not walk over me."

"Oh, right. I knew I had a reason." He hastily planted a kiss near her lips and set her down before she could punish him. "Villiers claims my grandmother may have dallied with spies or given succor to the enemy. Of course, she would have called them friends and family, silly woman."

Clare rubbed a soothing hand over his hard chest. "I do not remember the viscountess mentioning any such encounters in her journals. And what could she do, stuck here in the midst of rural obscurity with no funds? I do remember her regretting being unable to help her family."

"Yes, well, she may have done no more than give them beds or store their brandy, for all we know. But some of these acquaintances are still around, and Barbeau visited with them, which puts them under suspicion all these years later." He sounded aggrieved.

"His lordship knows Barbeau was murdered?" she asked with an innocence that wouldn't fool a child.

Hunt groaned. "That was not to be common knowledge." He gave it a second thought and shook his head. "Sorry. That was stupid. Meera told you, didn't she? Does everyone know?"

Clare shrugged. "They all speculate. What does the earl expect us to do about the death? We are preparing for wedding guests. Should we send everyone away?" As much as Clare was enjoying meeting family she'd never known, they might have a little too much of a good thing. Sending them away had a certain appeal.

"We may need to send away the Turbins, Jack and Elsa's new servants. Being French apparently puts them under suspicion, although Villiers has nothing on them."

Clare shook her head against his shoulder. "Elsa and Jack are accustomed to having a valet and lady's maid, and they are quite happy with the pair. We are not paying for them, they are. I doubt you can persuade them to turn them off for such a specious reason."

He rubbed her back. "My thinking, also. I cannot imagine how either of those old ducks would have killed anyone on the road. They're much too fussy for murder."

Clare laughed. "So who else does our suspicious earl suspect?"

"Avignon perhaps, but as I understand, he's behaved above suspicion for some years. Arnaud and Henri are most certainly on his list. Although, the lot I must suspect are my grandmother's unknown relations in London, people who have lived here long enough to be English, apparently. And Bosworth, if only out of spite."

Clare wrinkled her nose. "Henri has been schooled in

England for the better part of his life and might pass himself off as English if he tried, but his name alone gives him away. Have your relations changed their names?"

"English and French have intermixed for centuries. That my grandfather knew and married a French woman meant her family was known to his way back then. Her family name is Champlain, which is easily changed to Champ or Champin or anything similar. By now, they'll have married into English families. And if they're spies, wouldn't they use another name anyway? We just cannot hire any more servants until we work this out."

But every guest who arrived brought their own servants. The aunts had a maid. Avignon had a valet. Dottie had brought her maid. The earl and marquess had veritable entourages. "One assumes we don't count Villiers' and Spalding's staffs as suspicious?" she asked with just a touch of cynicism.

"I am not certain I even trust Villiers and Spalding, and I definitely don't trust Bosworth." With that, he bent and silenced her with the kisses she'd hoped for when she'd brought him out here.

At least his American mother and anyone in her company should be above suspicion!

TWELVE

PATIENCE: WEDNESDAY MORNING

Now that she had the occasional aid of an experienced orchardist—although surly Bergstein refused to work for the manor directly—Patience was more confident about developing a routine to rebuild the estate's orchards.

The only problem was that the men she hired didn't like taking orders from a woman. She wore her hair under a man's cap. She was taller than half the men in her employ. She disguised her great bosom beneath the leather apron Henri had purchased for her. But she still wore skirts.

"If I wore trousers, would they listen?" she grumbled to Henri after finding a pair of workers drinking behind the stable.

Henri had sent the pair packing when he came out to accompany her into the field. Even Patience had to accept that a woman alone with half a dozen male workers was not safe. She hated to think it, but some men never grew beyond their animalistic natures. She might be inexperienced but not naïve.

"They expect ladies to be soft-hearted and have no authority." Henri gave her one of his very French, appreciative looks. "And I do not believe trousers will do more than distract us into thinking about legs, so in my humble male opinion, trousers won't help."

"You tell me that because you don't like trousers. But that doesn't mean you're wrong." She was learning how he thought, which was not always comfortable—like now, knowing he was thinking about her legs.

She strode toward the orchard, hating that she loved having him at her side, even when he caused inappropriate. . . tingles. . . like now. She should be more independent, but she thought she helped him as much as he did her, so she struggled with the concept of sharing. "I like growing things. I like *learning* how to grow them even better. I do not like *managing* anyone." She kicked a stone.

"And in the best possible world, Bergstein would manage the men, inspect the trees, and report back to you. But he rightly understands that this crop will barely fill the village larders and will make no profit to pay him. So it is up to you to rebuild. I am understanding that trees are a long-term investment." He stopped when she did.

She inspected the blossoms for the first signs of fruit, delighting when she found tiny apple babies. "I pray every night that we can bring the manor to life again. Even though she misses my father, I've never seen my mother happier. And Paul is thrilled to finally meet his grandfather and have his own parish."

Her brother—she could never call him less even if they'd only just learned they weren't at all related—was educated and might move on some day. Patience would not. She'd do whatever she must to stay in the village where she'd spent her first years. After all the years of wandering, she *needed* a home and a place of her own.

"If we must pay the bank loan, it will be difficult," always honest Henri admitted. "I'm of half a mind that we should take the ramshackle place apart to find the jewels and rebuild a more modest edifice."

Patience glanced back at the sprawling manor on top of the hill. The heavy gray stone walls blotted half the sky from this angle. The staircase towers jutted upward to resemble a medieval fortress.

"It's part of history, *our* history. I've only just learned that I'm descended from earls! You can't understand how special it is knowing one has family where there has been none. I like to imagine my ancestors marching back through all the centuries. And yes, your idea is far more practical and mine is romantic. But what if there are no jewels to be found? How would we rebuild?"

"You have caught the flaw in my argument." He held a ladder so she might reach a higher branch.

"Clare says we must pay attention to all the strangers joining us, especially their servants and all the new hires. I am not very good with people. Mother tries to listen, but she's so busy opening unused bedrooms for visitors—she can't be everywhere." Deciding the gnawed leaves she'd spotted were not an insect problem, she climbed down.

Henri caught her waist and swung her against him. She gasped, but he merely pecked her cheek and set her down, grinning at his audaciousness. She was slowly growing used to his French ways and enjoyed them a little too much. She no longer thought him a rake, but he was much too bold.

And she *tingled* even more.

"Anyone digging holes in the cellar or knocking down walls is suspicious," he declared. "Beyond that, we can only watch and listen and share notes. That last is important. I might not think anything of the Turbins showing up in the tavern and talking to strangers, but if you tell me they had a private conversation with Avignon before doing so—then we know to watch closer."

Heat flushing her cheeks, Patience nodded and strode toward the walnut trees. "Mother is keeping an eye on the Turbins. She is wary of foreigners."

Henri snorted. "We are all foreigners to this village. Perhaps we should keep an eye on the *locals*, who once knew the earl and viscountess."

Patience halted and turned to stare at him. "You are correct. Only someone familiar with that hidden footpath might know to set a trap there."

Henri rubbed his rather arrogant nose. "How do we learn who knows about it? A race?"

She lit up. "That can be arranged!"

THIRTEEN

HUNT: WEDNESDAY NOON

HUNT RUBBED HIS WEARY HEAD. "A RACE? YOU WISH TO HOLD A race for the wedding breakfast? To see who will break their necks first?"

Henri bounced gleefully. "We'll start at the church. The hidden footpath is out of sight, in the overgrown field behind the chapel. The drive is the only *visible* route to the manor. We offer some small prize for fetching something the bride left at the house or some such. It will look like an idle pastime. Everyone will take the drive, except the one who knows the shorter path."

"I'd far rather have it done before Sunday, but you're right, we need to have the entire village gathered. Although there is no guaranty that our culprit will actually attend services."

"True. But they may attend the breakfast festivities. Every little bit we learn is useful. With staff bustling about at all hours, it is difficult to remark on odd behavior. Although Villiers' fancy secretary seems to be spending an inordinate amount of time in the library with Bosworth." Henri disdainfully pronounced *Villiers* as Hunt had originally, giving the "i" it's own syllable, instead of *Vill-yers*.

Hunt ignored his cousin's disdain and pondered his information. The secretary would be Jones, the generals' former liaison Hunt was supposed to consult, should he ever find the time. "Poor fellow doesn't have much space for writing correspondence in the cubbyhole we've provided in the attic. I'm more concerned about Bosworth and brandy smugglers, people who know that hidden footpath. I will now suspect anyone who arrives claiming to be family." Hunt grumpily followed Henri out.

Quincy met them in the main corridor. "Sir Oswald Champlain and Lady Champlain to see you, captain."

Speak of the devil. . . *Damnation.* Villiers was practically prophetic. His grandmother's relations had English titles now? And were rude to boot, arriving without invitation. At least they hadn't ridden up by the hidden path.

"I don't know them. Let them cool their heels in the great room. Send for Clare, if she can be found." Irritated with the unexpected intrusion, Hunt turned to his cousin. "Presumably, Lady Reid's distant family. Fetch Arnaud. I'm not going in there alone."

Henri whistled in surprise and trotted off toward the gallery. Arnaud was the easiest member of the family to find. As long as there was daylight, he was in front of his easel.

Hunt dashed upstairs—although dashing with a limp was crippling. His Aunt Elaine, Lady Spalding, sailed into his path before he reached safe harbor.

"A carriage arrived," she said crisply, belying her plump, cuddly appearance. She was a dowager marchioness, after all, and accustomed to giving orders. "If it is your mother, I must go down with you."

Hunt tried not to show his shock. He had thought his mother and her sister at odds. "I will be certain to let you know the moment she's introduced. This is a Sir Oswald and Lady Champlain, presumably your mother's family. Do you know them? If so, I will be grateful if you will attend on them with me."

Hunt had never had to deal with a large family until he arrived in England. His American father's family might be large, but they were scattered over distance and separated by poor roads. Here, everyone was within a day or two's drive.

"The Champlains?" she asked in suspicion, sniffing. "I do not recollect my mother associating with such. If you wish to interrogate them, wait until dinner so I may have time to study them."

So much for friendly family.

"I appreciate that." Leaving her to take that as she would, he threw himself into the hands of his new batman. He had a hard time calling the rough ex-soldier a valet.

Hunt had spent these last months dealing with the eccentric Reids, his purported grandfather's family. But the Champlains were his *mother's* family. He knew his mother would be eager to meet them when she arrived. He had to be polite and not heave them out for arriving without invitation.

"They's French?" James asked, forgetting to imitate his haughtier peers. "We'll be consorting with the enemy!"

"Their lordships know of them, apparently. Villiers says the Champlains are more English than French. I'm American-French. Am I the enemy?" Impatiently, Hunt flung off his work coat and waistcoat.

His batman-valet struggled with that concept as he located proper attire. "*You* are not abetting the enemy," he grudgingly conceded.

"Not these days, anyway. And I will not accuse you of murdering the Frenchman in the lane." Although now that he thought it, Hunt had to add that as a possible motive. . . had someone killed Barbeau simply because he was French? Carrying a message from France? A spy?

"That is generous of you, sir." Not unintelligent, James shut up and performed his duties.

Clare met Hunt in the upper hall as he emerged from his chamber. She patted his starched and itchy neckcloth. "Very nice, captain. You shall astound our visitors with your gentility—if you do not speak. It won't be much fun, though." She beamed saucily.

He growled at her assessment of his incivility. "You are looking very pleased with yourself."

"Mrs. Upton has accumulated furnishings for several new bedchambers. We are prepared for guests, even if they are impolite enough to arrive without warning. This would not have been possible before our new housekeeper's arrival." She took his arm and let him lead her down the stairs. "Let us see if your family is as obnoxious and demanding as mine."

"Except for the aunts, the earl's descendants are amazingly pleasant, actually. Mad, perhaps, but easy to go along with." Apparently, eccentricity suited him better than propriety. He hadn't known that about himself, but he should have.

Arnaud and Henri had already taken chairs in the great chamber where Quincy took guests he thought needed to be impressed. The two-story cathedral ceiling of solid oak, massive iron chandeliers, and the dozens of gold-framed paintings certainly dwarfed anyone thinking highly of themselves.

Sir Oswald rose at their entrance. Graying thin hair, pompous nose much like Hunt's own, jowly and portly, he appeared to be of middle age—old enough to have met Lady Reid as a viscountess, but young enough not to have known her prior to her marriage. The viscountess would have been in her late sixties now, had she lived.

Sir Oswald bowed and held out a hand to his wife, raising her to her tiny feet.

Lady Champlain was tiny all over, barely five feet, if Hunt was any judge. Pouty lips, dark eyes rimmed with some cosmetic, she was younger than her husband but most likely in her thirties now. She smiled prettily and curtsied.

"You are much like your grandmother!" Sir Oswald exclaimed.

Since he'd never known Lady Reid, Hunt couldn't attest to that as fact or fiction.

Hunt waited until everyone returned to their seats and were sipping tea or coffee, indulging in small talk, before he asked, "We had no notion of your existence. How did you know where to find us?"

He thought Clare might pinch him for his rudeness, but she merely nibbled delicately on one of Elsa's delicious scones. Henri and Arnaud stuffed their maws and waited expectantly.

"Your mother wrote us, of course. She realized that you didn't know our side of the family," Sir Oswald said.

Ah, Sir Oswald would be about Hunt's mother's age—cousins, presumably. But they hadn't invited people they didn't know. Why were the Champlains here?

"I had not realized anyone from my grandmother's side of the family lived in England—besides Henri and Arnaud, of course. Did you not know of each other?" Hunt was trying to sort out the French family tree, but it wasn't neatly embroidered and hanging on his study wall as the English Reid tree was.

Henri and Arnaud were Lavignes. Their Grandmother Champlain had been Lady Reid's sister, if he recalled correctly.

"Foolish boys." Lady Champlain tapped Arnaud's knee with her fan. "They never sought us out. The families have not been in touch for decades, of course."

"We were unaware any of our grandmother's Champlain family had left France," Arnaud said. "There was no mention of you."

Hunt sat back and sipped his coffee, watching warily. Arnaud did not speak often in company, but he did so with much thought. He'd obviously been searching his memory banks for these people.

"Our family left before you were born," Sir Oswald explained. "I'm a seafarer, earned my fortune in the Caribbean in my youth, knighted for capturing a pirate brigantine and returning it to the English crown with its gold intact. I lost touch with our family after Lady Reid died. Napoleon put rather a crimp in my seafaring days."

If he was a smuggler, they couldn't prove it one way or another, although Hunt thought he might consult Villiers and Spalding about the knighthood. Dinner tonight might be interesting if everyone attended.

"Well, we are delighted to make your acquaintance, sir, my lady," Clare said politely. "I'm sure Mrs. Huntley will be thrilled to see you when she arrives."

Was that a flicker of alarm? Had they counted on his mother *not* sailing the Atlantic?

Hunt continued, without giving away his doubts, "I assume you knew my mother while she was presented to society?"

"My lady and I weren't married at the time," Sir Oswald said. "I was at sea and didn't meet my lovely wife until after Cousin Frances married her American and sailed away to her new home. I must congratulate you on your upcoming nuptials! I understand they're to be this Sunday?"

Villiers' warning of French spies came back loud and clear.

His mother didn't know of their impending marriage. How did this stranger?

77

FOURTEEN

ELSA: WEDNESDAY DINNER

"The Champlains arrived with a valet, a maid, a coachman, and a footman," Elsa whispered as the family gathered in the great hall before dinner. "Their servants are already asking questions." Given her rule over the kitchen, she had a unique perspective on any newcomers.

"The more I think on it," Clare whispered back, "the less likely it seems that new arrivals might have murdered that poor man. It had to be someone already here."

"The Turbins?" Elsa asked in alarm. She liked her mostly silent new maid. At least, Marie knew how to fix her horrible hair when she needed it, like tonight. "Surely not. They have been busy setting up our new suite, mending and cleaning our ragged clothes. We truly have become careless about such things since arriving here."

"I cannot fathom the Turbins climbing trees," Clare agreed. "It would more likely be one of the new men working in the orchard."

"Would any of them have known the footpath? I hate to think it of a local." Elsa pursed her lips and tried to recall all the new hires, but they mostly ate in the barn. Their rooms were over the stable.

"Hunt sent locals to assizes for murder just last week," Clare reminded her.

Elsa winced. That had been a painful episode for the humble Uptons. But Gravesyde Priory was simply too small to harbor entire nests of evil.

Most of the people working in her kitchen had been hired from elsewhere, including her estate in Newchurch, so she was free to believe that they were not involved. "Locals would have known Lady Reid and the stories about missing jewels, so perhaps you're right." Elsa nodded toward the entrance. "There they are. I will politely meet Hunt's relations tonight, but tomorrow, you're on your own."

"Meera has all but deserted me," Clare said mournfully. "If you abandon me, I will have to enlist Dottie in my detecting."

"You will have to drag Dottie out of the library first. She and Jack's father have chosen to dine there tonight. Enlist Lavender." Although their seamstress cousin was too young for this gathering of elders and looking decidedly bored. She needed young men like the curate or the tutor to entertain her. "Meera is a newlywed. She and Walker must be left to establish their own customs. They have all but taken over the empty offices in the back hall, even setting up a parlor and dining table. They deserve a break from us—and from being stared at by rude strangers. Go forth and greet your guests and dubious in-laws-to-be."

Elsa knew that Hunt's African friend had amused himself at first by defiantly showing up at the dinner table with haughty aristocrats, but the Reids weren't very haughty. They had spoiled his fun by accepting him as the brilliant man he was. And Meera. . . didn't much care if people accepted her brown skin. It was her ability as a physician she hated questioned. Elsa assumed Clare's friend simply preferred Walker's intelligent company to that of unknown guests. Smart lady.

With a pasted smile, Clare strode away to greet the newcomers.

Elsa smiled in relief as Jack finally left the men in their corner to join her now that she was alone.

"You are looking particularly splendid this evening, my love. Although I do miss the flour on your cheeks and your delightful *eau de* vanilla." He brushed a kiss behind her ear.

She was glad she'd taken time to have her hair curled properly so he could blow on the ringlets. "That is because you went hungry too long while soldiering, and you are trying to make up for it." They'd been friends too long to indulge in polite flirting.

"Well, there were other needs neglected besides my stomach," he whispered, proving her point. "Do we need to test our new bed?"

"And scandalize the Turbins? Shame on you." She tapped him with her fan. "Clare believes you and I are in a particularly good situation for learning more about our new guests from their servants and about any murderous locals. I might speak with their maid and valets but the coachman and footman are all yours."

"Already done, my dear. I asked about Champlain's horseflesh, and their coachmen and I are now the best of friends. I expect to meet them at Henri's tavern this evening. These gatherings were far more entertaining when you wore flour, and Walker glared menacingly. We are too polite these days." He bowed to their guests as they arrived, before Elsa could hit him again.

She had loved Jack since he'd been no more than a schoolboy who hadn't minded a bossy, chubby child following him about. She adored him even more now as the man of integrity he'd become. But that mischievous boy still lurked beneath the sophisticated façade and brown curls.

"Lady Elsa, so very pleased to meet you." Tiny Lady Champlain dipped a deep curtsy, meant to impress the daughter of an earl. "And your mother is the delightful Mrs. Turner standing with the Comte Avignon, is she not? They make a lovely couple."

Actually, since her mother was probably years older, the comte was shorter and more rotund, and the only thing they had in common was most likely poor finances, Elsa wasn't in agreement. But perhaps they were both *shallow* enough to be a couple. She didn't know Avignon well enough to judge.

"You know them from London?" she asked politely.

"Oh, no, we do not move in the same circles. We have seen them at the opera and about town, of course. It was an exciting Season. And now Napoleon is back, and we are preparing for war again! Will you be joining Wellington, Mr. de Sackville?" She batted long dark lashes at them.

The lady's husband clucked his tongue. "Now, my lady, we mustn't bring up such unpleasant topics at dinner." He spoke again before she could. "We hear you are to be wed this Sunday. Our congratulations. Will Lord Villiers be here to give you away?"

"We thank you. He has agreed to attend, yes," Jack replied. "I understand you were acquainted with the late Lady Reid?"

Testing one's shared acquaintance was a time-honored tradition, but Jack's query was fraught with nuance. Elsa hid a smile and squeezed his arm in approval. They had yet to solve the puzzle of how this pair knew of the nuptials. Only family had been informed. Even Hunt's mother had not had time to receive her invitation, so that excuse was spurious.

"The viscountess was my cousin, of course," Sir Oswald said with confidence. "Lovely woman, raised two wonderful daughters. I hope to see them again."

"Your wish is to be partially granted. Mrs. Huntley has yet to arrive, but her sister is here." With malice aforethought, Elsa nodded at the door where Lady Spalding and Lady Lavinia opportunely prepared to make their grand entrance.

The Champlains glanced up in what appeared to be shock. Had they not realized the ladies had taken residence in this rural outpost? Or had they thought the family would shun the viscountess's illegitimate American offspring?

Usually, the aunts stayed in their suite rather than bother dressing for dinner. Tonight, Elaine, Lady Spalding—the viscountess's eldest daughter and of an age with Sir Oswald —had garbed herself in a deep maroon taffeta of French origin from a different era. The taffeta parted over an elegant, white silk underskirt. Her plump bosom sported the famed Reid Diamond pendant she'd no doubt worn to her presentation many decades ago.

Family tradition was to flaunt the Reid jewels on special occasions. Each of the third earl's descendants had worn a different set of the famed jewels for their presentations, flagrantly defying custom by flaunting the full array of earrings, tiaras, and necklaces in front of royalty. But the original jewelry had vanished into the earl's vaults and, other than the pendants, had not been seen in decades.

Lord Wycliffe, the fourth and last earl, had given the pendants to his sisters and daughters, who passed them on to their offspring. Elsa's mother was wearing her ruby tonight on a chain with some diamonds Elsa's father had given her. Elsa had worn it for her presentation.

Lady Lavinia, Lord Wycliffe's sister, wore her emerald. Tall and thin, her gray pompadour pinned with diamonds, their great-aunt was elegant in gray silk. The emerald was large enough to bend her neck, had that appendage not been so stiff.

If one of their guests was a thief, he or she had full view of the few remaining family treasures. Elsa silently cheered the old ladies' appearance. They had very definitely known the late viscountess. Did they know these supposed relations?

The Reid family had scorned the viscountess after she'd returned from France with a child most obviously not her husband's. The Champlains may have assumed the ladies would not acknowledge Hunt. Had the Champlains felt safe introducing themselves because they thought no one from the earl's family would be present? Even Hunt had been caught by surprise that his mother was willing to travel the Atlantic.

Had they actually received a letter from Hunt's mother or simply pretended communication?

Elsa watched in interest as everyone else in the room presented themselves to the pair of aristocratic gorgons, but the Champlains sank into the shadows behind Jack and Elsa.

"We should greet them," Elsa said cheerfully, tugging Jack's arm. "The ladies so seldom deign to join us." She turned to their guests. "Will you come with us, sir, my lady? I'm sure they will be delighted to greet you."

"No, really, we could not," Lady Champlain demurred.

"I had no idea that they visited," Sir Oswald muttered. "They have enormous estates of their own, do they not?"

"They have no family living at their estates to boss around. Come along, this is what weddings are for—families meeting families of the newlyweds." Elsa sailed confidently across the great hall on Jack's arm. She could hear him chuckling.

Chubby and bullied by those older than she, Elsa had lacked authority when she'd been young. Since then, she'd learned to run her own estate and command kitchens. . . and the love of this man who wanted her just as she was, plump and frumpy and not docile. Surrounded by friends and family who appreciated her, she no longer cringed at presenting herself to her proud relations.

She curtsied and planted kisses on their rouged cheeks. "I am so glad you will be joining us this evening!"

They patted her fondly, kissed Jack boldly, then looked over their shoulders. "And your companions?" Lady Spalding, Hunt's aunt, asked with an innocent look on her plump, rouged face.

Elsa turned to observe the Champlains attempting to blend in with the woodwork. "I am rather convinced you have not met them. He claims to be Lady Reid's cousin, I believe, come to visit his dear. . ." She wrinkled up her nose and consulted the plump dowager. "Would that make you and Mrs. Huntley his second cousins?"

"If so, I never met him," the dowager Lady Spalding said quite firmly. "My mother's relations were a seedy lot, admittedly. I may have met an uncle or two, but that was over thirty years ago. They did not linger long once my grandfather cut off access to his fortune. I do not recognize them as part of Society, if they are claiming that."

Elsa had not realized that the aristocratic Reids had scorned the viscountess for her *family* as well as her scandalous affair. Interesting. Poor Lady Reid. And it was not as if marrying a Reid had improved her position. The late viscount's madness had made him a murderous, immoral lecher—although the Reids never acknowledged that either.

Adam, Quincy's son and their only footman, appeared in the doorway to announce dinner. Elsa prayed her assistant cook had the meal in order. She'd planned a simple menu, one that would not task her inexperienced staff.

Hunt led both of the older ladies in, seating them on either side of his chair at the head of the table. Taking Clare's arm, Henri, garbed in his elegant second-hand clothes, accompanied by Arnaud, in his shabby remnants from France, seated themselves at the opposite end. Elsa giggled at their foolish attempt at precedence, took Jack's arm, and beat her mother and Avignon to a place near Clare, leaving her mother to choose Hunt's end of the table.

Lavender settled in the middle, with her pup probably at her toes.

Villiers and Spalding had declined to join them, as had their banker, and Patience and her brother were most likely dining with their mother below, keeping an eye on the kitchen. Elsa was grateful for their diligence.

By the time everyone found a seat, the Champlains were nowhere to be seen.

"Do I send Adam to be certain they're not absconding with the silver?" Jack asked in a whisper when he made the same realization.

"Hunt has already asked Ned to watch the door," Clare whispered back. "We are hoping to train him to help Walker. He and Adam are learning to communicate using a sign language Meera is teaching them from a book she found in the library."

"Ned cannot hear anything the pair are saying," Elsa said worriedly. Deaf-mute, adolescent Ned usually helped her in the kitchen, but he was exceedingly bright and eager. Washing pots was a bit beneath his capabilities.

"He reads lips well," Henri informed her. "That's how he knows what we are saying when we did not think he understood."

"That's most impolite of him." Jack speared a spring green. "Now he knows all the endearments I call Elsa and can steal them for his own purposes."

"I will have him teach me," Henri declared with a laugh. "French endearments are unwelcome in these times."

While the men fell into discussing the gathering war clouds, Clare and Elsa kept an eye on the great-aunts conversing with Hunt, Avignon, and Elsa's mother.

"I do believe they are enjoying themselves," Clare murmured. "I have not seen Lady Lavinia laugh, ever. What is Hunt telling her?"

"My mother spent half my season trying to attract their attention. She's in her element." Elsa studied the tableau. "Avignon doesn't seem intimidated. Didn't Dottie say he once courted her? I assume that's why she's declining to eat with us."

"I wonder if Avignon knew Dottie was here and inveigled an invitation so he might see her? She has a considerable dowry."

"And my mother has run through most of hers. So if Avignon is not wealthy, they both need to look elsewhere. The younger marquess my mother was leading along must have found better pastures." Elsa hated being cynical, but her mother simply played a role learned in her youth and never unlearned. She'd snared an earl at twenty. Over forty. . . She really couldn't hope for someone looking for heirs.

As the last dinner plate was removed and the delicate strawberry trifle presented, Elsa allowed herself a sigh of relief. Anne had accomplished the impossible—a dinner almost of London standards despite the antiquated stove and inexperienced staff. She'd prepared the trifle herself, so did not worry about the final course.

Clare led the applause as the first strawberries of the season were delivered. Hunt actually remembered to send his congratulations down to Anne for a job well done. And toplofty Lady Lavinia condescended to look down her lorgnette and the long table in Elsa's direction. "You have trained the staff well, my dear. I trust when you return to your estate as a bride, you will be prepared to take on your proper role as lady of the house?"

Elsa blinked in surprise. Jack grabbed her hand beneath the table and squeezed. What had her mother been telling the old lady? She'd obviously been toadying to Lady Lavinia's preferences.

Before she could formulate a reply, the butler appeared in the doorway with his silver salver of visiting cards. "The Comte and Madame Lavigne, sir. They say they are expected?"

Arnaud was the Comte Lavigne, was he not?

FIFTEEN

CLARE AND HUNT: WEDNESDAY EVENING

SEEING ARNAUD'S FIST CLENCH, CLARE PUT A CAUTIONARY HAND on his coat sleeve. "It may be a ruse." She nodded at a stormy Hunt on the other end of the table, who had already flung down his napkin. "Go with him, please. Tell him you are both to behave until you have the story."

Henri pushed back his chair when his brother did. She didn't have to tell him to behave. Henri was a charmer who knew how to pacify tempers—and how to deal with those who wouldn't pacify. She was grateful he hadn't departed for his tavern this evening.

"Clarissa, you should go with them," Lady Lavinia commanded. "One cannot leave Madame Lavigne alone to deal with male tempers. She is a guest."

Clare sighed, set down her napkin, and muttered, "After my mother died, I missed having someone to tell me what I should do. It's been a few years since then. Don't let them take away my trifle."

"I'll go with you, although we could call Mrs. Upton instead." Elsa rose with her. "She is family as well as housekeeper."

"And have her flee when the men come to blows?"

Grateful for Elsa's company, Clare led the way down the corridor to. . . the shabby parlor? Not the great hall? Interesting choice for titled guests.

Wide and long as the formal dining room, the front parlor —although well-worn—was large enough to entertain in comfortably. Except Hunt and his large cousins blocked all view of the interior with their height, broad shoulders, and intimidating stances.

Irritated, Clare tapped Hunt with her fan. He brushed her off as if she were a fly. Obviously, his temper had overcome his wits.

"Uncle Jules?" Arnaud was asking incredulously.

He rattled off a spate of French Clare loosely translated as *What the devil do you think you're doing?* Only less polite.

She and Elsa both poked him in the ribs with their fans. Arnaud glanced down in surprise, obviously so caught up in this encounter that he hadn't noticed their arrival. They took advantage to sweep around him.

Past the barrier of masculinity languished two weary women, one young, another most likely her mother, given the resemblance. They wore black bonnets and cloaks that might be a hundred years old for all anyone could tell from their threadbare state.

The distinguished gentleman was no less shabby, enhancing his resemblance to ragged Arnaud, except for the threads of gray at his temples and the deep furrows in his brow. At sight of Clare and Elsa, he bowed deeply.

"Introductions, *s'il vous plaît*," Clare demanded, before turning to Elsa. "Make certain Quincy has called Mrs. Upton. They will need rooms."

Elsa nodded understanding and swept out to direct their meager army of servants.

The younger woman wept and clung to her mother's arm as if frightened. Given the intimidating males looming over them, Clare couldn't blame her.

"Jules Lavigne, my ladies." Undeterred, their guest gestured at his family. "My wife and daughter, Adele and Sofia. We have traveled an immense distance under turbulent circumstances. I would be most grateful if you would see to them while I. . ." He glanced at Arnaud. "Barbeau was supposed to explain!"

"Barbeau?" Hunt straightened. His voice echoed that of his cousins.

Oh dear. Clare prayed their guests weren't close to the dead man laid out in the crypt below.

"We sent him ahead, over a month ago," this unknown Lavigne protested. "He was to speak with the solicitors and learn if anyone in either family survived. We were told you were killed, monsieur! We did not know of young Henri's whereabouts. We are looking for Lady Reid's family. Barbeau sent a message saying he'd learned the last known location of Lady Reid, and he was to come here. When we did not hear. . ."

"Explanations, later." Clare nodded at Mrs. Upton, who'd just appeared in the doorway, still tying on her apron and narrowing her eyes at the unexpected visitors. "Mrs. Upton, these are the Lavignes, relations of the late viscountess. Are there a few rooms ready where they may rest?"

Clare turned back to the visitors. "Do I understand you have just traveled from *France*?"

"Oui, mademoiselle." The older woman curtsied and finally spoke. "An old friend smuggled us out. War has taken our sons. I could not lose Jules as well. We thought. . ."

"I will explain," her husband said curtly. "Go with the ladies. I will be with you shortly."

Clare would have liked to listen in, but she knew the men wouldn't converse until the women left. She would rely on Henri to keep them from blows.

"We just freshened the tower suite Oliver was using," Mrs. Upton said, leading the way up the marble stairs. "The rooms

89

are not fully furnished, but they are clean. I've had a maid take hot water up since the grates aren't lit. We'll have fresh linens on the beds shortly."

"The manor has been empty since the death of Lady Reid," Clare explained as they traversed the long upper corridor to the back hall. "Most of us here are relations to the late earl, including Mrs. Upton, who has performed wonders in opening up unused rooms since her arrival. We cannot offer luxury. Most of us are providing for ourselves. I will see if Lady Elsa's maid will help with your attire. Do you have trunks?"

"Only one. We did not dare pack much." The older lady Clare assumed was Adele Lavigne did her best to straighten her sagging shoulders and speak in clear English. "I am sorry Jean-Jacques did not warn you. He is usually most. . . reliable."

"Monsieur Barbeau was a servant?" Clare asked carefully.

"My fiancé," the younger woman said with a touch of pride. "He has been wonderful in assisting us."

Oh dear. Clare panicked.

HUNT OPENED THE SIDEBOARD WHERE THEY STORED THE BRANDY. He poured snifters for everyone. "I assume you were introduced as Comte Lavigne because you thought Arnaud had perished with his parents?"

Arnaud snatched a glass and paced. Hunt's artistic cousin normally avoided strong spirits, so Hunt knew he was in turmoil. Neither of his cousins had greeted this relation with enthusiasm.

"Oui." The older man accepted the glass gratefully, helping himself to the bowl of nuts Elsa's staff had set out.

They'd normally bring in other refreshments after dinner, but the intrusion had upset routine. Hunt wondered if he could have the strawberries delivered in here. He'd been looking forward to them.

Jules Lavigne turned to Arnaud. "We were told you died in prison. We could find no trace. And Henri. . ." He shrugged and glanced apologetically at his nephew. "We had not heard from you in years. It seemed expedient to claim the title while the Bourbon king sat on the throne."

"And not so expedient when Napoleon returned." Arnaud glared at a smoke-darkened oil painting on the wall while he sipped his brandy and explained to Hunt, "Jules is my uncle, my father's youngest brother. Also a descendant of the Champlains. Our grandfather married Lady Reid's sister."

He turned back to his uncle. "Captain Huntley is Lady Reid's grandson."

Jules shook his head wearily. "Titles are meaningless these days. It is family that matters. It is good to meet you, Captain Huntley. I am grateful for your hospitality."

Henri was the first to take a seat. He sipped his brandy and regarded his uncle. Feeling this might be a long evening, Hunt followed suit. He waited for Arnaud to explain about the messenger.

Henri spoke instead. "This Barbeau you sent ahead, how do you know him?"

The older man waited politely for Arnaud to sit. When he didn't, he dropped into an armchair. A maid hastened in with a tray of crackers, cheese, and fruit. He didn't even wait for her to leave before grabbing a handful, as if starved, which he no doubt was.

Hunt gestured at the maid. "Have a meal sent up to the ladies and a plate brought in here for Monsieur Lavigne, please."

"I apologize." Jules gestured at the tray. "We have gone without for so long, that it is habit to take when it's available. You do not need to go to trouble for us."

"Don't be an ass, *mon oncle*." Henri helped himself to a

wizened apple. "We left France for similar reasons. Tell us of Barbeau."

Jules looked mildly puzzled at this insistence. "He is a neighboring lad of good family. Hard working but a younger son. He did not wish to follow his father into law, so he has been helping us restore the fields. He and Sofia would make a match of it if they had the money to do so. That is why. . ."

"He came here hunting Grandmother Gabrielle's pearls," Arnaud said in disgust, finally settling in a wing chair by the cold grate. "Barbeau mentioned pearls in his last breath, remember?"

Hunt remembered, but he had no words to take away the shock on the face of his guest at Arnaud's crude reference. He wished Clare were here.

Henri flung a walnut kernel at his brother. "You are a clod, *mon frere*. You came here hoping for the same, so do not expect less of the rest of the family. The Champlain pearls were worth a king's ransom and were probably the reason the English pig married our great-aunt."

The argument apparently gave their uncle time to recover from his shock. "Last breath? Jean-Jacques, he is. . ."

"Dead, yes." Arnaud threw back another swallow of brandy. "Murdered, most likely by some other fool who is seeking easy fortune."

Jules buried his face in his hands and shook his head. "We sent him here in hopes of saving him!"

"Take Monsieur Lavigne upstairs," Hunt ordered. "Let him eat with his family. I don't think the loss of the pearls is the problem here."

The loss of hope, a future, and a good friend would destroy any man. He'd been in a place to know.

SIXTEEN

CLARE: THURSDAY MORNING

THE NEXT MORNING, HAVING SPENT A NIGHT RESTLESSLY TOSSING and fretting, Clare carried her morning tea toward her office in vague hope of finishing her copying job. Last night, she'd taken the coward's way out and let Monsieur Lavigne break the news of Barbeau's death. Her strawberry trifle had been soggy by the time she returned to it, but she'd eaten it anyway to hide her tears. This morning she was too distraught for breakfast.

Before reaching her desk, she noticed the door to the unused withdrawing room was open. Odd, since the cluttered chamber hadn't been used in decades. Vaguely remembering recommending it to Dottie, she wandered across the hall to see what was happening.

Anything was better than thinking of that weeping child upstairs, mourning the loss of her beloved. The Lavignes hadn't been in the breakfast room—Bosworth had been. Clare didn't know why he was lingering, but she was in no humor to speak with the banker.

It took a bit of study to even find Dottie amid the abandoned tables, chairs, desks. . . draperies? Cobwebs and dust weren't as bad as they could have been. At some point, Mrs.

Upton must have attempted to put it in order—before guests began arriving.

Clare noted a gold silk sofa buried under an upside-down game table, which in turn held a three-legged stool. It was furniture purgatory, where unusable pieces went to wait assignment to the attics or the fireplace.

And every surface was now covered with open books— Lady Reid's journals?

Apparently, Dottie had taken her suggestion seriously. Clare winced and located the younger woman reading a page she'd marked with a long piece of red yarn. "Are you having any success?" Clare asked, out of politeness.

Dottie wrinkled her brow. "I cannot know for certain. The room is drafty." She gestured at the single drapery hanging over the ancient windows—blowing with the squall outside.

"The whole point of heavy draperies is to prevent drafts." Clare picked up one of the velvet ones laying across a battered desk, but it was moth-eaten. "And these old fire-places are no better. It's the reason we've kept the wings closed. We cannot possibly heat all these rooms come winter."

"Or dust them," Dottie said dryly, picking up a journal and brushing off the grime before showing it to Clare. "I took out the journals written during Lady Reid's last years. I left them open mid-book, with yarn to mark the page. Most of them remained untouched, but a couple have had their pages turned. I just cannot tell if a draft might have blown them over."

"This is the page it opened to?" Clare had skimmed many of the journals over the past weeks since they'd been found, but they were in poorly spelled, badly written French. The early ones had been fascinating, but the later ones had mostly been tedious. She hadn't paid attention to details. "On this page, she is complaining about English food, as usual. She says C came to tea. I had not thought she had many visitors, but Mrs. Upton stayed here at one point, so I suppose she visited occasionally after marrying the curate. There may have been others. I don't know why everyone used initials instead of names. It's most annoying."

"I should imagine they had so few acquaintances that the abbreviation made sense at the time. I doubt she's trying to conceal the identity of anyone having tea." Dottie took the book back and ran her finger down the tiny scribbles. "There's a passage at the bottom. . . *The G's tell me the cart arrived. C was pleased.* A cart?"

Clare glanced at the date. "1792, I was still in the nursery, but I recall from my history reading that was the year the revolution spilled from France, and the continental war began. Perhaps we need to do as the boys are doing and read these journals with the news of the time in mind? Although I daresay the G's are the Gaithers. They were here as caretakers when we arrived and had been servants since the days of the viscount." Elderly and suffering dementia by the time she and Hunt arrived, but she did not need to speak ill of the dead.

Dottie's frown deepened. "Since the messenger was murdered, the ghost is even more agitated. Or perhaps it's our new guests. I'd hoped that the page might tell us something useful. Could this be code, like the scratches in the earl's paintings?"

"Code? She wished to be reminded that the cart arrived on that date? That C visited? I'm sorry, I cannot see it. I think you need to remove the books from drafts." Clare looked up at the arrival of Roberts, the Earl Villiers' young valet, if she remembered rightly. Generally, she had little to do with other people's servants. She waited for an explanation of his appearance.

Tall, blandly blond with a forgettable face, he glanced around at the jumble of furniture and scattered books. Being an imaginative sort, she almost felt a frisson from the ghost.

He seemed to be paying too much attention to a storage room.

Or too many deaths and talk of jewels and pearls had left her entirely too suspicious.

He bowed perfunctorily. "I was sent to find Mr. Jones. I cannot find him in his chamber or the kitchen, and the library is locked."

"I am sure we have not seen him," Clare said frostily. "Perhaps he is exploring places where he doesn't belong like everyone else." Good for the baron, locking the valuable library with all these strangers roaming about.

"My pardon." He bowed and hastened away.

"That was rather rude," Dottie said absently, studying another tome.

"I am not fond of strangers on a happy day. When a gallant young man is murdered on his way here, I'm even less so. Ask Hunt for a key to this room and keep it locked. Perhaps you might move all the journals in here for safety. If there are any clues in them, we don't need killers finding them." Clare's insides ground like broken glass even as she admitted this.

She was afraid. She had hoped she'd overcome her timidity, but obviously, she'd just hidden it well. What if it had been Hunt who had caught that twine between the trees? With his weak knee. . . What if the twine had been meant for *him*? Or even Arnaud? Perhaps Bosworth meant to eliminate the heirs. Horror squeezed her lungs, as it had those months after her sister had been blown up before her eyes. She caught a table to steady herself, and it rocked.

Dottie glanced in Clare's direction, nodded, and returned to her ghost hunting.

Now she had a need to know where everyone was. Gritting her teeth at her idiocy, Clare checked the breakfast room again. Bosworth was still there, reading through a stack of

96

documents. She hated speaking with the disagreeable man, but she supposed she must.

"Have either of their lordships come down? Have you, by any chance, seen the Champlains or Lavignes? We have a houseful of guests and fewer people at the table than when the manor is empty." She picked up one of Elsa's breakfast rolls and noticed the serving platters were almost bare.

"Villiers and S-sp-palding are arguing politics in the library." Bosworth didn't bother glancing up. "Or p-perhaps they've found more dead bodies and are looking for a p-place to conceal them."

Three more days to Elsa and Jack's wedding, and she might have to kill a man. Clare forced a smile. "Thank you for your help." A pity that they knew the banker had as much right to live here as everyone else—unless, of course, the courts decided against illegitimacy. The earl's will had not specified. That was a battle for another day.

She disliked descending to the chaos of Elsa's kitchen. The servants didn't appreciate the intrusion on their territory. Perhaps she could find Mrs. Upton upstairs, overseeing the daily housekeeping routines. Nibbling on her sweet roll, she checked the formal dining room first, then proceeded to the family parlor.

There, she discovered Elsa's mother—the former countess of Villiers—playing the mutual-acquaintance game with the tiny, mysterious Lady Champlain. Elsa's mother would easily win points for knowing the best society. But the petite, vivacious Lady Champlain was winning by wooing an earl's widow and potentially gaining entrance to that society. They both glanced up expectantly at Clare's arrival.

"We missed you at dinner, my lady." Clare had no reason not to be polite, although she still wasn't entirely certain why the Champlains were here.

"Travel is so wearing," the dark-haired lady said with a

sigh. "I did not wish to be a bore. But I understand we missed the excitement of new guests?"

Both women waited for the gossip.

Clare hadn't heard anything from the men yet this morning—one of the many reasons she was trying to run them down after her panic spell. But from what little she'd learned, she assumed the impoverished, grieving Lavignes did not have proper claim to any title, not that Arnaud wanted it either. She played it safe. "Relations of Hunt's. Weddings bring together families. It's all quite exciting, isn't it?"

She left them to chew on that for a while. It wouldn't take long for them to work out that any relation of Hunt's was more likely to be related to his French grandmother than his American father. And since there was some connection between Sir Oswald and the Lavignes a generation or so ago, it should be interesting to learn if the newly-arrived French Lavignes might know the mysterious London Champlains no one else knew. The arrival of both couples did seem a tad conspiratorial.

That the Champlains hadn't packed their bags and fled after learning Lady Reid's daughter was in residence said they were determined to carry out their game—or their claim was genuine.

Clare located their housekeeper in the gallery ballroom, talking with Lavender and studying a box of second-hand gowns. Henri brought back good quality garments for Lavender to adapt for those who needed them. Many of the maids had arrived with only a single dress. Lavender and her ladies had started making uniforms so the servants need not use their meager wages to buy clothes for working in.

Even the usually happy adolescent Lavender looked solemn when Clare joined them.

"It is so terribly sad to come all this way to escape war, hoping to find family and a future, only to lose one's beloved," Clare's young cousin said mournfully. "We are looking for more mourning clothes for the Lavignes. Their trunks were meager."

"That is what I've come to find out. Are they still in their suite? Is there aught we can do for their comfort? I simply don't know what to say or do in the face of such tragedy." Clare hoped Mrs. Upton, a former curate's wife, would have words of advice.

"Mr. Lavigne has gone down in the crypt to verify the young man's identity and arrange for his funeral. I carried up breakfast for them earlier since they brought no servants." Mrs. Upton handed a drab black bombazine to Lavender. "This is sturdy and will suffice for the lady, for now."

She turned back to Clare. "Paul is building the coffin. The Lavignes are Catholic, but he thinks he can provide a service for their loved one. As Lavender says, it is horribly sad. My heart breaks for them."

Mrs. Upton's son was their new curate and also a carpenter, which was extremely convenient given the decrepit state of most of the manor and the village. Buildings constantly needed work, and the manor's maintenance budget kept the young curate in food and clothing.

"We must take comfort that the Lavignes left France before war overtakes the land again. I understand Napoleon is even conscripting married men now. Is Arnaud in the crypt too? He did not seem pleased with the arrival of his uncle's family." Clare rummaged in the box and found a black shawl with a ragged hole. "I will see if the aunts can repair this. It is a very fine weave."

"Arnaud is with Hunt. Henri is entertaining the Lavigne ladies. He seems pleased with the arrival of family. He took up a bouquet Patience gathered to brighten their room. She is arranging funeral flowers now." Mrs. Upton frowned a little at the mention of her daughter and the peddler/tavern owner but did not comment on how often they were found together.

"We really need more ladies' maids. Marie cannot do everything."

"Elsa's mother brought her own, and the aunts share one. Our guests can learn to share with others, as the rest of us must. This is not London, and we are not wealthy as lords. I will speak with them." One more item to add to her list. Her book would never be finished.

Clare hoped she'd have time to marry. Despite the frustration, perhaps it was providential that Hunt's mother was delaying the nuptials until all Elsa's guests departed.

Except the baron's book auction was scheduled for next week. She sighed and stopped back in the parlor to ask Elsa's mother about sharing her maid, a suggestion quickly accepted since it meant a source of gossip.

She was debating tackling the aunts upstairs or sneaking off to her office, when Hunt stomped in from outside. The access to the crypt/dungeon had been sealed off above-stairs when the new manor was built. It could only be accessed by an outside door, and she assumed that's where he'd been. He smelled of spring rain as he rubbed at his damp hair. He hadn't bothered with a hat.

"You are up and about early. Have you broken your fast?" She handed him her handkerchief so he could wipe cobwebs and raindrops off his face, while she surreptitiously admired the rugged, masculine cut of his jaw. James had managed to shave him far better than he once did on his own with sight in only one eye.

"I could take more." He aimed for the breakfast room, tucking her hand into the crook of his damp coat. "I feel as if I've climbed a mountain already this morning. Lavigne is truly stricken by all that's occurred. He's a lost man. Arnaud is not being patient with him."

"Arnaud must be fifteen years younger or more, but he spent how long hiding in the attic, recovering? He ought to be more sympathetic to his uncle's circumstances. Is he really that upset about the poor man using the title to aid his escape? It seemed the least he could do to protect his wife and daughter." Clare poured coffee for Hunt while he cleaned off the rest of the platters.

"It may be a long ago feud, possibly over pearls. From what little I've ascertained from Arnaud, the Champlains were probably pirates but definitely seafarers, as Villiers told me. They brought back fortunes in spices and gold and had a particular penchant for pearls. Pirating is probably how the Reids and Champlains knew each other." He tugged her down in the seat beside him and fed her a bite of cold bacon.

Her tea was tepid, but the story held her fascination. "But Arnaud and our new guests are *Lavignes*. Lady Reid was the Champlain, and perhaps Sir Oswald is also. Wouldn't the Champlains be the heirs to any pearls?"

Clare winced as her vivid imagination connected the coincidence of a pearl-loving Champlain arriving at the same time as a young man who spoke of pearls with his dying breath. Connecting the two stretched credulity.

"Besides, we know the viscountess spent all her pearls presenting her daughters to society and trying to pay off her husband's debts." She reassured herself with pragmatism.

Hunt washed down cold eggs with his coffee before replying. "You are speaking of current generations, but the matter most likely lies in the past. As I understand it, Lady Gabrielle Champlain *Reid* was sister of Jeannette Champlain *Lavigne*. Gabrielle was the eldest, and we know from her journals that she was given a rope of pearls as her dowry when she married my purported grandfather. But according to Arnaud and Mr. Lavigne, there once were more. I'm afraid the Lavignes are on a treasure hunt, just like Wycliffe's heirs."

Clare chewed on a bite of toast and thought that through while Hunt cleared his plate. "You are saying there is possibly a treasure trove of pearls somewhere just waiting for someone to claim them?"

"Possibly," he emphasized. "Because of the war, there is uncertainty in the inheritance and no ability for any of the family to ask each other. Arnaud and Henri had no knowledge of any legacy, for instance. They assumed Lady Reid used her wedding pearls, especially after we discovered she was selling them to pay the mortgage. Which, come to think of it, ought to make them partial owners in this derelict edifice."

"You're just trying to be shed of the responsibility," she laughed, before returning to the subject. "So you're thinking that their Uncle Jules is older, has access to family papers—possibly through the Barbeaus, the family lawyers—and thought to claim any Champlain pearls in his grandmother's name, but why *England*? That is far-fetched. Especially since there seem to be Champlains already in England who would have claimed them first. How does one go about interrogating guests?" Clare sipped her tea and tried to puzzle out how many ways a fortune could be lost.

"Mr. Lavigne claims the family had a solicitor in England, and that Barbeau sought him out. Arnaud knows nothing of this."

Clare went straight to the point. "So, who inherits if they are found? Sons? Cousins? The younger brother, Jules, who survived, or Arnaud's father, who did not?"

"First, they need to speak with this solicitor to see if the inheritance exists. If it does, the heirs may depend on who can prove they are who they say they are. Barbeau was supposed to deliver the Lavignes' papers to the solicitor, make inquiries, and bring any release forms here, to the viscountess's last known residence."

And Barbeau's pockets had been empty.

SEVENTEEN

HUNT: THURSDAY MORNING

As they traversed the hidden lane, the slight, blond Marquess of Spalding kicked a rock with his expensive knee boots, undoing an hour of his valet's polishing. "I came here because of my stepmother's wild tales, to be certain she is safe. And to work with Bosworth in moving the manor's investments to sound harbors with greater returns. And I'm presented with murder and potential fraud and. . ."

"You are hiding here from spying eyes while you receive missives about Wellington's movements. It's not as if your communications go unnoticed," Hunt said dryly. "I was once an officer. I'm not ignorant. I assume the fate of the army determines the fate of our investments. You might want to consider investing in the future of America." He limped down the unmarked path the Lavigne's messenger had inexplicably taken.

"Napoleon's army is on the move. Villiers is in a position to keep us abreast of the news. But you are right, London is full of spies these days. For all we know, your Champlains and Lavignes are among them. Villiers has sent Jones back to the city to look into them."

"That will be useful," Hunt conceded. "Everyone is being

polite at the moment, but I fear daggers drawn once the topic of the pearls is engaged. As the titled heir, Arnaud is the most logical beneficiary of any family pearls, but he fled with the shirt on his back and has no documents. He claims no knowledge of the English Champlains."

"Speak of the devil. . ." Spalding studied the scene under the tree where a man had died. "What are they doing?"

Hunt watched Clare's young cousin, Dorothea, spinning slowly on the path, while Arnaud leaned against a tree and stoically watched. Hunt thought the frail young lady in black might be the Lavigne's grieving daughter. She merely stood to one side, weeping into her handkerchief.

"Are you sure you want to know?" Hunt asked. "That is the spot where we found Barbeau. We've thoroughly canvassed the area and found no indication that anyone hid in the shrubbery. But we did not find the documentation he'd promised to bring."

"I wanted to see if the path might be useful for my purposes or a danger to others. I am assuming it is not so hidden or secret anymore." Spalding shook his head as Dottie, dressed in sprigged muslin and a flowered bonnet, quit spinning and appeared to go into a trance. "That young lady needs a keeper."

Hunt snorted. "The whole blamed Reid family need keepers then. Your stepmother brought Dottie here evidently for just this purpose—to talk to spirits."

"How do you tolerate the flummery?" Spalding asked in disgust, turning around to return up the lane.

"Accept the family as they are, eccentric but extremely intelligent. I am waiting for Lady Spalding and Lady Lavinia to work out the earl's codes and shower us in jewels. They knew him and must understand his thinking better than any of us."

"I am more than grateful that you are keeping them busy. My wife threatened to run away if I allowed my stepmother to interfere again, and she left my daughter in tears over the dower house situation."

"Well, the estate has been hers for decades," Hunt said mildly. "It was cruel to move her out."

"But practical, as my business agent pointed out. My new son-in-law is likely to be prime minister some day. They need to entertain. The dowager does not."

Despite his appreciation for the aid the elderly aunts had brought him, Hunt couldn't argue that. Besides, he had his own battles to fight.

Jack and the new curate were waiting impatiently on the front steps. "Paul and I have drawn up a list of where everyone was the evening Barbeau died. I'm inclined to turn off the lot, including *your* servants, my lord." As a former soldier, Jack did not have a high opinion of government authority.

"Just because they are not who they claim to be does not mean they intend to cause harm," Paul Upton remonstrated. "It simply means we must question their motives."

"*My* staff?" Spalding asked ominously. "They were thoroughly vetted before I hired them."

"Your secretary, Norsworthy, is new, is he not? As is Villiers' valet, Roberts?" Paul asked as they entered the two-story vestibule. "They did not come up through the ranks as usual?"

Spalding practically growled. "They were *recommended.*"

By which Hunt assumed they were government agents of some sort. He raised a finger to his lips and indicated the vestibule ceiling, two stories above them. Clare had discovered a listening post on the upper wall.

The bats that came and left through the broken transom had plenty of holes to dart through.

Perhaps it was time to employ the unused study in the rear wing, away from prying eyes and ears. Gesturing, Hunt led the way.

He was unsurprised when Earl Villiers stepped from the library to join their little parade. Hunt might have been more surprised had Jack's father abandoned his books. Next to the slender marquess, the younger earl was a tall, imposing man.

"Settlements signed?" Hunt ventured. A year ago, he had been fighting an army sent by these British nobles. He had been forced to learn diplomacy these last months for Clare's sake.

"Signed under duress," Villiers agreed, glaring at Jack. "You will regret it when Elsa chooses to give her wealth to her mother or orphans or a horse academy. Women have no concept of money."

Jack shrugged. "We are happy without the wealth. She has set aside funds for any offspring. I currently survive on *no* funds better than her mother does *with* them."

"Do you have any idea at all how much our father left Elsa?" Villiers asked. "You could be living a life of ease if you moved back to her estate, instead of dealing with murderers who might poison your food next."

"*Elsa* fixes our food," Jack said with a laugh as they strode through the drafty main corridor of the old manor. "She only owns that estate for a lifetime. I am building one we can pass on to our children. Be happy for us and apply your considerable expertise to the problem at hand."

The small party halted as they reached the back of the manor while Hunt unlocked the massive double doors into the new west wing. The corridor here was smaller and less drafty but unadorned by aging paintings. In his latter days, the earl had evidently ignored the new additions his son had built. Hunt gestured for his toplofty guests to enter the enormous study no one had ever used.

The tall earl and slender marquess examined the sturdy— empty—walnut shelves, the enormous—unused—mahogany desk, and the decided lack of chairs.

"If the viscount ever furnished this office, the furniture has migrated elsewhere," Hunt explained without apology. "But the walls are solid and there is only one door to block."

"We're not old men. We can stand." Despite his slighter size, the marquess radiated authority as he leaned against the desk and crossed his arms. "Now what is the meaning of this meeting?"

Hunt propped himself against the door, crossed his arms, too, and left the moment to Jack and his cohort, the curate.

"Our resident physician believes Barbeau was struck down on Sunday night. He was barely alive Monday morning, when we we found him. You may ask her for details, if so inclined, but Meera tends to be reasonably accurate." Jack waited for argument.

Glad that he didn't have to deal with bigots or misogynists who might question Meera's skill, Hunt moved the conversation on. "I asked Jack and Elsa, and the Uptons, to discreetly question the servants. They are all in a position to see and hear more than the rest of us do."

"Why? They are family, not servants," the marquess protested.

"This is a rather egalitarian household," Paul admitted. "Proximity, not class, matters. Henri and Arnaud added to our information."

"For all we know, they and their relations are French spies! I am to trust their word over *my* staff, approved by honorable British gentlemen?" Spalding glared.

"Hear them out," Hunt insisted.

The earl leaned against the massive desk as well. "Jack is an idealistic fool, but I'll vouch for his honesty. It will be up to us to examine what he presents. That's only fair."

The marquess grunted agreement and waved them on.

The curate produced a notebook from his pocket. "Our first problem is the timing. Coming from London, most people overnight in Stratford rather than risk riding at dark. But the Lavignes claim Barbeau left them early Sunday morning. He must have thought himself able to reach us to keep riding. This time of year, the journey from London might be made in a day if one sets out at dawn, changes horses, and doesn't mind risking the dangers of dark roads. That might leave him riding up the path near sunset. At that hour, almost everyone in the manor is accounted for."

Jack interrupted. "But no one had to be there to watch him fall. We have no idea how long the twine has been tied to the trees. If Barbeau carried documents from the London solicitors, then those documents vanished overnight. Someone had to have gone out after dark Sunday evening—and possibly every night since the twine was installed."

"That is only if we know Barbeau was the intended victim," Hunt reminded them.

Jack shrugged. "His papers were missing, so we work on that assumption. We limited ourselves to tracking people on the night Barbeau died. We have a list of everyone on the property Sunday evening. We cannot vouch for villagers. Henri intends to announce a race after services this week to determine who among them might know of that path."

"At this rate, every man from here to London," Villiers said grumpily. Glancing at the long list, he handed it to Spalding. "Your lot wasn't here yet. Presumably, they are not suspect."

"Neither were the Champlains nor the Lavignes," Jack added. "That leaves Avignon, family, and staff, including yours, Villiers."

"If someone stayed in Birmingham, might they have ridden down here one night, set up the trap, and rode back?" the earl asked.

"We've debated that. This is a small town. Strangers are noticed. It's possible, perhaps, but not logical if they were coming here anyway," Hunt explained.

"Our theory," Paul interceded, "is that the villain knew

Barbeau was in London and knew Wycliffe Manor was his destination. They simply arranged to be here first."

"I am the one who decided—" Villiers halted his protest and gave it a second thought. "*Jones* recommended we come early when we learned Spalding was meeting Bosworth here. I had already been notified of Barbeau's inquiries. As my secretary, Jones looked into him. But he was with me. . ."

The earl frowned and thought about it. "Jones or Roberts rode ahead of the coach to arrange inns and meals. But I hardly think that gave either of them time to tie twine."

But Villiers' secretary and new valet had been seen wandering around at night, and they'd been here before the body was found. Hunt tried to recall what the servants looked like, but he didn't pay attention to anyone outside of family.

Having arrived after the victim's death, Spalding was less concerned. "I was delayed by business matters and my staff was with me. Is there any possibility one of *us* was an intended victim? Wouldn't that make more sense?"

"We're not here to speculate," Paul reminded them. "All we are doing at this stage is gathering information. Our intent is to determine who might have removed papers from the victim on the night he died."

The marquess tightened his thin lips but gestured for them to continue.

"No one on our list was where they were supposed to be that night," Jack reported. "Elsa heard the valets arguing, so we started there. Once we began questioning, stories unraveled."

"The servants all claimed to have been in their respective rooms or employers' chambers all evening," Paul explained. "Avignon told us his valet, George, was with him, choosing the next day's wardrobe."

"But Elsa heard George claiming to have seen the earl's man, Roberts, in the library that evening. Victor, my new valet, claimed to be in his quarters, but Elsa overheard him confirming the library encounter, which means all three of the manservants were downstairs after we sent them off for the evening." Jack sounded aggrieved. "I like Victor. He works hard. But I cannot tolerate liars. I have sent off letters to the agency that sent him and to several of his references who might still be alive, as I should have done at the first."

Villiers crossed his arms over his elegant waistcoat and studied the ceiling. "As I recall, on Sunday evening, I was responding to some missives I'd received earlier that day. After Roberts carried in my tea and hot water, I told him he wouldn't be needed any longer. That was probably around nine. His time is his own then, although he should have asked permission to explore the library."

"Did you send him to speak with me?" Jack asked. "Because that's what he told us. Victor complained Roberts was in our new suite before the library incident. Elsa and I are using our old chambers, but the Turbins have been fussing over the new one and are in and out at all hours. I can think of no conceivable reason for Roberts to look for me there."

"I wouldn't have sent for you at that hour," Villiers admitted. "He's new. My trusted man left rather hastily, and I didn't have anyone in position to step up, so I took Roberts on a recommendation. Perhaps he was learning the household to better aid me. I'll speak with him."

"Did your Turbin follow Roberts to the library?" Hunt asked, wearying of tedious details about wandering servants. He'd never had servants until he arrived at the manor. Did they often leave abruptly? The idea of replacing them made his head ache, and he rubbed the scar on his temple.

"Victor claims he was suspicious and followed him." Jack didn't appear as if he believed anyone.

"And your aide, Jones, my lord?" Paul addressed Villiers. "Was he working with you that evening as he says?"

The earl rubbed his jaw to unclench it. "As I said, early on in the evening, yes. But I sent him off at nine too. I had private correspondence to write and did not need prying eyes. But he's an experienced army man, recommended by a highly placed general. He is privy to government secrets. I cannot believe him capable of wrong doing. If anything, he may have been following one of the others."

"So all three valets and a distinguished aide-de-camp were all wandering around Sunday night after the family went to their chambers?" Hunt demanded, consolidating all the rattle.

"And Avignon, captain," Paul added. "The stable lads say he rode out early in the evening and returned late. He says he was at the tavern. Henri closes the tavern early on Sunday nights."

"I might remind you, captain," the marquess said bluntly, "that your cousins are far more likely involved in this family feud than servants. Have you verified their whereabouts?"

Both Jack and Paul glanced worriedly at Hunt. He knew his cousins' habits. With sinking heart, he nodded for them to continue.

Jack read from his notebook. "Arnaud and Paul escorted Patience back to the manor from the tavern at eight and weren't seen again. After leaving Patience and Arnaud at the manor and visiting with his mother, Paul went back to the parsonage. Henri closed the tavern at ten and has no one to vouch for him after that."

Hunt shrugged. "By ten, we were *all* in our individual rooms—with no witnesses, and that includes me and you, Jack."

EIGHTEEN

CLARE: THURSDAY NOON

BY LUNCHEON, CLARE GAVE UP ON FINISHING HER FRESH COPY. The men had been closeted in the west wing, shouting, all morning. Elsa was in such a state of wedding nerves that she was sending up test dishes to anyone poking their nose outside their door—and some who were not. Lavender had stopped by three times to show Clare different adornments for the bridal gown she might never wear at this rate.

And now timid Patience was standing in the office doorway, wringing her hands, and repeating nonsense.

Clare removed her spectacles, rubbed her nose, and tried to refocus. "Dottie wishes us to hold a. . . *spirit circle*? Is that like summoning demons with candles and pentagrams and smelly herbs?"

Tall, awkward Patience shook her wispy blond curls, while wearing a dubious frown. "It is about the ghost becoming increasingly agitated and flinging her journal about."

Clare sighed and nibbled the final bits of the most delicious ham and cheese toast she'd ever encountered—one of Elsa's experiments. "Can we persuade Elsa to join us? If we leave her in the kitchen much longer, there won't be any supplies left in the larder, and we'll all be fat."

Patience nodded a little more eagerly. "And Miss Lavigne. Her mother has taken to her bed, and Miss Lavigne is hoping Dottie might help her speak to her betrothed's spirit. If naught else, it might distract from her dismals. We mean to meet in the blue salon so the aunts may attend as well."

For a clergyman's daughter, Patience was exceedingly open-minded. . . and naïve. If they allowed the use of their salon, the old ladies had engineered this.

"And Mrs. Champlain?" This was beginning to sound like such a delicious farce that Clare was willing to be diverted. Their petite intruder had taken to having her meals delivered to her chamber. That needed to stop. They didn't have enough staff.

"I had not thought of her! I have not seen her about. Do you think she will brave the aunts?"

"Don't tell her they'll be there," Clare said wickedly. "Will Lavender tear herself away from her sewing? She needs to rest her eyes, or they'll fall from her head."

"If you will fetch Lavender, I'll attempt Mrs. Champlain." Looking unusually rosy-cheeked, Patience ran off on her self-imposed errand.

Living with insanity was apparently healthy for the late curate's daughter.

Lavender left her sewing ladies and gathered up her puppy to eagerly follow Clare. "My grandmother believes in spirits?" she whispered in awe.

"Oh, I seriously doubt that," Clare said, drawing Lavender out of her hideaway with the temptation of irritating the supercilious baroness. "But she'll want to control events."

"What about Mrs. Upton?" Lavender ran up the marble stairs ahead of Clare.

"Patience tried to draw her mother out, but she doesn't approve."

"And Elsa's mother?" Lavender reached the top, nervously petting her puppy. The master suite was only a few steps away.

"I suppose Mrs. Turner is a Reid, but she is showing Comte Avignon about the grounds. I think she is more interested in courting than socializing." Clare checked a corridor lit only by oil sconces and saw no one else. They must already be in the salon. "I cannot imagine any two people more different than Elsa and her mother."

"Me and grandmother," Lavender said direly, hesitating outside the door. "I fear she will bite off my head."

"Lady Lavinia is rather like a praying mantis, isn't she? But she's the earl's sister. If anyone knows family secrets, she does." Clare took Lavender's free arm and shoved her inside.

"Take that creature out of here," Lady Lavinia commanded the instant they entered. For the occasion, the baroness had donned a grayish-brown visiting gown. Her gray pompadour towered so high, her tall, thin figure did give the appearance of a praying mantis. And her command was as likely to be for Lavender as her puppy.

"The puppy is well behaved," Clare admonished, taking the more positive path before Lavender could flee. "Perhaps the spirits like puppies. Who doesn't?"

That answer was obvious from the lady's glower, but Patience arrived with the slender, dark-haired adolescent in black and diverted the argument. Sofia Lavigne's eyes were red from weeping. Clare's heart went out to her. Clare had lost her father at a slightly younger age. The shock could be no less.

Leaving Lavender to settle in a corner, out of sight behind her formidable grandmother, Clare introduced Sofia to the company.

"Did you know that your great-aunt Gabrielle married at

seventeen?" Clare asked, tucking the girl into a chair by the only fire in the house. The ladies liked their rooms warm.

"And my mother lived to regret it," Lady Spalding retorted, looking unusually grim. Hunt's aunt, the plump dowager marchioness, normally wore a pleasant expression. "You must read her diaries while you are here. I have only just learned what a terrible man my father was."

"All Reid males were spoiled," Lady Lavinia sniffed. "My brother was the only boy in a sea of girls. He doted on his son. Those were different times."

"How so?" Lavender demanded from her corner. "Sons still have everything their hearts desire. Women still must rely on men for everything. We cannot even inherit our own estates. Your husband's property passes to his heirs, not to you. I shall earn my own way and never marry."

"That is sadly true," the marchioness said with a sniff. Since her stepson's agent had suggested she leave her beloved home and move into the dower house, she'd been in a snit. "But I would not have missed those years with my darling Spalding for all the world."

Lady Lavinia rolled her eyes. "Spalding ate too much beef, drank too much port, and died falling down the stairs in front of the guests at your daughter's come-out ball, leaving everything in his son's hands, which is why you're here today."

As a distraction from argument, that shocking anecdote worked remarkably well. Even poor Sofia stopped wiping her eyes to stare wordlessly. Clare covered her mouth as she imagined the horror of such an event—the ladies watching their beloved husband and father dying at the very moment of their headiest triumph. She wanted to hug poor Lady Spalding and comfort her over an incident years past.

With amazing timing, Dottie emerged from one of the suite's bedrooms wearing a colorfully crocheted shawl Lady Lavinia must have finished. She carried one of the late viscountess's journals. "You are correct that we need to own our own property and funds." She set the journal down on the tea table. "The problem, of course, is that we cannot earn money, and men will not let us control the funds we do possess."

Elsa swept in with Patience right behind. "Have we missed anything?" She set down a tray piled high with little cakes and biscuits.

"We will need to send Henri to haul back a cartful of chocolate to replace what is in those," Clare said dryly, studying the array. "Patience, did you find Mrs. Champlain?"

"Her maid says she is still not feeling well." Always hungry, while remaining slim, Patience helped herself to a scone and jam and settled on an empty loveseat. She placed a napkin over her generous bosom to protect her gown from crumbs.

"Your cousins apparently believe owning your own property instead of being owned is the secret to happiness," the dowager Lady Spalding answered Elsa, keeping up with competing conversations. "The shawl looks good on you, Dorothea."

"It is very dramatic." Dottie held it out like wings, showing off the various shades of pink and red, then added ungratefully, "I'd rather have that pretty black Lady Lavinia is repairing."

The preying mantis held up the frail shawl and scolded, "This is for a *widow*. You are not in mourning. Miss Sofia may use it when I am done."

Refusing to play placating hostess when they were all family, Clare helped herself to a chocolate confection and a cup of tea before settling next to Patience. "How are we to summon spirits?" She thought that might make a most excellent scene in her next book, should she ever be given opportunity to write it.

"I have no notion, really." Dottie opened the journal to a page she had marked. "I have only heard about such things. I thought we might draw the draperies and light a candle. I asked Meera for some incense, so we might use that."

"Jasmine," Patience corrected. "If you wish to draw the viscountess, she loves jasmine. I smell it all about. I mean to learn how to grow it."

The black-clad waif pulled a pouch from the pocket of her old-fashioned gown. "We make the perfume." She handed a vial from the pouch to Dottie, who sniffed it and passed it around.

It was exceedingly strong. Clare raised her eyebrows and passed it to Elsa.

Sofia continued quietly. "I brought seeds as a gift. I will show you what must be done to grow the vine, but I cannot help you with perfume. That is my mother's domain—as it once was Mademoiselle Gabrielle's before she married."

The viscountess had been a perfumer! That explained a good deal.

While Dottie arranged the room to her satisfaction, Patience pulled a chair next to Sofia so they might talk seeds. Clare settled back and waited for the entertainment. London had nothing so interesting as her insane family.

Which was worrisome, if she thought about it. Her family managed to get themselves killed on a regular basis. Her sister had run off to Egypt and had herself blown up. Clare did not want to be responsible for any more deaths.

While impulsive and unusual, surely, a spirit circle could not be harmful?

Once the room was darkened with only the glowing coals in the grate and the candle on the table for light, Dottie insisted they form a circle. The aunts remained on their sofa, while everyone else moved their chairs closer, and, at Dottie's direction, held hands.

Clare held Great-Aunt Lavinia's paper-thin hand on one side and Elsa's firm, work-hardened one on the other. Silence. Darkness. Jasmine perfuming the air. Lit only by a single candle, the journal lay open on the tea table, surrounded by an array of confections that ought to entice any hungry spirit.

"Mademoiselle Gabrielle, Lady Reid," Dottie whispered. "Are you here?"

A stronger jasmine fragrance wafted through the room, but that might be Sofia's vial.

"Your great-niece has lost her beau. Is he there with you?" Dottie frowned helplessly, then turned as the draperies rustled.

The salon was drafty. Had the aunts closed the windows tightly?

"I believe this is where I'm supposed to make up something," Dottie said dryly into the silence. "But all I sense is a presence."

Sofia murmured in French. From what little Clare could hear and translate, it was a plea to poor Barbeau and a prayer for guidance to his Maker. Tears ran down her cheeks.

The journal suddenly slammed across the table, taking a selection of tarts with it.

NINETEEN

PATIENCE: THURSDAY AFTERNOON

"And the book fell open to the same page it showed Clare and Dottie earlier, the one that mentions the cart and C being pleased." Patience concluded her tale as pragmatically as possible, although she'd found the spirit circle rather alarming. "I cannot see how anyone might have moved the book or even why they should."

Jack and Elsa joined them while Patience was explaining events to her mother, brother, and Henri. It was too early for Henri to open his tavern, and he didn't take his cart into Birmingham every day. His strong, confident presence made her feel more poised than she was.

The small housekeeper's parlor barely held them all, but it was convenient for Elsa, who could dash back to the kitchen should chaos erupt in dinner preparations.

"We really need to confront the Champlains." Jack tilted his wooden chair back on two legs and glared at the ceiling. "Hunt won't do it. They could be his grandmother's relations, and his mother might be looking forward to seeing them, for all we know. But their arrival without invitation is odd."

"They will not go anywhere near Lady Spalding, which is even odder, since one assumes she is their niece or cousin. It

119

seems to say that they don't expect her to recognize them. In which case, since she and Hunt's mother are sisters and grew up together, Mrs. Huntley is unlikely to know them, either," Henri pointed out. "Arnaud and I know nothing of the English branch of our grandmother's family. They've been in England longer than we've been alive."

"So, it is only Lady Reid's daughters—Lady Spalding and Mrs. Huntley—who might recognize the Champlains as family? Or recognize Sir Oswald, at least, since the lady is younger." Patience's mother sipped a cup of tea and frowned. "I never encountered Sir Oswald in my brief time here, but that was a long time ago. Their servants are prideful and do not mix with the staff. I've learned little of them."

Patience wished she could add to the investigation, but she only worked with the men in the orchard. She doubted they knew anything. Henri quit his pacing, frowned, and leaned against the cushioned arm of the chair she'd chosen. His masculine presence in this tiny room. . . was disturbing, in a good sort of way, she supposed.

"But this C in the lady's journal. . ." Elsa hadn't taken a chair but occasionally peered into the hall so she could listen for noise from the kitchen. "Is the spirit trying to tell us this C is *Champlain*? Perhaps as a smuggler, he brought her brandy, and that is the mention of the cart?"

"The Champlains didn't arrive here until *after* Monsieur Barbeau died." Paul studied his notes. "Do we need to question their servants to see if they stayed nearby? Or if the servants rode ahead and stayed. . . Where? The village has no inn."

"We should question Champlain's servants casually, ask how long they were on the road, did they come directly from London, that sort of thing." Jack rocked back and forth on his chair. "If the Champlains are frauds, they really are our best suspects. They may have feared Barbeau had caught them in their fraud."

"You are avoiding questioning the more obvious suspects, because you do not want to lose our most excellent servants," Elsa teased. "Marie and Victor have given no indication that they know either the Champlains or the Lavignes, but they were the ones who showed up on our doorstep a week before Barbeau."

"And then there is the Comte Avignon and his servants." Paul read from his list. "They were here that night. We have only spoken with George, his valet. Avignon has a coachman, I believe?"

"No, he's my mother's. They came in her landaulet. But it is odd that Avignon switched from courting Dottie, to my mother. The man is pleasant, and I would be thrilled for my mother, except how can one trust a capricious man like that?" Elsa winced at the crash of crockery in the other room.

"Despite his unassuming demeanor, Avignon's valet is a bit scruffy," Jack noted, wrinkling his nose. "I cannot see how a man who looks so rumpled can dress a count so elegantly, which is suspicious in itself. And they were here before Barbeau, which gave them time to tie the twine. We cannot confirm that either Avignon or his valet weren't out and about on Sunday night."

While Paul made notes, Jack continued, "I've talked with the coachmen of our nobles. The marquess came from his estate and stopped overnight in Stratford to pick up Bosworth. Elsa's brother came directly from London, but as he said, his men rode ahead to arrange private rest stops. If one of them rode further than expected, he wouldn't tell me. So his staff, Jones and Roberts, remain on our suspect list. Roberts is a new hire. He and Jones are not fond of each other."

"I know you wish to find who killed that poor lad, accidentally or not, but there is more than one problem here, isn't there?" Nettie asked. "You have Sir Oswald and his wife who showed up, uninvited, supposedly eager to see the captain's mother again, but hiding when they learn her sister is here. Then, you have the Lavignes, who claim to have sent the lad ahead, because why?"

Patience thought that a most excellent point. Her head spun with all the names and people she really didn't know.— possibly because they were all pretenders.

Beside Patience, Henri crossed his arms and shrugged. "My uncle claims Barbeau was to present documentation to the solicitors to prove they are Lady Reid's heirs. They say the solicitors gave them directions to come directly here. Both Hunt and Villiers have sent queries to London and their own lawyers, out of an excess of caution, but there hasn't been time for a reply. Arnaud and I know nothing of any other family solicitors." He frowned. "Although now I think on it, one of the solicitor's names on the London firm Lavigne said they used is similar to the one Hunt consults about the manor trust in Stratford. I will look into that."

Jack set his chair down and stood up just as more crockery hit the floor. "If that is all we know, I will speak to the coachmen again."

"I will see if I can ferret out Lady Champlain's maid. Henri, can you lure Sir Oswald's valet into your web? I will continue listening to chatter, but I need to go." Elsa dashed out to set her kitchen in order.

Paul rose, tucking his notebook into his pocket. "As a clergyman, I must speak with the Lavignes about the funeral. I will see what I can learn from them. I'm thinking it would be better if I were a valet and could join the gang of them that seems to be forming."

"I cannot do more than speak with poor Sofia about seeds and perfumes." Patience began to rise. Both her brother and Henri held out their hands to help her. Unaccustomed to so much attention, she took Henri's larger one. It was bare and warm and steadied her awkwardness.

"You might learn more than I will," Paul suggested.

"Innocent conversation can tell us a great deal, especially since the Lavignes had only a hired carriage, arrived without servants, and have not joined us for meals."

"Of all the beslubbering boil-brained flap-dragonery I've ever heard!" Elsa's voice rose from the kitchen in an hysterical pitch. "Do *not* tell me you have dropped that whole tray because a door won't open."

"No-o-o-o," the remarkably loud voice of Betsy, the rattle-pated maid, carried on a wail.

Alarmed, Patience tugged Henri down the hall. The sturdy maid was clumsy and thick-witted and overly creative, but usually imperturbable.

"I got it open," Betsy wept. "And a man fell out."

TWENTY

HUNT: THURSDAY AFTERNOON

ALERTED BY HENRI, HUNT LIMPED DOWN THE LONG EAST WING corridor to the theoretically unused service stairs near the stable. He'd thought the exits of all the faux towers had been closed off and locked. Built to allow in more daylight than the old fortress of a manor, the wing was bright and airy—and cold from lack of draperies or much in the way of furnishing.

When he reached the tower, half the household already stood about, shocked and weeping, in the circular area. They parted to let him pass.

A large male body sprawled across the stone transom, obviously lifeless. Hunt needed everyone safe, away from whatever had occurred here. Instinct said this death wasn't natural, even if he could not immediately see blood. Who the devil was it?

"We don't want the boys down here. Keep them in the schoolroom," Hunt ordered, knowing the command would send Clare running up a different set of stairs, away from this obscenity. Looking white-faced and grim, she nodded and fled.

How long had the door on these distant stairs been unlocked? Hunt clenched his molars over his own carelessness. The only possible reason to use this moldering rear tower would be to access the stables—except this wing was currently unoccupied. Which meant anyone using them did so clandestinely.

Surely the outer door was locked? He and Jack had verified the security of the thick oak planks not long ago, although they'd not bothered verifying the safety of the stairs. This new tower was probably only a hundred years old, unlike the stone manor towers it imitated.

Jack had run out to check the locks after hearing Betsy's story. Thank heavens for ex-soldiers who understood protecting their flank.

"I want all the servants who have rooms in the attic over this wing gathered in one place." Hunt had heard Clare complaining that they'd had to open the attic for the retainers their aristocratic guests had brought. He had no notion how many used the rooms. "Keep them from talking to each other, please."

Looking fiercely protective of her staff, Mrs. Upton snapped orders, and Quincy herded everyone in the direction of the empty guest rooms.

Hunt stood guard while Meera and Walker examined the body that had fallen out after Betsy shoved open the door. Why was the maid using these stairs instead of the main ones to the kitchen, on the manor end of the wing?

"That's Jones," Henri murmured as Walker turned over the body, revealing the blood that had previously been concealed. "Villiers said he'd sent him to London to find out more about the Lavignes and Champlains."

"Perhaps he thought he'd sneak down the back stairs so no one would pursue him?" Hunt knew there was a warren of interconnecting rooms in the attic above, but he hadn't studied how the servants had divided them. He would have thought most of them would have taken beds closer to the main manor, near their employers. "Is his room in the attic?"

"Probably. Let me take a look from the top." Stepping around the body, Henri disappeared up the tower stairs.

Hunt only knew of two sets of keys, his and the set the housekeeper and butler had in the kitchen. There was nothing in the manor worth stealing except the silver and books, so they'd never had need to guard any other keys. He'd have to check the keyrings.

Apparently expanding their guest list required more security. Hunt balled his fingers into fists and resisted shouting at everyone to mount their horses and decamp. He'd been living in fear of losing the manor. Perhaps he should be more afraid of *keeping* the blamed Gothic horror.

With the crowd cleared, Villiers and Spalding arrived, trailing a reluctant Bosworth. The banker glanced at the body, muttered an imprecation, and fled, looking pale. Not a soldier was their lordly banker.

Villiers cursed vividly at recognizing the corpse of his secretary. Spalding put a hand on his friend's shoulder.

"Meera's a lady," Hunt warned, wondering if he could fine an earl for blasphemy.

"I sympathize and second your sentiments, my lord." Taking Walker's hand, Meera pulled herself upright. "I fear Mr. Jones suffered before he died of his injuries. It is a very narrow staircase. He evidently tumbled head first, hitting walls and stairs as he fell. His wounds bled when he hit bottom, so his death was not instantaneous. Since no one heard his cries, perhaps he was blessedly unconscious."

"He had to have been there for a day, at least," Villiers said in a pained tone. "I gave him orders the night before last and haven't seen him since."

"Tripped?" Hunt asked, desperate to hear it was an accident.

Henri's voice called from the attic at the top of the stairs. "No sign of a tripwire."

"If there was a wire, someone could have removed it,"

Spalding suggested. "Or perhaps he was drunk and fell over his own boots in the dark."

Leaning on Walker, Meera shook her head. "The treads are too narrow for a man's boot and easily missed, but, unless he was very very drunk, he would have caught the wall and sustained fewer injuries. He does not smell of alcohol. It is more likely that he was shoved, forcefully."

They had a killer inside the house. Hunt had hoped Barbeau's death was some freak accident he might blame on outsiders. Mentally cursing as Walker led his wife away, Hunt no longer harbored that hope. He wanted all the wedding guests gone, *now*.

Meera was not supposed to be climbing stairs at this stage of her pregnancy, but she had warned them not to move the body until she'd seen it—for good reason, it appeared.

Quincy, their massive butler, returned in company with Adam, his equally large son. As a former prize fighter, Quincy had seen and sustained serious injuries over the years. Even he looked pale.

"Quincy, if you and Adam would. . . ?" Hunt gestured at the once dapper secretary crumpled without dignity on the floorboards.

They would soon have to open a mortuary. Barbeau's body was still in the crypt, waiting for the Lavignes to give orders for his burial.

"I vote we burn this hellhole to the ground," the marquess said as they traversed the corridor to the suite where the servants had been herded.

"Place doesn't belong to you," Hunt reminded him, even if he agreed. "If it comes to a vote, I will abstain unless there is a tie, but do you really think any of the ladies would vote to burn their ancestral home?"

"Elsa could take the staff to her estate," Villiers argued. "Between us, we could house the entire family on our various estates."

"But you haven't. And most of the staff has family nearby. Would you take them too?" Hunt shoved his hands in his pockets and faced his noble guests. "Spalding has even pushed his own mother out of her home. No one offered Clare solace or a helping hand when she lost her entire family and struggled to raise her nephew alone. Lavender would be homeless if we lose the manor. The village would die again. The manor is needed. What suits you does not suit all."

"I will offer my mother an entire wing of the main house." Spalding stomped off, presumably in the direction of the blue salon and the dowager.

Hunt waited while Villiers struggled with grief and temper.

"It is likely I have brought the killer here," the earl finally admitted. "Jones was following my orders. I had Avignon investigated when he started courting my stepmother, and then I had Jones asking questions of your new guests and inquiring into your French relations. All their backgrounds are questionable."

Hunt resented the implication, but the man had a right to his grief and anger. It just needed redirecting. "Even *Bosworth* has secrets. On top of that, I know he resents our conspiring to remove the manor's investments from his hands. If he had any notion Jones was involved. . ."

"Jones wasn't a money man. But I take your point. I employed Jones to uncover secrets, and he was very good at his job. Everyone in the manor has secrets, including the servants and your ex-soldiers." Villiers gestured at the suite. "Will you do the questioning? I wish to listen."

They entered to observe a roomful of staff cowering under Arnaud's stern regard. Hunt's cousin seldom made his intimidatingly large presence known, but when he did. . . The unacknowledged comte was far more impressive than the slender marquess and the graying earl.

Arnaud had secrets. He'd lived here when the place was

empty of all but caretakers. He was one of the very few who knew the ways in and out of the manor that the rest of the company had yet to explore. And he might know more of the pearls his family sought than he was telling.

Hunt shut down that train of thought. If he couldn't trust his cousins, he could trust no one, and he couldn't live like that.

"There's a dressing room through there." Arnaud indicated a decorated panel. The main chamber contained little more than a few spindly-legged tables and chairs, but the floors had recently been mopped and the smell of mold and mildew washed away. The staff had arranged themselves around the walls, leaving the older ones to take the chairs.

Apparently, Elsa had thought to send up a tea tray with plates of confections. Cups rattled uncertainly, but Hunt nodded at these men and women who served the manor so silently and competently.

"I simply need to write a report for the court," Hunt lied. "Help yourselves to the tea, but please don't talk among you until I've had a chance to interview everyone. We all see things differently, and I want what *you* know, not what someone else thinks they knew. I think you can all understand that."

Perhaps not Betsy. A big, frumpy woman of middle age, her apron consistently smeared from her work, she was rocking back and forth, weeping. Hunt started with her. The maids were the only people who should have been in this wing, cleaning the unused rooms, but it appeared every servant in the household had been nearby when the wailing commenced, including those of their guests.

In the dressing room, under the stern eye of the tall earl, Betsy practically wilted. Even her cap slid down over one eye, exposing her frizzy brown hair. Hunt wanted to fling Elsa's brother out, but a witness of Villiers' stature was good to have, and the man was evidently attempting to work out his distress.

"His lordship has just lost a good friend and secretary," Hunt told the weeping maid, hoping to draw her attention by gaining her sympathy. Clare had taught him, outside the army at least, kindness worked better than intimidation. "For your own safety, as well as others, we have to know what happened."

Betsy nodded and blew her nose vociferously into her handkerchief.

"Can you tell me why you were using the backstairs?" Without a chair, Hunt leaned against the wall so he didn't appear quite so threatening. Betsy had been with them since the first. She had a good heart if not a normal brain.

"I was taking a tray to those poor Frenchies what lost their boy." She sniffed and rubbed her chubby hand at her eyes. "But they wasn't answerin' their door. And then I stopped to ask Marie what I should do. She was a'cleanin' the fancy suite for Lady Elsa. She told me to take the tray back downstairs."

The Lavignes weren't answering their door? Damn. Their chamber was nearer the other wing, so it was possible they hadn't heard the wailing. He'd still have to check on them. *Damn and blast.*

And Marie. . . Hunt searched his memory. Elsa's new maid, perhaps. Likely, if she was fixing up the suite Elsa and Jack had chosen. "So you decided to carry the tray all the way to the end of the hall, *away* from the kitchen stairs?"

Betsy shook her head, and her cap teetered. "Marie said she'd been hearing the lady's ghost. For a Frenchie, she's a good sort. We thought maybe we should check the doors. Mrs. Upton says they's to stay locked unless there's guests."

Ah, efficient Mrs. Upton. He'd have to find some way of thanking her for what he'd neglected to do. "So you checked the doors to be certain a ghost couldn't get in?" He had to ask. The logic failed him.

Betsy nodded vigorously. "Yes, sir, captain. The spooks'd be playin' with us if we don' watch out."

Villiers remained grimly silent through this nonsense. Hunt continued as delicately as he could manage so as not to frighten the maid. "So you checked the doors. Were they locked?"

She shook her head. "The handle turned on the stairs, and it shouldn't orter."

The answer to the spooks then. Someone had been using this wing when it should have been empty.

"So I tried to pull the door a little and. . ." She began wailing again.

"It's all right, Betsy." Hunt wished Clare were here instead of glowering Villiers. "You did everything exactly right. Why don't you have a lie down for a bit? And have Arnaud send in the next person."

He didn't have much better luck with the rest of the staff. Persuasion and kindness could not wring answers from people who didn't have any. They were all eager to help, but their duties were mostly in the main manor, where the guests were, not in this empty wing. Marie and Victor Tobin were the only ones who worked here, when they had time—and at the far end from where Jones fell.

"It is spooky here," Marie admitted, showing little trace of her French accent. Frail, barely larger than a child, with thinning gray hair, she should have retired years ago. "Even the locked doors rattle. I do not go without company. Victor left to fetch a polishing cloth when Betsy stopped in."

Which pretty much summed up all the interviews with the maids. Mrs. Upton had the manor's female servants clean in pairs. They called on Adam and Ned for heavy lifting, since Victor was elderly and as slight as his wife. Only the servants of their guests wandered alone. Hunt had left them for last.

As the last housemaid fluttered away in relief, Villiers

growled, "We need to question your footmen. But how does one question a mute?"

"Sign language and lip reading with Ned. But Adam is Quincy's son and training to fill his father's footsteps. If he shoved Jones down the stairs, it's because the man deserved it." That had been a rotten thing to say. Irritable, Hunt needed a good whiskey. He was bad with people.

"Jones was not a ladies' man," Villiers admitted, apparently following his own train of thought. "Your handsome young footman may have been angered if Jones made a suggestion he found reprehensible, although I cannot see Jones doing anything so indiscreet."

Charming, one more motive to throw into the pot. Hunt rubbed his throbbing temple. "I'll sound out the valets, then call Adam and Ned. But I have never seen either of them in a temper, and except for yours, all the valets are small, old, or less than attractive to a man like Jones, to be blunt. I suppose Avignon's man might be sturdy enough to push Jones, but he's the ugliest of the lot."

Pacing the closet of a room, the earl nodded understanding. "Roberts and Jones did not get along so I doubt indiscretion is a problem there. I noticed Avignon's valet in the crowd of onlookers. Is there any reason for to him have been at this end of the house?"

Mrs. Upton had stashed the bachelor Avignon in the front of the manor, in the guest hall off the gallery loft, an acre or more away from the back tower. His valet had no business on the family end at all. But Hunt knew how the household worked. "Everyone in the kitchen seems to have run upstairs after Betsy's hysterics, including Spalding's secretary. It appears Elsa hung on to her kitchen staff, but she has no control over other people's servants. George and Norsworthy were most likely in the kitchen and heard the caterwauling. Which of the guest servants are out there besides those two?"

Avignon's pockmarked, squint-eyed, shabby valet was

memorable, at the very least. Norsworthy, not so much, although Spalding's middle-aged secretary might be stronger than he seemed.

"Jack's man, Victor," Villiers' replied. "He's even holding a polishing cloth. I don't know the names of the Champlain servants, but they're there. Spalding's valet, Ernest."

Victor had reason to be in this wing. The Champlains were housed in the main family corridor, but their servants, like the marquess's, had been downstairs with the others. Afternoon tea, perhaps. Spalding's valet and secretary could have been there as well and run up after the others. Did it even matter why they were here? Would a killer return to the scene of a crime?

Villiers glanced into the other room, counting heads. "My valet was supposed to be doing laundry in the cellar, but Roberts is young and excitable and probably followed the crowd. If I'd had time, I would have hired someone older. But he's presentable and has excellent references."

Hunt had no notion of how often servants quit. He'd never had any until recently, and it appeared his manservant wasn't with the rest of the crowd. James hobbled about on a wooden leg and didn't go downstairs often. As a former soldier, he was probably guarding Hunt's quarters.

"Since he's new, we should verify Roberts' references?" Hunt asked.

Villiers didn't look happy. "Jones did, I thought. I trusted him implicitly. I don't know who I'll send to investigate your nest of potential spies now."

If Jones had been killed for investigating all their French relations, then Hunt would prefer not to send anyone but himself—except he was expecting his mother and a wedding. A trip to London was not in his future.

"All right, let's interview Avignon's man next, simply because I don't like his smarmy looks. You will note I make a very bad magistrate." Hunt opened the door and signaled George to enter.

"Want to tell us why you are on the opposite end of the house from your employer's chamber?" Hunt had exhausted his limited supply of patience when faced with the pock-marked valet's mocking expression.

George shoved his hands in his pockets and shrugged. "I was carrying up water when ever'one come running and screaming. Thought it was a funny direction to run if there was a fire, so I followed."

"Have you ever used the rear stairs or seen anyone else use them?"

"Your man there unlocked them, my lord." He nodded at Villiers. "The lot of us have rooms overhead, and mighty poor rooms they be, sir." He glared at Hunt. "No windows and hot as the devil of an evening. So some been sneaking outside to sleep in the stable. You treat the horses better'n us."

Because Elsa's money paid for the stable, not the manor. Her trustees were sticklers. Hunt studied the slender little man with suspicion. "Do you speak to Avignon this way?"

"Keep my mouth shut around that one. See and not heard works best wit' gents like 'im. Soldiers like yourself, cap'n, like the facts."

"You're not a valet," Villiers said in accusation.

"I'm what I need to be," George countered. "Your new man ain't no better 'an me. He runs about all hours o' the night, taking up with questionable personages."

"Roberts?" Villiers shrugged. "I send him on errands when Jones isn't about."

"Was it Jones or Roberts who unlocked the door?" Hunt asked, deciding George might not be much to look at, but he wasn't averse to gossiping about his fellows as the others were. He just lacked clarity.

"Don't rightly know which of 'em did it first. They both been using the stairs to the stable, following one another looks to me. Or they could just be meeting up with the lasses. The men got rooms overhead. The maids are in the other side. No easy way to get from one attic to the other wit'out goin' outside or downstairs."

"Well designed," Villiers conceded grumpily. "Keep the cocks out of the henhouse."

But the deceased Jones had more likely been seeing a stable hand than a maid, Hunt assumed. Either way, this wasn't getting them anywhere. "Jones was supposed to ride out yesterday morning. Did you see him leave?"

"Nah, he left the evenin' afore, sneaked out like always. Counted your horses yet?"

They'd not had any reason to do so until now. No one had known Jones was missing.

"I don't suppose by any chance you followed Roberts and Jones when they were following each other?" Hunt asked, not hiding his cynicism about this nosy badger of a man.

"Aye, I tried a time or two, but they knew I was there. I slipped out another door one night and saw that Champlain fellow in the garden, but weren't no one wit' 'im." George's accent came and went, possibly revealing agitation.

Sir Oswald may have been enjoying a smoke in the courtyard. Or he could have been plotting with one of the servants for reasons unknown. Hunt lacked the patience to find out. He'd prefer to heave them all into the street.

"How long have you worked with Avignon?" Villiers asked, so casually that Hunt suspected he already knew the answer.

"Not long a'tall. His man up and quit for a better position just afore he got this invite. Wouldn't hire a cove like me unless he weren't desperate. And he don't pay enough to keep one of them fancy fellers."

Hunt was suspicious by nature. Two new valets for two of their guests and a new secretary for Spalding? He'd have to ask how often valued servants were inclined to quit.

"What do you know about the Champlains' servants?" They'd been as reclusive as their employers. Hunt had no idea who they were.

"Hoity-toity. Don' speak to us. Not sure they's even English. 'er name's Nadia. 'e's Leon, but they don't pronounce it that way. May be married. They're sharing a dressing room insteada sleepin' in the attic. Can't say I blame 'em." He glared at Hunt again.

"Half our guests suffer from windowless rooms." Hunt glared back. "The manor was designed as a fortress, then used as a hunting box until recently. It's not meant for luxury. Have Avignon speak with our housekeeper and see if she can place you anywhere else. He's the one you should confront, not me."

"Do you have anything else of relevance you wish to convey?" Villiers asked wearily.

"Aye, I think from somethin' what was said, old Victor knows Champlain, may have worked wit' 'im afore. They don't like each other much."

"Victor?" Villiers asked.

"Jack's valet. Wasn't Jones supposed to investigate him?" Hunt definitely wanted a drink now.

Staring down Avignon's bold servant, Villiers didn't reply to that. "All right, let's bring Sir Oswald's man in here, next. Any good reason he should be in this wing?"

"Not a one," George said cheerfully, heading for the door. "Anytime you got questions, ask away. I'm at your service."

"Send Leon in, please," Hunt ordered as the man departed. Before the door opened again, he muttered, "That one is looking for a new position." Hunt had always despised gossip, but he had to admit, George's loose tongue was useful.

"I'm about ready to hire him," Villers returned. "He's got his nose to the ground for some reason."

"Not one of your men?"

"Not mine. Without Jones, I don't know how I'll investigate him. Jones remembered the Turbins from an earlier search and intended to look into them, as well, when he reached town. Elsa should have told me she hired a new maid." Villiers pulled a notebook from his pocket and jotted down a reminder.

Hunt felt his headache building. The dead man had known something about Jack and Elsa's servants that needed investigating? Surely the elderly couple could not have pushed a man the size of Jones down stairs. Or tied twine between trees.

Sir Oswald's valet, Leon, entered. He was a paunchy, dapper, blond man of indeterminate age, although not young. Nervously, he bounced up and down on the balls of his feet. At least he knew not to speak unless spoken to.

"How long have you worked with the Champlains?" Hunt was weary of the usual questions and decided to learn more of their odd visitors.

Leon puckered his brow in thought. "Year, maybe more? Since his lordship got married. I worked for her ladyship afore that, as her footman."

"And Nadia is your wife? Did she work for her ladyship also?" Villiers jotted another note.

"Yes, my lord. We been with her for some years."

Had he been in the valet's shoes, Hunt would have demanded an explanation of this interrogation. But unlike George, Leon was apparently a well-behaved servant, unlikely to question authority. "And why were you in the east wing this afternoon?"

"His lordship said he remembered a painting here he'd like to see again. I was looking for it."

"Sir Oswald has been here before?" Hunt didn't bother hiding his surprise.

Once they ascertained Leon knew nothing more, Villiers closed the door behind him and glared at Hunt.

137

"These murders cannot continue. I'm taking Elsa and my stepmother out of here and calling in people more capable of rooting out criminals. I advise you to have your soldiers prevent anyone from leaving until this matter is settled." Looking grim, the earl reached for the door.

Hunt blocked him, fury boiling up with no release in sight. Clare would no doubt leave if Elsa did, but he couldn't stop a man from protecting his family. If he had anywhere to take Clare, he would. He didn't. And his mother might arrive in the middle of the confusion. He had no choice.

"Gravesyde Priory is its own law unless you can persuade a magistrate from Shropshire down here, where he knows no one and can do nothing. Leave, if you must, but this is *my* jurisdiction. I will not have benighted thugs bullying my people. I'll have the soldiers shoot anyone who dares attempt it."

Villiers glared and stormed out. So much for having a noble ally.

TWENTY-ONE

PATIENCE: THURSDAY DINNER

PATIENCE STEADIED THE HAND HOLDING A SMALL GLASS OF canary. She was very bad at small talk, and the gathering in the parlor before dinner was too grim for pleasantries. She'd almost stayed below stairs with her mother, but Elsa had returned, weeping, from an argument with her lordly brother. And Clare was decidedly unhappy. Patience needed to support them, if she could.

If both brides fled before their weddings. . . The manor would surely close up, and she panicked just thinking about it.

This was her home. Now that her father was dead, she had no other. She'd lived in Gravesyde as a child, loved the manor library, and the orchards. . . The orchards desperately needed her. And yes, so many people dying was awful, but people died. It wasn't the fault of the family, surely. Captain Huntley was doing everything within his power to secure the grounds. They'd been locking doors and locking up keys all afternoon.

The poor dead man's horse had apparently never left the stable. Patience was quite certain that meant the guests were the problem. Nervously, she surveyed the gloomy parlor, hoping their unexpected company might come down of their own accord so they might be discreetly questioned. But neither the Lavignes nor the Champlains appeared. Even the aunts remained in their suite.

Looking elegant in his embroidered waistcoat and tailcoat, his neckcloth neatly starched, Henri whispered to his far less elegant big brother. Arnaud shook his head in obvious ill humor. They were directly related to the Lavignes and possibly related to the Champlains. None of them were Reids. Patience could almost hear Henri persuading his brother that their French guests were their responsibility.

Arnaud was the only one who could resist Henri's charm and persuasion. Henri walked away, looking disgusted.

If she wanted to stay at the manor, she must behave as if she belonged here. What would Clare do?

At the moment, Clare was with Hunt, discreetly arguing with an earl and a marquess. Surely, if she could do that, Patience could visit the ill and grieving. As a clergyman's daughter, she'd been trained to do so. She was awkward, but she knew how it was done.

She met Henri halfway across the parlor. "We cannot leave the Lavignes to mourn alone. Paul will be holding the funeral for their loved one tomorrow, but someone should be with them this evening. They are in a strange country, among strangers. You at least speak their language."

Henri's smile was brief and wry, but he nodded. "I have been telling my thickwitted brother this, but he is in a snit. I think he fears someone wanted to kill him, the true heir, and Barbeau died in his place. Arnaud knows he is the comte, that the lands are his. He does not want them, but he feels guilty for having abandoned them."

"There could be many reasons the messenger died, if only that he took the wrong path at the wrong time. Perhaps we might ask who else knew where he was or when he'd arrive."

Daringly, she took his arm. "We must speak with your relations."

His grim visage brightened, and he covered her hand with his big one. "Are you offering to go with me? I thought to carry up meal trays."

His touch went straight to her dizzy head, and it took a second to register his words. She took a deep breath and reminded herself that he was simply being sympathetic.

"If we go now, we may not miss too much of Elsa's dinner." She wrinkled her nose. "Although it's likely to be very salty with tears. Villiers is insisting that she return to her estate as soon as the vows are said on Sunday."

"I think after the vows are said, Jack will be in charge, not the almighty earl. But Hunt is thunderous, and I'd rather not see everyone at daggers drawn. Let us invade the kitchen. You will be my excuse for going down there!" He ushered her out the door. If anyone noticed, there was no outcry.

Once they'd acquired the necessary trays, they fumbled them inexpertly up the service stairs to the family floor, where the Lavignes had been installed in the old tower suite. "I should have worn an old gown and pretended to be a maid," Patience whispered, watching wine glasses wobble.

"I love you in that gown," Henri whispered, pushing the staircase door open with his broad shoulder. "Do not deny me the pleasure of seeing you in silk! The dark blue makes your eyes even lighter. Can I balance this tray and knock at the same time? The maids must be jugglers."

Trying not to giggle at his nonsense, Patience helped him hold the tray while he rapped peremptorily. "*Dîner!*"

The door opened a crack, revealing the pallid Sofia. Her eyebrows raised, but she wasn't brave enough to shut them out. Henri pushed the door wide and nodded for Patience to enter first.

"Madame, Monsieur, how are you faring?" he asked cheerfully. "You remember Miss Upton? She is sister to the clergyman who will speak your words on the morrow." He set the tray on a game table evidently being used for dining.

He was laying on the accent pretty thick, but Patience hoped it was comforting the grief-stricken family. "We've all been so worried about you," she murmured, setting out plates. "You really must let us offer our condolences. This has to be frightening."

"You are kind," Adele Lavigne said, taking a chair her daughter pulled out for her. "We are lost without Barbeau. He was to take care of everything."

"And now we are here, beggars, with no documents, no nothing, at the mercy of my brother's family." Jules Lavigne paced instead of sitting. "We should have never come."

"Papa," Sofia pleaded. "We had hopes. We can still go to the solicitors and learn what Jean-Jacques learned. He must have had a reason for coming here."

"I daresay it was because he learned Arnaud is alive and lives here." Henri pulled out a chair for the elder Lavigne. "But there are mysteries we should resolve."

"Mysteries, ha!" A gentleman even in hunger, Jules hovered over the dinner table without taking a seat.

Patience hurriedly took a chair beside the grate so the gentlemen might sit too. "We are very much afraid someone else was the intended victim. It seems odd that Mr. Barbeau should take a hidden path that even the family was not aware of. Someone he met must have known of it."

Or someone already in the manor, who may have meant to harm Arnaud—the heir to lands these people evidently wished to claim. It was all very confusing.

Henri didn't sit but opened the draperies on the last of the sunlight in the west-facing window. "Your solicitors—Browning, Dryden, and Hallewell, correct? They would have told Monsieur Barbeau many things, perhaps. Captain Huntley may write them, but a letter would be far better from you, *oui*?"

"I have been attempting to compose in English," Jules Lavigne admitted. "But what proof have I of who I am when our documents were in Barbeau's keeping?"

Patience thought such trust a trifle foolish, but she did not know what they'd had to do to escape a country on the brink of war. "Arnaud can vouch for you. You truly do need to know what the solicitors know. Monsieur Barbeau may have left them your documents."

"I'll help to write the letter and make certain my stubborn brother identifies you. Solicitors are particular, but I cannot think there is any reason not to tell you what they told Barbeau. Although if they gave him papers. . ." Henri took a seat beside Patience and shook his head.

"France and England are at war again," the older man reminded them. "We are outcasts everywhere. Once upon a time, our family was celebrated on two shores. These days, there is just us, and we are nothing."

"Papa!" Sofia protested. "You are not nothing. The king returned our land. We have that."

Not necessarily, with Napoleon returned from exile, but no one in the room dared say that.

Henri squeezed Patience's hand before speaking. "The papers Barbeau gave to the solicitors—were they just passports or more?"

"Birth and death certificates, deeds and wills, to show we are the heirs to the Champlain properties as well as the Lavigne land." Jules glared defiantly at Henri. "He was to inquire into your whereabouts. We had no death certificate for Arnaud, but we had an eyewitness account." His shoulders slumped. "I should be grateful to know that my brother's sons are alive."

Patience certainly thought so, but she understood the desire for a home of one's own. Henri squeezed her hand again, telling her he wished to speak. Relieved, she needn't think of anything soothing to say.

"We are grateful to know we still have family," Henri assured them. "But why was it necessary to prove all this to English solicitors? You could have gone on without us forever, and we'd likely never know."

"Because of your Champlain great-grandparents, dear," Adele Lavigne said. She raised her slim neck so her fading blond curls dangled stylishly. "Jules's mother and Gabrielle were their only heirs."

Patience timidly raised her hand. "Then who is Sir Oswald?" Did the French do things differently and leave their property to daughters and not the males in the family?

"A distant cousin." Jules waved a dismissive hand. "His branch were my grandfather's younger brothers and went to sea. My Grandfather Champlain owned the land adjoining the Lavigne property. He left it to his eldest daughter, Jeanette, and her husband, my parents. He had thought Gabrielle, his youngest daughter, taken care of when she married into an earl's family."

That would be the viscountess, Lady Reid, who'd led a tragic life trapped in England with a violent husband. Patience sighed. At least the rest of the Reid family lacked his propensities.

"Still not understanding," Henri admitted. "English solicitors cannot prove your ownership of either property, especially the Lavigne land, since our father was the eldest, and Arnaud, as heir, is alive."

"It was not the land." Jules ran his long-fingered hand through thinning hair. "It is the Champlain pearls. The land is worthless without money. We cannot rebuild. We cannot even hire peasants to plow the fields. We'd hoped the entail on the pearls could be broken."

"Arnaud said the same of the land's uselessness," Henri acknowledged. "But we thought the pearls were gone. What entail?"

Jules Lavigne stiffened. Patience took that to mean he did

not wish to tell his nephews. But it was a little late for that. She said carefully, "It is possible poor Mr. Barbeau was murdered for pearls, since he mentioned them before he died. Wealth does not buy happiness. It must be used to heal wounds."

Sofia broke into tears. "Tell them, Papa. They are meaningless now!" She jumped up from the table and fled into the anteroom.

"Not meaningless," Jules said harshly, burying his face in his hands. "Our only hope of a future. We must return to London and inquire of the solicitors."

"Quite possibly. If you are prepared for a journey after the funeral, I will ride with you, but Hunt is to marry soon. And we now have two deaths to solve. Until a killer is caught, it may be dangerous for us to ride anywhere." Henri did not use his usual charm in starkly explaining the circumstances.

Reminded that the Lavignes had not been in their tower when they'd discovered the second body, Patience timidly diverted the conversation, giving time for emotions to settle down. "You are aware that the earl's secretary died on the stairs last night? Did you hear anything?"

Adele nodded diffidently. "Today, we took a walk in the pretty courtyard while the sun was out, and when we returned, all was great. . . confusion. The maids, they tell us of the poor man. But at night, we hear nothing. Do you think this. . . connects to Barbeau?"

"We can't know until we find the killer," Henri said. "But it's unlikely to have two different killers on the loose."

That brought frowns all around. Two killers. . . did seem unlikely.

But why would the same person murder a French stranger and an earl's secretary?

Lady Lavigne. . . Well, perhaps she wasn't a lady if Jules wasn't a count? Patience gave up on titles. Sofia's mother reached across the table to pat her husband's hand. "We should stay for the funeral and perhaps, for the wedding. We must help these generous people find the asp in their bosoms. We may be the reason that poor Mr. Jones died."

Jules shook his head. "We did not know the Englishman. Barbeau, as you have said, must have been in the wrong place at the wrong time. Perhaps it was the Englishman who was supposed to ride that lane. This has nothing to do with us."

"But everything to do with pearls you wish to claim that might belong to the entire Champlain family?" Henri asked with an edge of impatience.

Pearls might be why the other Champlains arrived? And Hunt's mother! His grandmother was Gabrielle *Champlain* Reid. Lady Reid had owned an enormous string of pearls— which she'd sold, hadn't she? Patience rubbed her brow trying to sort it all out.

Jules gave a rather Gallic gesture and sipped his wine. "They are probably tall tales anyway. We are clinging to illusions. You are aware that the Champlains, Lady Reid's family, were seafarers and collected pearls?"

"Not just the wedding pearls?" Henri stood and paced impatiently. "I don't know why—if they still exist—they would be in England."

"Safekeeping, of course. Browning, Dryden, and Hallewell are a very prestigious firm, recommended by my father, your grandfather. The Lavigne sons looked after the Champlain daughters as much as we were able."

Patience thought sleeping with another man's wife might not be her definition of "looking after," but that had been a different time and place. Would Hunt's mother be recognized as a descendant?

"A Mr. Browning in Stratford is one of Wycliffe Manor's solicitors," Henri noted with a frown. "A relation?"

Jules shrugged. "I cannot know. I only know what my father told me, and that is the pearls were to be distributed evenly over a period of twenty years to the daughters and their children. The value of pearls goes up more certainly than that of risky investments in times like these. It must have made sense to our Grandfather Champlain. I do not ask for all of them. A single pearl might pay the labor on plowing a field with perhaps a little left for a wedding offering to the church."

Not that the offering was needed anymore, Patience thought sadly, wringing her hands.

"After Père Champlain died, we were unable to collect his share," Adele whispered. "With the war, we had no way of presenting our documentation. After all these years, Jules should have more than one pearl."

"When the king returned, I stupidly thought it better to claim the land first. Then we'd have something on which to build. And then Napoleon escaped and conscription began again. . ." Jules gestured helplessly. "This time, it was decided that we should leave. I am too old to fight more. Barbeau was too young. We wished to farm, nothing more."

And years worth of pearls would have given them a little fund to start anew. Patience wanted to weep along with the Lavigne ladies. She knew how hard it was to scrape by on nothing. It had to be worse for people raised in wealth.

"Did Barbeau's message to you say that the pearls are still in the vault?" Henri demanded.

"His message said to meet with him here before attending the solicitors. So we hired a carriage and came here straight away, hoping for good news."

"Instead, Barbeau had discovered Arnaud and I are alive and also claimants to those pearls," Henri said in disgust. "How did he intend to be rid of us?"

TWENTY-TWO

CLARE: FRIDAY MORNING

"YOU ARE BEING R-R-RIDICULOUS." BOSWORTH THREW DOWN THE volume he'd been examining and glared at Hunt. "Garret B-b-browning the Third is a fine solicitor, the grandson of the Garret B-b-browning in London. The one in London is a d-doddering old fool, as is the entire firm. It's the reason the viscountess moved her business to us."

"So she was not selling off her rope of pearls to pay the mortgage but using the pearl a year she inherited?" Clare tried to sort it all out, but pearls were meant to be worn, not used as money. She shook her head at the ways of men. Bosworth was in an important library, surrounded by knowledge, and he was examining the books for monetary value. She did not understand it at all.

"Exactly. W-we have no idea what h-happened to the pearls in her possession. By the time we were informed of her d-death, the s-servants had all absconded. Your late Mr. Upton had s-seen to her burial but was remiss in s-sending us notice of her d-death." Bosworth picked up the next volume on the table.

"Perhaps Upton did not know her bankers," Hunt said dryly. "It's not as if he were family or even her clergyman.

She was a recluse. One would think you might have inquired about her health upon occasion."

"That is not my task. F-family should do that d-duty. She had no f-family except those F-frenchie cousins of yours. Go ask them what became of the pearls. Perhaps she hid them with the earl's missing jewels." The banker made a note of the title and details of the next volume he chose.

"But you visited upon occasion, did you not? You were familiar with the caretakers. You had to oversee the trust property. I assume you cut that path from the road to the drive." Hunt picked up the volume Bosworth set down, just to irritate him.

Clare rolled her eyes at this antagonistic approach, but Hunt understood men better than she did. Bosworth returned his attention to Hunt. Mission accomplished.

"I d-did not scramble up trees and tie twine to h-hang a m-man who did not belong there in the f-first place. Lady Reid was a client. My f-father sent me out to v-visit with her twice a year. I continued that policy after her d-death, to be certain the property did not f-fall to r-rack and r-ruin."

Clare noticed the banker stuttered more when upset. She set a hand on Hunt's arm and spoke before he could. Sometimes, soothing worked better than irritating. "We are grateful that you did. You say you visited with Lady Reid? I did not know that! We are trying to determine who may have visited with her who might have known about the pearls. Or who her servants might have been?"

Bosworth finally leaned back in his chair to study them. "Y-you d-do not accuse me of s-stealing the p-pearls?"

"That accusation is almost as shocking as if we actually had accused you," Clare retorted. "Of course not. But someone who knew of that path told poor Barbeau to take it, then murdered him. Unless they meant to murder you. Arnaud knew of it, but he goes nowhere. Who else uses it?"

"Perhaps your F-frenchman meant to murder me, then."

149

Hunt balled up his fingers, but Clare shook her head at him. Bosworth had a point, even if it was irrelevant.

Folding his hands over his belly, the banker sat back with a frown that wasn't directed at them for a change. "The lady had s-servants, of course. The trust allowed for them. There were never as many around as I thought the trust paid to be, s-so I tried to pay attention."

Hunt wisely held his tongue and perused the stack of books on the table, although Clare knew he listened. The banker so seldom spoke without hostility that she paid attention when he did.

"There were the Gaithers, of course, b-butler and house-keeper. The viscountess had a F-french cook and a lady's maid, but I s-seldom saw them. I believe the maid was married to a f-footman. I'd have to look in the accounts to see if there was a list of names."

"Walker can do that," Hunt agreed. "An excellent thought. I'm not sure that her servants would know of the path, but anything might help. Did she ever have visitors?"

"She didn't acquire that b-brandy from local merchants," he said dryly. "But I never met them."

"That's all useful to know, thank you. We'll let you return to your work." Hunt took Clare's arm and led her out before whispering, "What exactly is it he's doing?"

"I think Jack's father gave him the earl's codes to play with. It seems to keep him occupied while Jack and Elsa's brother argue over settlements and what is invested where. Are we going to see Walker now?" She hurried to match his long footsteps.

"He'll have finished his breakfast. I'm thinking I should ride into Stratford and interview this Mr. Browning. Perhaps he visited the lady?"

"One would think, if she had a banker and solicitor at her disposal, she'd have sold some of her wedding pearls to help her nephews." Clare puzzled over the possibility that the necklace had been in the manor but never sold, as they'd assumed.

"Do we need to read her entire library of journals? I recall we found no mention of selling pearls to pay the mortgage. We have only the ledger records to know she did that. Betsy told us she was seen wearing a rope of pearls. They existed and she had them in her possession, but did she write about them?" Hunt stopped in the wide corridor under his gas lamps.

"If they were stolen before she died, I'm sure the journals would have mentioned it. She had histrionics over missing chocolates. I will talk to Dottie about reading the journals more thoroughly than we have, and in light of our current knowledge. Have you written the London solicitors?" Clare lifted her skirt to climb the marble stairs.

Hunt sent her ankles an appreciative glance that stirred a thrill she probably shouldn't notice in a house of mourning. She hastily lowered her skirt.

He continued in his usual pragmatic tones. "We've sent off a package to London with letters from Lavigne, me, and Arnaud, with a reluctant verification from Bosworth. I cannot know when to expect a reply. To keep him from calling in troops, I have Villiers working with Jack on the notes Jones took of his investigations. He's really at a loss without the man. The two funerals are at noon?"

Clare knew he was furious at the earl for reasons he hadn't explained. She hoped this meant they'd settled their disagreement. But her beloved was tense and more irritable than usual. She supposed he had a right to be. Two deaths in a week—on top of all else. She stopped to give him a peck on the cheek, then darted back when he reached for more.

"We thought two funerals expedient, before the rain comes again." A little confused by all her emotions—two funerals and two weddings?—Clare ran off to look for Dottie.

Her cousin was usually with the aunts when not in the with-drawing room, communing with spirits.

She was startled to discover the handsome young curate also closeted with the old ladies. Shouldn't he be preparing for the funerals?

A man of middle height, with a shock of auburn hair, Paul Upton rose and bowed at Clare's entrance. "I had hoped to speak with the bereaved, but Lord Villiers claims there is nothing to be said about his secretary other than that he was a good man."

"A good soldier, a good secretary, always a gentleman," Clare suggested, remembering far too many funeral services.

Dottie spoke up from the table where she sat with the aunts at a table of books, papers, and pens. "I diverted Mr. Upton to ask about spirits. Thank you, sir, you have been most helpful."

"My pleasure." He bowed and Clare noticed he gave Dottie an appreciative glance similar to the one Hunt had bestowed on Clare. Was that the scent of jasmine filling the air? Oh dear. She would start believing the lady's spirit was matchmaking—except an heiress trained to run a wealthy household, and an impoverished curate whose wife must be a housekeeper and cook, made a very bad match.

"Do you need help in finding the Lavignes? They're at the far end of the corridor." Clare preferred to stay here and ques-tion the meddling aunts, but she had to offer.

"No, thank you. Patience and Henri have introduced me to them." Paul bowed to the ladies and departed.

Clare studied the table of books and swept up a list in unfamiliar handwriting. "Paul gave you his list of possible suspects? You are solving mysteries and not codes?"

Lady Spalding waved her plump, beringed hand. "The codes are quite impossible. My grandfather had a labyrinthian mind. Sir Oswald and his odd wife, however, avoid us, which is suspicious. I must have met my mother's English relations at some point, but I don't remember them."

"Another of the journals fell open to a reference of C visiting." Dottie produced the volume. "I have asked the tutor to draw up a timeline of France's revolution and the war to match against the journal entries. He is setting Davy and Oliver to it. As I understand it, Lady Reid died in 1801, after Napoleon began his reign."

"You should talk to Arnaud. He'll know actual dates better than these journals. The lady's news might be weeks late." Clare took a seat to study the book. Her French was improving, but the lady's handwriting and spelling had not. "She does not seem so pleased with her mysterious Mr. C in this passage." She checked the date on the volume: 1795. A tumultuous year for French aristocrats, if she remembered her history correctly.

"She calls this C an ingrate but does not say what they talked about." Dottie took the book back. "They were executing aristocrats in Paris. She must have been grieving."

"I cannot fathom why it matters now. Henri and Arnaud were schoolboys at the time. They were sent to the safety of school here during that era. I don't know the exact dates." Clare picked up the list of suspects. "Arnaud returned to France after the death of his parents. Henri did not. So, yes, the lady still had people she knew in France."

"We are trying to understand what happened to Mother's pearls," Lady Spalding explained. "While my sister and I were being presented in London, she sold them one at a time to pay modistes and so forth. She replaced them with fakes so no one could tell. I have no notion how many she might have had left when she retired here."

Perhaps not many if she had to sell her annual inheritance to pay the mortgage.

"We are trying to determine how many people on this list

may have known about her pearls," Dottie added. "Did they visit? Did she use the remaining pearls to rescue her family?"

Brandy smugglers might have those kind of connections. So might Sir Oswald, the seafarer. Clare shivered. Since they had been inherited through the female line, might those pearls belong to Hunt's mother and aunt? None of this had much to do with Barbeau or Jones.

"If we could find Lady Reid's servants. . ." Lady Lavinia picked up the list of suspects with her frail, age-spotted hand and studied it through her lorgnette. Today she wore a large cap instead of her usual formal pompadour. "We might learn more. Although, I suppose the servants may have stuck their spoons in the wall as well."

Clare refrained from rolling her eyes at the euphemism. "Walker is looking up the account entries for that period, but mostly, they use initials or just say 'Paid domestic quarterly wages" and give an amount. I don't think they'll be useful."

Clare picked up another copy of Paul's list. Personal servants made up the majority. The curate would not suspect a lord of murder, rightfully so. They'd have hired someone to do their dirty work.

None of them really knew the servants of guests—or noticed them. They could have been almost anywhere at any time. The men attempting to pin them down were acting in frustration.

"Are you reading the latter journals, the ones from her years after she exiled herself to the manor?" Clare asked. "We read the ones from her marriage to the viscount, but only skimmed the last ones. I did not think to look for references to staff."

"I am trying. I originally hoped to find references to the codes. Now I am noting visitors and will add servants. Generally, she does not mention names, unless they irritate her. She complains about the cook's plain English cooking or if M doesn't curl her wig properly. Mostly, she leaves domestics to the G's."

"The Gaithers, the butler and housekeeper. I thought Bosworth said the cook was French, and possibly her lady's maid as well." Clare noted the French Turbins were high on Paul's suspect list. Jack and Elsa wouldn't appreciate that.

Dottie hastily flipped through pages she'd marked with various colors of the ladies' threads and yarns. "I believe—" She stopped to skim a passage, then passed the open book over. "Her French cook quit. Apparently 'A' offered her a better position in London. Lady Reid was furious."

"Not an oddity," Lady Spalding, her daughter, murmured. "Mother had a temper. But really, a good cook would want an audience, and there would be none to appreciate his creations here."

"And then, several pages later, 'C' brings her an English cook. The viscountess is certain the cook is a spy. Does that mean the lady doesn't trust C?"

"We need to bring Henri and Arnaud in here!" Clare studied the pages. "They would have been old enough to notice a different cook, even if they didn't visit often."

"What would that serve?" Lady Lavinia asked in irritation. "It's not as if they might recognize a cook as one of our current guests."

Clare studied the suspect list in resignation. "And none of this has to do with the deaths of two young men, one English, one French. Although one assumes Barbeau, at least, knew of the pearls. Do you propose *we* question all these people? Hunt already has, without much success."

"We wish to speak with Sir Oswald and his wife," Dottie said decisively. "They are purportedly of French descent, relations to the viscountess. He could be a smuggler. His name begins with C, and they behave suspiciously."

"And one of the servants mentioned Sir Oswald was

looking for a painting he'd seen here before," Clare added excitedly.

"Except they arrived much too late to set a trap for Barbeau," Dottie pointed out.

"Not if they sent someone ahead." Clare stood up. "There are quite a few new servants on that list. Put the ones who were here at the beginning of the week at the top of the people to be questioned."

"That would include Jones," Lady Spalding said, with a frown. "Surely Villiers' secretary—"

"Knew something that got him killed!" Clare declared in triumph.

TWENTY-THREE

ELSA: FRIDAY MORNING

ELSA RAN UP TWO SETS OF SERVICE STAIRS FROM THE CELLAR kitchen to the family floor where Jack had closeted himself in their new suite, away from prying eyes. The service stairs hid the servants from the guests as well—a fact that Jones's death made horribly clear. She was grateful the kitchen was beneath the manor end of the east wing so she need not pass the landing where Jones had died.

She hated the idea of having to move their bridal suite back into the dark fortress of the main manor—but if killers were now traipsing up and down this empty corridor. . . She shuddered.

They'd been leaving the windows open in the suite to air it out. As she entered, a damp draft lifted the rose-patterned damask draperies. Elsa hoped the breeze would remove any musty odor from the ancient fabric. The maids had polished the dark mahogany of the poster bed and wardrobes to a gleam, and the blue bedcover with embroidered roses almost looked new after a good laundering and some minor patches.

She could buy new, but she saw little point. One simply slept in beds. Well, and other things that didn't require entertaining anyone but themselves. She and Jack had come very close to anticipating their vows, but not in that bed. That was for their wedding night—only two more nights away! It was good they were too occupied to think about the enormous changes ahead.

They'd decided they didn't need a private salon with fashionable decor. They had an entire manor full of rooms for entertaining in. Jack had simply come in here so he wouldn't be interrupted as he worked through Jones's notes. She hated bothering him now. He wasn't much at bookwork and preferred to be with his horses, but two murders. . . They couldn't leave Hunt and Clare to deal with such crime on their own.

At her entrance, he glanced up with a smile that heated her all the way through. She was still growing accustomed to being loved by this gallant man she'd adored since childhood. She'd never felt particularly lovable. She was bossy and eccentric and a little too plump and hated primping and frivoling about in lace. She liked pretty clothes well enough. She simply hated being idle. Lace and horses and kitchens did not work well together.

Jack rose and took her in his strong arms. An ex-soldier and a bruising rider, he had muscles on top of muscles, and he used them to shelter her and make her feel safe when she'd thought all the world against her. She hugged him back, relishing the closeness and the scent of masculine musk. . . and jasmine. She'd be jealous, but the perfume permeated everything.

"To what do I owe this rare pleasure?" He kissed her neck and nibbled at her earlobe. "Surely it is not time for the funerals already?" He glanced at the window. "Although the rain hasn't started yet."

"No, they're still scheduled for after luncheon. I just had a little time between meals and. . . I cannot even say for certain how you can help. I simply needed to sort out my thoughts by talking to you."

Jack kissed behind her ear, then stepped back, understanding that clarity of thoughts did not occur while kissing. "Tell me all, my dearest dear."

Elsa took a breath and tried to bring her cascading thoughts into order. "Hunt has enlisted the entire household in his search for a killer, and the *Turbins* are on the very top of his suspect list. And he's right. It is very suspicious that they turned up here before everything started happening. But we'd sent requests to the staffing agency and. . ." She paced about, touching the pretty oil lamp on the night table, circling the small table Jack had set Jones's notes on.

"The Turbins had a perfectly proper letter of reference from the agency," Jack added, when her words paused. "They gave a list of previous employers and a letter from their most recent one. It's not even coincidence that they showed up when they did. We were the ones requesting a maid and a valet."

Jack opened one of the wardrobes to reveal neat stacks of linens, trousers, and hooks of coats. "They are obviously well trained and experienced."

Elsa twisted her hands in her apron and faced him. "Clare says Lady Reid had a French maid who was married to a footman. The journals don't reference them often, and she only has the initial M for the maid so far. But what if. . ."

He grimaced and nodded toward the notes he was reading. "Jones asked the same question, although he didn't mention the journals. He was just generally suspicious of the Turbins because they were French. He tried questioning them, but as we've noticed, they're elusive. They stay pretty much exclusively to their own room and ours. Do they dine below with the others?"

"Good-hearted Betsy carries trays up to their room, as well as to Hunt's valet." Elsa nodded at the dressing room where the Turbins had set up cots for themselves. "She says the Turbins have what she calls the rheumatiz and can't climb stairs. We'll have to give her an extra wage for that."

"The manor is large enough to conceal an army," Jack grumbled. "I suppose we need to speak with them. But even if they admit to working for Lady Reid in the past, what does it matter? They can't climb trees! And I doubt the two of them together had the strength to push Jones down the stairs. He was a pretty strong man."

Elsa brightened. "But they may know who worked here during the lady's time and who visited! Where are they now? This is where they usually are."

"I left them mending in our old rooms. They may have rheumatism, but they still manage to sew. Shall we tackle them together?" He offered his arm.

"Oh, yes, please. I don't even know where to start." Elsa took his arm, and they traversed the faux tower where the back halls and stairs intersected and opened into the older portion of the manor. They found both Marie and Victor in Elsa's rooms.

Sitting near the windows with baskets of mending, the servants glanced up in surprise at their entrance. Victor stood, bowed silently, and awaited orders.

Marie bobbed a hasty curtsy. "My lady, what can we do for you?"

Tongue-tied, Elsa looked to Jack to respond.

Jack was never hesitant and always blunt. "Captain Huntley is gathering a list of Lady Reid's servants and guests prior to her death. There is some reference to a French lady's maid named Marie, who is married to a footman. Would that be you, by any chance?"

Elsa hid her wince as he blatantly made up that little detail about the maid's name.

"That was many years ago, monsieur. Of what matter is it now?" Victor asked, his narrow, wrinkled face creasing even more with his frown.

160

"We don't know for certain," Elsa managed to collect her wits to speak. "The captain is trying to discover who might have known about that path where the poor messenger died. Mr. Bosworth says it is an old path, before the time of Lady Reid's presence. So he's interested in knowing who might have visited back then and may have known of it."

The couple exchanged nervous glances. Again, Victor spoke for them. "We do not wish trouble, my lady. My Marie and I, we grew up on the lady's estate in France. We were young, no more than scullery help. She brought us to London with her and her new baby daughter. We stayed with her in the city, where we learned what pleased her. Later, we followed her here. After she passed, everyone was turned out. We had to go to the city to find positions. Then we hear the manor has opened again, and you are looking for help. The country reminds us of home, so we thought maybe we find positions here and look for a little place where we might retire on our small savings. But we are not yet ready to retire, *vous comprenez?*"

"You knew Lady Reid?" Elsa asked in astonishment. "How fortuitous!"

"We were servants, my lady," Marie murmured. "And young. We barely spoke the English. She was very tragic when she visited her family. She wanted people she knew to be with her. For us, it was an opportunity."

Elsa did a hasty mental calculation. The viscountess had fled her abusive husband and bore a daughter outside her marriage nearly fifty years ago. The Turbins had indeed been very young and must be nearing seventy now.

"So you worked for her in London while she was raising her daughters?" Jack asked, apparently also doing the math.

"Oui," Victor admitted. "She did not have many staff. We did a little everything, pushed brooms, carried trays. Much later, we worked up to our place now."

"We really need to call for Hunt and Clare. I cannot even

think what to ask." Elsa twisted her apron and tried to imagine the life this couple had lived. "How did you find new positions after Lady Reid died? Did her friends help you?"

"She had no friends, my lady," Marie said softly. "She had people who wished to—how you say?—*use* her. Her cousins, they brought the. . ." She darted a look at her husband. "Can I say?"

"If you mean they brought the brandy, we've already surmised that," Jack said impatiently. "Her cousins, you say? Would that be the Champlains?"

"Oui, Monsieur Champlain would visit and count the bottles."

Monsieur? Before he was knighted? Elsa gripped Jack's arm tighter.

"The lady told us to pretend he was not there, so we stayed away from her rooms then." Victor kneaded his upper arm and looked uneasy. "We have seen this man and stay out of his way again."

Definitely Sir Oswald! And he had been at the manor as little as fifteen years ago?

How much could they trust the Turbins to tell the truth? And did they endanger the pair by asking questions? Elsa had learned to dodge and hide from her bully of a stepbrother and stepfather, but that wasn't quite the same as avoiding a potential killer.

Jack took the matter out of her hands. "You recognize Sir Oswald as the man who once visited the viscountess? What about his wife?"

Marie shook her head. "He only came himself. He spoke poor French. We spoke poor English. He did not stay long when he came."

"This was when?" Jack demanded. "*After* Lady Reid returned to Wycliffe Manor? Did he ever visit when she was in London?"

"No, non," Victor said emphatically. "There was not a revolution then. War brought the émigrés much later."

Ah, the viscountess's daughters had married and moved away *before* Lady Reid departed London for the manor. So her daughter, Lady Spalding, most likely had not met Sir Oswald and would not recognize him. So why had they avoided her?

Had Sir Oswald been avoiding the *Turbins*? "You said he did not speak French well. He could not be an émigré."

"No, our lady, *she* helped the émigrés when she could," Victor explained. "This Champlain, he was a sailor. He brought the brandy and the émigrés and the messages from France."

"And took back what in return?" Jack asked harshly.

Victor shrugged. "We do not share in her talks. Money from the brandy, perhaps."

"The pearls," Marie murmured, twisting her fingers together and looking worried. "She cried over the pearls each time she cut off another. I had to repair the knots."

Sir Oswald had said he was a seafarer. He had not lied. *But he knew of the pearls.* He'd gone to France during the revolution. He could be a spy. Fear seeped into Elsa's heart. Could they throw out a guest based on this knowledge? No. He hadn't been here when Barbeau died.

But what of Jones? The Champlains had been here then. Had her brother's secretary learned Sir Oswald's secrets? Did they have two different killers?

"You know of the pearls?" Jack asked before Elsa could formulate the question.

Marie nodded. "My lady's dowry, from her family. She say they were all she had of home. This Champlain, he brought word of the death of her parents. She cried and gave him a pearl to take back for their funerals and for prayers in the church."

Which left the obvious question. . . "What became of the pearls after her death?" Elsa asked, almost holding her breath.

Marie wiped her eyes with her handkerchief. Victor held her shoulders and finished for her. "The priest, he looked at her letters and books and found names. He wrote to them. A man came, said he acted for her family. We'd seen him here before, with the Champlain rogue. He was an émigré, an important one, an aristocrat. He said the solicitors told him everything belonged to the earl's estate except the pearls, and they belonged to her family. What could we say? Who would we ask? Her family in France was dead. Her daughters were gone. He offered to take us to London where we might find new positions."

The *priest*—the late Mr. Upton, the local curate. He'd admitted to writing to the solicitors about the lady's death. He'd been all she'd had by then. Mr. Upton had been a bit of a rascal, but Elsa was fairly certain he had never been a thief. His family had been much too poor to be living off stolen goods. If the solicitors took the lady's only possession, then they must have known all else belonged to Bosworth's bank. Presumably, they believed the bank already knew of her death. And the earl's estate was no concern of theirs.

"You were just servants and could not argue," Elsa murmured, trying to see that awful time through their eyes. They would have been frightened, helpless, and a man, presumably of authority, one who spoke their language, offered aid. "Do you know this man's name?"

"The lady called him Avril sometimes, Charles when she wasn't angry with him," Marie offered tentatively. "He was too young to be her lover. We thought. . . perhaps he knew her family, but we did not know him."

Charles Avril. Elsa could think of no one of that name.

That did not mean everyone here used their real names.

TWENTY-FOUR

HUNT: FRIDAY MORNING

"I BLOODY WELL WANT WHOEVER KILLED JONES STRUNG UP AND drawn and quartered," Earl Villiers growled, pacing the larger study Hunt had finally resigned himself to using.

It was either that or have people form a line outside his old one. If he must play the role of general, he ought to at least be paid like one. With a sigh, he leaned back in the chair he'd rescued from Clare's furniture purgatory. His knee objected to standing while the earl threw his weight around. A pity one couldn't shoot nobles for being annoying.

Jack flung his stack of notes on the mostly empty desk. "We can't know who did it from these notes of his. Jones suspected everyone, but he was relying on documents, not interviews. Did he never actually *talk* to anyone?"

"He was a secretary," Villiers retorted. "He sent letters. That's what he did. Could some of his correspondence have been removed?"

Jack and Villiers bickered like fishwives when frustrated. Hunt would rather shout them down.

As Henri and Arnaud entered, Hunt gestured at the arguing almost in-laws. "Sorry to drag you away, but Jack has learned a few things about Lady Reid's household. We're hoping you can verify them."

Impatient with the argument, the slender Marquess of Spalding had wandered off. Now, he dragged in a leather chair from the billiard room across the hall and set it in a corner near the empty bookshelves. Taking a seat, he crossed his leg over his knee and tapped his fingers in irritation. "Are we, or are we not, dealing with French spies? All I've heard is talk of missing jewelry. Are thieves likely to kill? I'd think they'd be more likely to run."

Arnaud leaned his wide shoulders against a shelf and shrugged in his usual taciturn manner.

Henri set down a brandy decanter, but the new office had no glassware. He threw up his hands in disgust and said what Hunt was thinking. "One kills for money, revenge, passion, or defense. Or any combination of the above. If Jones threatened a thief. . ." He left the insinuation hanging.

Walker entered with an armful of old bookkeeping ledgers. "Lady Reid left her butler to keep accounts. You will not find much in here. If you do not need me, I am helping the curate with the coffins and setting up a memorial service."

This was the reason Hunt needed the enormous study and the massive, empty desk. One more occupant, and the room might explode. At least they had room for the huge ledgers.

Hunt thanked Walker and waved him off, knowing if anything useful were to be found in the books, his friend would have found it. But the bloody noble aristocrats weren't likely to believe without seeing for themselves. He let them study the cramped, fading handwriting and turned to matters at hand. "Jack, tell Arnaud and Henri what you've learned."

Jack explained about the Turbins having previously worked for the viscountess and the émigrés who came and went, possibly with brandy shipments.

Arnaud shook his head. "I returned to France as soon as I was old enough to find transportation, so I was only here for a few years while she was alive. I remember nothing of brandy or émigrés. Our aunt was happy for our company and glad to see us during school breaks, but she did not engage us in conversation. We fished. We shot game. And we ate everything in the larder. I vaguely remember a French cook when we first visited."

"She made chocolate pastries," Henri crowed. "And then she was gone and we were given solid English bread. It is not as if we complained. We never had enough to eat at school."

"And Lady Reid never explained why she lost her cook?" Hunt asked. His grandmother was an enigma to him. As far as he was aware, his mother had seldom corresponded with her. The distance was great. Perhaps he should question his aunt, Lady Spalding. She had at least been in the same country. He waited for the marquess to suggest they speak with his stepmother. The slender aristocrat simply glared at the ledgers, wanting to find spies.

"We were energetic boys. She barely knew how to talk to us." Henri picked a ledger and sat cross-legged in a corner to examine it. "You are asking us to remember nearly twenty years ago!"

"Do you remember if she had a lady's maid and a footman?" Jack asked.

"They were French," Arnaud recalled. "We did not see much of them, but the butler would order them around in a loud voice, as if they would understand English better if shouted."

Henri brightened. "I remember that! And Victor would mutter French curses under his breath while smiling as if agreeing with whatever Gaither shouted. I started doing the same, until our aunt caught me and scolded."

"*Victor?*" Jack pounced on the name. "The footman was called Victor?"

"And his wife was Marie." Henri turned the ledger so

others could read it. "Gaither called them the Turds. Here they are, V and M Turd, bonus."

Villiers grabbed the book, then passed it on to Spalding. "A Christmas bonus just for her personal servants? That must have generated ill feelings."

"Victor and Marie Turbin." Jack sat back with a frown. "They appear to be telling the truth, then. But are they telling us all of it? And who is this Charles Avril who took the remaining pearls?"

"And are they in danger for telling us this?" Villiers asked. "We need to interview the Champlains. It seems rather obvious that he was the one who delivered the brandy and knows more than he's telling. Why the devil is he here anyway?"

"Purportedly to see me wed and greet my mother," Hunt said dryly. "But if he will not even speak with my aunt. . ."

Henri stood up. "I'll have Adam fetch Sir Knight. I doubt the lady was with him back then. And I'll look for snifters while I'm out there."

"And chairs," Arnaud growled.

"Fetch your own, *mon frere*," Henri called over his shoulder.

"It's before noon. We need lunch more than brandy," Hunt protested.

"Murder hasn't spoiled your appetite?" Arnaud shoved himself off the wall. "I'll send someone down to the kitchen and have a tray brought up."

"Don't you think Elsa has enough to do?" Villiers grumbled.

Arnaud ignored him and departed with Henri.

The crowd was growing testy. Hunt thought he ought to send them all on maneuvers to work out their frustration. At least Villiers had quit shouting about bringing in invisible authorities. For now.

"The servants are the ones who have been prowling about

where they don't belong," the marquess remarked idly, as he flipped through the ledger. "I've had Norsworthy keeping track of who is in the kitchen when, and anywhere else he might see them. Only a few of them spend time below stairs, where they should be attending laundry and boot cleaning and such."

"You think one of our guests' *servants* visited Lady Reid and was privy to her secrets? Took the pearls?" Hunt couldn't imagine it, but Clare had informed him that he lacked imagination. She had more than enough to spare, He'd consult her later.

"The Turbins knew about the brandy," the marquess said. "Why not? Most of the current staff aren't old enough to have met Lady Reid, but I'm tracking suspicious behavior. The ladies have been sharing maids, so Lady Elsa's ancient maid is often with the Lavignes, presumably because she speaks French."

"And because Lady Champlain refuses to share her maid, Nadia," Jack added. "Elsa has complained. Nadia and Leon appear to be as reclusive as their employers."

"I can't comment on the other servants, because my batman has difficulty maneuvering stairs with his pegleg and doesn't go to the kitchen. He has sweet-talked one of the maids into delivering trays to his room and does not sleep in the attic with the others." Hunt studied the list of suspects Paul had created. "James has, however, struck up a friendship with this Leon, Sir Oswald's valet. I believe an exchange of boot black and formulas was involved, so boots are being polished somewhere."

"Documents," Jack said abruptly, putting his chair back on four legs. "Barbeau was bound to have the Lavignes' documents and letters from the solicitor. Has anyone had fires in their grates?"

"They'd stink the house up if they did. We haven't had a chimney cleaner out. The Gaithers said they had them cleaned last spring, but they died this year before it could be done this year. Most of the rooms have been closed until recently," Hunt twirled his pen nub and worked out who had been stored where. The guests were all housed in the old portion. The smaller rooms had no grates.

"Ask the maids if any of the guests had ashes in their fireplaces," Villiers suggested. "If they're like my chamber, your formidable housekeeper has all the brass polished and not a speck of dust dare settle. There is no fuel, either. Very inhospitable of you, Huntley. Spring mornings are chilly."

"Aside from the small matter of possibly burning the place down. . . The aunts filched all the coal to keep their fire going. I'm waiting to see what they do when they run out," Hunt said dryly. "I don't know if the trust will cover fuel for the entire wretched household come winter."

"The dowager has an allowance. She can afford to fuel the entire manor if so inclined." Spalding sounded surly. "If she stays here this winter, she won't be needing to fuel the dower house."

Hunt stayed out of that argument. He'd hovered over campfires these past winters. He knew nothing of fueling enormous manors. He jotted a note. "I'll ask Mrs. Upton about the fireplaces. It's a valid point. Pity we can't search all the baggage. The documents may be useful for forgery and the thief may have kept them."

Arnaud returned with a maid bearing a tray of food—and Mrs. Upton, with mugs of ale. She evidently overheard this last.

"The Lavignes and Champlains refused to have their trunks removed to the attic, although the Lavignes only have one. The Champlain servants keep trunks under their beds. All else is in the attic storage room. Insist that everyone attend the memorial service and have people you trust check trunks and wardrobes." Mrs. Upton started to depart, but Hunt detained her.

"Have any of the maids reported fires in any of the grates?"

She frowned in thought. "Only in the ladies' blue salon. I trust no one is likely to start lighting fires." She sailed out, her small nose in the air.

The late curate's wife was definitely a Reid, Hunt mused, reaching for a mug. She knew how to give orders like a general.

Arnaud frowned, helped himself to a sandwich, and headed back for the door. "Henri was supposed to be finding the Champlains. Let me see if he's having difficulty."

Hunt recognized Arnaud preferred to work on his own—and to protect his younger brother. Not that Henri needed much protection, but they worked well together. He appreciated that they didn't need his orders.

"The question becomes, who do we trust to do the search?" Jack asked, grabbing a plate of sandwiches after Arnaud's departure.

"You." Hunt snatched thick brown bread laden with mutton and relish. "Arnaud and Henri have to attend the funeral for Barbeau, but you have no reason to. Although one hopes the Champlains join the Lavignes. I fear they won't be persuaded from their chamber."

"No reason for servants to leave their rooms either." Unfazed by Hunt's order, Jack drank his ale.

"I doubt the Champlains will obey if the dowagers request a visit." Villiers drank his ale and studied the ceiling. "Searching Avignon's trunk would make me happy. He, at least, was here when young Barbeau died. I had Jones investigate him when he escorted my stepmother here, but he didn't have time for a full report—which places our noble Frenchman high on my suspect list."

"Elsa's mother has no reason to attend the service. Mrs. Turner can invite the Champlains to *her* chambers. They seem thick as inkle-weavers these days," Jack suggested.

Hunt had reservations about searching private property, but if English nobility with knowledge of the law didn't quibble over it, he couldn't. And he damned well wanted to catch a killer. Or killers.

"Damn, I miss Jones." Villiers tilted his chair back. "If Jones were here, I'd have him search the trunks in the servants' quarters. I don't trust young Roberts to do so. Who else wouldn't look out of place wandering around up there?"

"Our footman, Adams," Hunt said with regret. "Honest as the day is long, but we need him guarding the doors with his father. I'm not sending any of the maids to search, and Ned sleeps in the stable. We need more male staff."

"I trust my valet," Spalding said. "Ernest has been with me for years. But he's not the world's brightest fellow. And my secretary is a recent hire, which makes Norsworthy as suspect as any of the other servants, although I cannot imagine how or why he'd be involved. He isn't French and doesn't know the victims."

"I suppose I can ask Walker to guard the garden door this once. We'll set Adam to searching servant trunks while Jack does Avignon, the Lavignes, and the Champlains. Perhaps we'll have some response from London in this afternoon's post. I'd really like to hear from the solicitors, see if they've learned anything about Sir Oswald. I doubt there's been time to look into the Lavignes." Hunt stood, needing to check on the funeral and memorial service arrangements.

"What about Bosworth?" Jack asked. "He's not likely to attend, but he's spending all his time in the library. Do you want him searched?"

"Bosworth is your bloody banker," Spalding answered. "Try not to insult him before we finish the trust affairs."

"I'll have my man James take a look where he can," Hunt murmured to Jack as they left the nobles plotting in the study. "He has made friends of several of the valets who room with their employers."

"Like pretty-boy Roberts, Villiers' man?" Jack grinned. "I'll vouch for anything James does to that lout. I've never wanted to be a spy, but there are some people who just need to be watched."

"I'd start with Avignon and the Champlains, not the servants," Hunt said grimly. "But hanging a count and a knight might be difficult."

TWENTY-FIVE

CLARE: FRIDAY NOON

WEARING AN OLD, LAVENDER, SEMI-MOURNING GOWN OUT OF respect for their guests, Clare checked on the arrangement for the memorial services in the great hall. The Lavignes were Catholic. The village's tiny chapel didn't match the grandeur of a cathedral, but the great room had been built along the lines of the former priory's massive chapel. The towering ceiling and pointed, Gothic windows might be more familiar to the family.

The servants had turned this hall into a meeting room so many times, that she didn't even need to direct them anymore. A long table that normally stood under the windows was set up like an altar in the area that would have been the nave, with a book pedestal from the library in the center. Sofas and chairs were turned to face the table, and someone had even thought to place small stools by the front seats, so their guests might kneel in comfort.

Patience had provided giant bouquets for the altar and the pianoforte. They did not know any French hymns, but Clare could play a few simple English ones that Patience had chosen as suitably funereal. With a voice like an angel's,

Patience would bring tears to the eyes even if she sang in ancient Greek.

"It will be a very small service," Clare murmured as Patience joined her. "I don't believe anyone but immediate family will attend. Villiers will be here, since we mourn his secretary. But Lavender and Dottie have no interest. And the aunts appear to be plotting."

"It is something to do with Elsa's mother inviting the Champlains to join the aunts' for a tea party." Patience laughed at the older ladies' machinations. "They asked for a bouquet as an excuse for visiting."

"Even the Champlains aren't attending the service? How unkind. Hunt has so few family members still alive, that one would think they'd support each other, even if they are strangers. None of us knew one another, but it's been marvelous to see how we work together." Deciding the chamber could not be improved upon, Clare followed Patience into the corridor.

"I have given up on the captain's family tree," Patience admitted. "I understand that Lady Spalding's mother is the captain's grandmother, and that the Lavignes are somehow descended from. . . Lady Spalding's aunt? Hunt's great-aunt? The connection is not close."

"It is apparently close enough to share the family pearls, should they ever be found, which I doubt." Clare didn't wish to consider the fight that would ensue should they be uncovered. How much of Lady Reid's family would be entitled to them?

The men had scattered to their various roles after luncheon. The coffins had been carried out of the crypt and set in wagons, ready to be moved to the graveyard at the end of the service. The curate was no doubt changing into his robes in the small room Mrs. Upton kept for her son's use. Clare glanced up the stairs, but Hunt wasn't on his way down yet.

Quincy arrived in the corridor just as the front bell clamored. A hasty knock followed. Alarmed, Clare pulled Patience back into the great room.

"We aren't expecting anyone, are we?" Patience whispered. "Everyone is already here."

"Other than Hunt's mother, and I cannot think she'd make such a clatter. I suspect if it were her, Quincy would be outside, greeting her carriage, even before she climbed out. I don't know how he knows about visitors before they arrive." Clare peered around the doorway, but she could see nothing from this angle.

"I think Quincy pays the soldiers to warn him of approaching visitors," Patience whispered back. "I've seen them sitting in trees."

"If they are the ones who prefer drinking to working, I hope they don't fall out. And I hope he's paying them in food, not money for ale. I suppose it's useful." Clare was dubious, but she did not rule the world.

Quincy apparently left their guest cooling his heels in the vestibule while he carried the visiting card tray to the great room. He always knew where to find Clare and Hunt. Spooky.

She took the card and frowned. "Garrett Browning III, esquire?" Her eyes widened. "The solicitor from Stratford! Oh, my. Quincy, you'd best fetch Hunt and install Mr. Browning. . ." She couldn't bring him to the great room. And the baron and Bosworth had practically taken up residence in the library. The old study was too cluttered. . . "It will have to be the parlor. Patience, will you send for a tea tray?"

Clare was relieved she was dressed appropriately for a change—as was Hunt, she noted, when he clattered down the marble stairs. He had donned the new coat and waistcoat Lavender had tailored for him, plus a crisp neckcloth, to honor their guests at the service. It probably would not do to examine his aging buff trousers and boots too closely. When Quincy apprised him of the visitor, he frowned.

Rather than speculate about why their solicitor might have arrived, unannounced, Hunt drew Clare's hand around his elbow and simply stormed the parlor as if anticipating battle.

"Browning." He bowed as the solicitor stood. "You've met my fiancée, Miss Knightley, I believe. To what do we owe this honor?" He gestured for the man to retake his seat.

"I apologize for imposing on you like this." A vigorous man in his forties, with a full head of brownish-blond hair, the solicitor accepted the teacup Clare handed him. "But I did not trust the post to arrive as swiftly as I would like. I just received this stack of documents from my grandfather in London."

He removed a pouch from his coat pocket and set it next to the tea tray. "I believe you have requested information on some of Lady Reid's family? When I looked at these, I became concerned. My grandfather, unfortunately, is reaching his dotage. I'm not at all certain he understands what he has here. Our services with the Reid family date back half a century, at least. Routine, unfortunately, replaces thought over the years."

Hunt removed his monocle from his vest pocket, glanced at the papers, and handed Clare half of them. "We probably need to have Villiers and Spalding look at these."

For the poor man to have arrived from Stratford by noon, he had to have left early this morning. Clare quickly skimmed the papers, understood Hunt's concern, and rose. "Mr. Browning, let me have Quincy take you to a room to freshen up while someone prepares a luncheon tray for you. We are about to hold a memorial service for the gentleman who visited your grandfather. We'll have to look at these later."

"Of course, Miss Knightley." The solicitor rose with her.

"We appreciate your concern. These papers may have a

significant impact on Lady Reid's family. Please make yourself at home. The library is open, if you wish to visit it. Mr. Bosworth is generally in there." Hunt took Clare's arm and led her out as Mrs. Upton hurried down the corridor at their signal.

Leaving the housekeeper and Quincy in charge of their guest, Hunt hurried Clare down the corridor to his private study. Jack was already there, practically bristling, whether with eagerness or frustration was difficult for Clare to discern. The men were obviously up to some nefarious plot they had not told her about.

Hunt flung the pouch on the desk. "Solicitor just brought the information on the Lavignes and the Champlains. He's concerned. I don't have time to see why. Villiers will be at the memorial service, so we need Spalding to go over this. He's a neutral party. We don't have more than an hour to search those trunks. You may need to enlist Ned."

Search trunks? Clare widened her eyes but she wasn't about to argue. What did they expect to find in trunks?

Jack grabbed the pouch, glanced quickly at the documents, whistled, and headed out of the study. "Find some way to keep everyone in the service for as long as possible."

"What is going on?" Clare whispered as Hunt led her back to the hall. The backward clock chimed nine, so it was most likely almost noon. "Those papers include the Lavigne's official documents. Shouldn't we take them to the family? It might give them ease of mind."

"The top letter from the senior Browning says the Lavignes are *impostors.* Since receiving word of the death of Comte Lavigne, he has filled the requirements of the Champlain/Lavigne trust by distributing the pearls to his remaining family." Hunt halted in the double doorway to examine the occupants of the massive hall. "*Arnaud* is the Comte Lavigne, and he is not dead."

Paul Upton, their curate, was speaking with the grieving

Lavignes at the front of the great hall, near the makeshift altar. As relations of the family, Arnaud and Henri had taken chairs behind the sofas the family was meant to take.

Villiers had joined them as the only mourner for Jones, his aide.

Off to one side, the Comte Avignon was perusing what appeared to be a prayer book. His knee bounced impatiently. At the arrival of Elsa and Jack's French maid and valet, his knee stopped bouncing, and he frowned.

The Turbins took a dark corner. After casting anxious glances at the rest of the company, they were whispering worriedly to each other. What was that about?

Patience flipped through music sheets at the ancient pianoforte. Clare squeezed Hunt's arm and left him to find his own place. Hers was with the singer.

Impostors? Were her instincts all wrong in believing the little family was truly grieving the loss of their friend and future in-law?

The pearls were already gone? To whom? Surely not Arnaud.

Half expecting Dottie to burst in declaring Lady Reid's ghost was on a rampage, Clare settled on the pianoforte bench. "We are to delay the service as long as possible," she whispered to Patience. "The men are up to skullduggery."

"I will speak to Paul. Start with this song." She opened a page, then slipped to the front, waiting for the Lavignes to take their seats before whispering to her brother.

Their curate was an extremely understanding young man. He glanced at Hunt, who nodded curtly. Message received, she assumed. The prayers and sermon would be lengthy.

Clare itched to know what was happening literally behind her back, but she would simply have to hope and pray that all went well.

If the Lavignes were impostors. . . would they have killed Barbeau? Jones? *Why*?

179

TWENTY-SIX

ELSA: FRIDAY AFTERNOON

"I'LL BE QUICK. DELAY AS LONG AS YOU CAN." JACK KISSED Elsa's cheek and abandoned her outside the door to the aunts' spacious suite.

Jack had explained their search plans earlier. His new warning that the Lavignes and Champlains might not be at all what they seemed was a concern. . . especially if the dowagers had already determined that without even seeing the solicitor's papers.

The aristocratic old ladies awaited in their salon, wearing their best visiting gowns, their hair made up as if to impress the best of society. Elsa's mother hid a wry smile as Elsa entered. The aunts had never given her mother a second glance until this turn of events.

"This may all be for nothing," Mrs. Turner, the former Lady Villiers, warned.

Elsa's mother was slender, as Elsa was not. She wore the latest fashion, as Elsa did not. She had a maid who dressed her blond hair to perfection, with dangling curls and smooth chignons. Elsa's hair refused confinement. They lived in two different worlds that seldom collided. But in this moment, they were in collusion.

Her mother picked up the bouquet Patience had arranged earlier and joined her daughter in the doorway.

Elsa gestured for her to proceed toward the Champlains' chamber. "I see no reason for the Champlains to resist our invitation. She, at least, seems eager to enter society. We simply need to remove them from their chambers so Jack may see if they hid any of the documents Barbeau carried."

Nadia, Lady Champlain's maid, answered their knock. Behind her, the knight and his lady appeared to be arguing. Their trunks spewed clothing, as if they'd never been fully unpacked.

"Tell your mistress that Lady Spalding and Lady Lavinia have invited us to a small tea party while the rest of the household attends the funeral services," Mrs. Turner said with a smile, handing over the bouquet. "Do not leave us to attend alone!"

Lady Champlain evidently overheard. She cut off her discussion to come to the door. "The ladies, they have asked us before. Are they very bored?"

That was a cynical question. Elsa duplicated her mother's deceptive smile. "I rather think they are looking for an audience. Do you suppose they may have worked out a clue to the whereabouts of the jewels? Or perhaps Lady Reid's pearls?"

The petite lady's dark eyes widened. "Oh, a mystery tea! How very exciting. And will the other gentlemen be present?"

"I'm afraid everyone is attending services at the moment. Jack has been invited, but he is with an ailing horse, last I heard. But Sir Oswald is certainly welcome. How can we turn down such an invitation? The ladies hardly ever entertain." Elsa bobbed a curtsy as the older man came over to listen.

He appeared on the verge of rejecting the invitation, when his young wife placed a hand on his arm and turned pleading eyes to him. "Please, dearest? It is so seldom we have such an opportunity. And on such a sad day! We should help the ladies pass the time while everyone is engaged elsewhere?"

"The staff is having a small gathering in the kitchen, as well. If your servants would care to join them? I believe the captain has provided a keg of ale as he does on special occasions." Elsa stepped aside, indicating that everyone should proceed her.

While her mother chatted with Lady Champlain and led away a grumbling Sir Oswald, Elsa remained in the doorway, waiting for Nadia to depart. She did not see Leon and hoped he did not return to interfere with Jack's invasion.

As lady of her own estate and commander of the manor's kitchen, Elsa knew how to order servants about. Learning deceit and trickery took more practice, but she'd done that as well, as a defense against a brutish stepbrother and stepfather. Ushering Nadia toward the back service stairs to the kitchen, Elsa grabbed an opportunity when she saw Dottie peering from her room.

Making certain Nadia continued on without her, Elsa gestured at her cousin while the others entered the ladies' suite. Once Dottie joined her, she whispered, "The men are searching trunks. Could you stand guard and warn them if anyone comes upstairs?"

"Should I disguise myself as a maid and pretend to be dusting?" she asked in amusement.

"No time. Turn up the sconces and pretend to be examining the atrocious artwork?" The walls were adorned with remnants of the late earl's collections, removed from the estates he'd given to his family.

Dottie wrinkled her nose in distaste but produced a notebook and pencil from her pocket. "I can do that. Perhaps I will spot more concealed codes!"

"One hopes more helpful ones. Thank you!" Elsa entered the spiderweb the old ladies wove, hoping to come out alive.

No one looked up as she entered. Searching for a good seat, she noted a flask hidden in the folds of Lady Lavinia's voluminous skirts. The late earl's daughter came from an era not so mindful of propriety. Oh dear. Elsa settled on a blue satin chair with gilded arms where she could keep an eye on the flask. The ladies had already served their guests tea. Elsa took the cup poured for her, sniffing to be certain nothing had been added.

"I do believe I remember you, sir." Lady Spalding reached for a sugar biscuit. "I was quite young, of course, and you were only a little older. At that age, I noticed all the handsome men, of course, but Mother made it clear I must marry money."

Lady Spalding and Hunt's mother had been presented in London shortly after the American revolt but before the French tried to overthrow their king. One assumed Sir Oswald had not been helping emigres at the time.

He looked wary but brushed at his thinning hair as if recalling his younger self. "I don't believe I remember the occasion. You would have still been in the nursery when I brought Lady Reid and her babe to London. I was no more than my father's sailor then."

Ah, the relationship was earlier than the Turbins had said. Had they lied? Or not made the connection? Or someone was weaving tales.

"I could be wrong, of course." Lady Spalding waved her chubby, beringed hand, indicating she might be the tale weaver. "Mother and I had a difficult relationship. I spied on her dreadfully. Although, surely, if you were family, you must have visited when you were in town?"

"I married, had my own children," he said with a shrug. "It is possible I ran an errand when we were in port, but we did not visit an earl's household as more than the deliverer of packets from France."

Before the lady could harass their guest more and drive him from the room, Elsa spoke up. "You have children, sir? How old are they? Are you raising them at sea?"

Lady Champlain smiled thinly and sipped her tea.

Sir Oswald squirmed. "My daughter is married, with babes of her own. My son. . . he does not love the sea as I did. He works for a counting house these days." He patted his wife's hand. "We hope someday to have children who will follow in my footsteps."

Ah, this was a second wife, of course. Interesting that they did not make much of their connection with Lady Reid's family. Then how did they know of the wedding and the arrival of Hunt's mother? The question slipped out before Elsa could bite it back. . . "You must have kept up your correspondence with Mrs. Huntley if she wrote you about the wedding."

Sir Oswald held out his cup for a refill. It clattered slightly until Lady Spalding took it. "I suppose I took an interest in little Frances after transporting her across the Channel as an infant. She was always about the house when I made deliveries."

"After she married, she asked him about the best ships for sailing to the Americas, and his advice was so sound, that she asked him again for this return journey," Lady Champlain said, more smoothly than her husband. Perhaps she believed it.

Elsa wasn't certain she did. He'd just gone from an occasional delivery of packages from France to ones frequent enough to be acquainted with a protected daughter of a viscountess. It was possible, she supposed. Hunt's mother was scorned as a by-blow and not a Reid. But avoiding these probing questions about their connections—or learning that Mrs. Huntley would actually arrive—might be why the couple avoided the company. Were they liars?

Elsa hid her surprise as the two old ladies tipped the flask into the knight's teacup under cover of an enormous bouquet of blooming tree branches. How often had they performed that trick?

They did the same when they filled Lady Champlain's cup.

Elsa began to see the purpose of serving ale to the staff while the footman searched their rooms. Once bosky, the servants might be more inclined to linger and talk. Would honest Mrs. Upton know how to lead them into gossiping about their employers the way the conniving old ladies led their soon-to-be-drunken guests?

Elsa suddenly had an itch to know what was happening elsewhere. She wasn't helping much here. She'd let the more experienced society ladies dissect their guests.

Rising abruptly, she apologized. "I really must check on the pies. I'm afraid the maids may partake too much of the captain's ale and forget about them. Excuse me, and I hope to return quickly."

"She won't, you know," she heard her mother say as Elsa fled out the door. "Once she's in the kitchen, she forgets all else."

There might be a reason for that.

Dottie was no longer loitering in the corridor pretending to admire art.

The door to the Champlain's room was closed. Elsa tested the knob, locked.

What did she do now? Fretting, she didn't even know whether to take the main stairs down or try the service stairs to the kitchen.

She was afraid of the service stairs when the house echoed so emptily. Normally, the halls bustled with people going to and fro. Not a soul stirred upstairs or down. Where was everyone? Was the memorial service over? She couldn't hear music. Surely they hadn't left for the burial already? The ladies wouldn't. They'd be in the parlor.

The parlor it was, then. Perhaps check the great hall first. But where was Jack if the memorial service had let out?

TWENTY-SEVEN

PATIENCE: FRIDAY AFTERNOON

PATIENCE DEARLY LOVED SINGING. IT DELIGHTED HER THAT SHE could provide the solemn music to commemorate any occasion. She hoped her songs helped the grieving family.

But she nearly dropped from the strain of worrying about killers roaming the halls as Clare played the notes of the final song and Paul offered up the last prayer. She wanted to run away instead of standing with Clare, waiting for their audience to file out. Except she knew what was proper. She had to wait until everyone left.

Henri didn't bother being proper. He skirted around the mourners and headed straight for her. Her heart danced a little and some of the exhaustion lifted.

"Your singing is so brilliant I am amazed angels did not come down to join you." He glanced to Clare. "And you did a marvelous job of coaxing music out of those ancient keys. I suppose the maintenance trust does not replace musical instruments?"

Clare offered a faint smile. "I'm fairly certain it does not. Even if it did, instruments would be far down our list. We will all have to be rich someday. . . or persuade one of the aunts to buy new."

"I know I am supposed to help carry the coffin, but I need to borrow Patience, if I may. Tell Hunt I will catch up." Without batting an eyelash at what was proper and what was not, Henri took her elbow and steered Patience out the door before she was surrounded by people departing.

"They will all want to thank you for having them in tears." Henri steered her down the corridor, glancing in the family parlor. Finding no one, he kept going to Hunt's old study. "I don't have time to wait."

"To do what?" Patience asked helplessly. She loved being part of whatever he was up to, but it would be nice to know what it was.

"I thought you might want an excuse to escape. You always flee the tavern the moment you're done singing." In the study, they encountered Lord Spalding with a stranger Patience assumed was the solicitor she'd only caught a glimpse of earlier.

Yes, she'd much rather flee than smile politely as people complimented her voice. Everyone could sing. It embarrassed her to be praised for so silly a service.

"Sorry to intrude." Henri didn't sound sorry but impatient. "I have only a few minutes. I don't know what you've found in those papers, but I'm fairly certain the Comte Avignon has just recognized Lady Reid's former servants, the Turbins. And they have recognized him. One or the other of them may try to escape while we're at the graveyard. Do you know where Jack is?"

Timidly, Patience offered, "Quincy should."

Spalding frowned. "Jack is investigating. We have learned that young Barbeau inquired about the whereabouts of all Lady Reid's relations after he presented his documents to the solicitor. Presumably, he hoped to reunite them with the Lavignes."

Patience didn't understand the significance, but Henri did.

"He may have alerted a killer?" Henri clasped her hand tighter. "Who rode directly here and set a trap? Why?"

"Someone besides you, your brother, and the Lavignes has been receiving the pearls. The solicitor had been told you were all dead. There is only a small portion of the inheritance left to distribute. Thieves are hanged," the marquess said curtly. "Find the thief, and I wager we'll have our killer."

Patience hid her gasp. The slender marquess seemed harmless, but his expression was cold. She hated to think any of the company might be hanged over *pearls*. It seemed so senseless. But a killer. . .

"Arnaud and I must carry the coffin, as does Hunt. That only leaves Quincy and Walker to guard the doors. We can't trust the servants, even yours, my lord. With Adam helping Jack search, you and Villiers will have to prevent anyone from escaping." Henri placed Patience's hand on his arm. "Patience can have the ladies gather in the parlor for safety. I'll have Walker send Meera to join them."

Frowning, the marquess conceded his point, grabbed a document folder, and gestured for them to precede him. "Villiers should be in the library. We ought to lock the servants in the cellar until this is done."

"My mother is in the cellar," Patience reminded him. "I don't think locking her up would be wise."

"Your mother belongs upstairs with the nattering ancients. And I suppose we can't persuade them down to join you and the other ladies in the parlor?" Spalding followed them into the corridor as the remainder of the memorial participants departed the great room. He obviously didn't expect an answer. Prying the dowagers from their chambers would alert the household that something was amiss.

Who else was with them? Were they in danger? "I will warn Clare, if you will warn Lavender and Quincy on your way out." Patience released Henri's arm, praying the men knew what they were doing.

Wouldn't it be easier to allow the killers to ride away? She knew the answer to that.

Patience couldn't think clearly with men throwing around their authority and experience. Henri reduced her to quivering insensibility with just his smile. Learning to stand on her own required walking away.

She hurried to join Clare, who was leading the mourning ladies to the parlor where they might watch the funeral procession pass. Patience caught one last glimpse of Henri casting her a worried glance before he joined Hunt, Arnaud, and Monsieur Lavigne exiting the great hall. The look heated her in ways it shouldn't, confusing her even more.

The men filed toward the carriage exit to meet the wagon carrying the coffins. Avignon joined them. Paul hurried in their wake. They would pass the gallery where Lavender and her ladies worked. Since the gallery was between the portico exit and the front entrance, perhaps Quincy might guard that door.

Patience mentally counted heads. After the funeral procession left, the Champlains, the ladies, and all the servants were left in the manor. Jack was supposed to be somewhere. She didn't think the Turbins had joined the funeral procession. While Clare ushered everyone from the memorial into the parlor, Elsa left the parlor to guard the stairs. What was that about?

Before they joined the company in the parlor, Patience signaled for Clare and Elsa to join her. "Henri and Lord Spalding believe the Lavignes' pearls have been stolen and Barbeau was killed to prevent anyone learning that. Or maybe so the thief might escape?" She was unsure of their theories. "They want all of us to stay in one place. They think the thief might use this time to flee."

Clare widened her eyes as she grasped the problem. "The aunts are upstairs. We have no notion where Dottie is." She turned to Elsa. "Jack is searching the upper floor, near the aunts and the Champlains. Did Adam go to the attic? Do we need to bring the boys down here with us?"

Elsa glanced anxiously up the stairs. "I'm hoping Dottie went to the schoolroom. She was supposed to be watching the bedchambers, but she's not, which worries me. I think I need to go to the kitchen and count heads. Everyone is accounted for except the servants, correct?"

"I have no notion at this point." Clare glanced despairingly at the stairs. "I cannot think that anyone would harm the boys and their tutor. Would a killer take a hostage? I should probably run up and tell them to lock the doors."

Patience could see they were both torn between their different duties. She was the most expendable—and she'd far rather be in the attic, than with weeping ladies in the parlor. She'd had enough of that with her father's death. "Let me run up to the schoolroom. I'll look for Dottie along the way. I imagine that's where she's gone. I'll tell them to lock the doors, then I'll run right back here."

Elsa and Clare looked relieved, which made Patience feel as if she might be useful.

"I'll do the same with the kitchen," Elsa said. "I'll see if I can persuade your mother to join us, although I think it unlikely that she'll come to harm surrounded by our staff."

Meera hurried down the corridor toward them, looking puzzled.

"I'll explain in a minute," Clare told her friend. "With guardians nearby, the parlor is safest. If you see anyone else, Patience, herd them this way." Clare led Meera in to join the Lavigne ladies. Elsa hurried toward the kitchen stairs at the rear.

Still thinking it would be far simpler to let scoundrels run away, Patience took the marble stairs up. People intimidated her. But on the whole, she thought most folks would go their own way if left alone. Why would a thief bother with small boys? But Dottie. . . was an heiress. Would she be foolish enough to attempt to stop a thief—and potential killer?

The voices from the aunt's chambers were a trifle loud. Should she check on them first? Not until her father died had Patience needed to make her own decisions. It was daunting, if lives truly were endangered. She just couldn't believe anyone could come to harm with so many people around.

Laughter followed a loud outburst, so the aunts must be fine. She slipped past the main stairs in the direction of the gallery loft, then hurried down that narrow hall, toward the attic steps.

James, Hunt's valet, slipped from one of the rooms by the gallery and headed for another. Was he a thief? Or one of the men searching? With one leg, he couldn't flee anywhere easily.

Another decision made, she ignored him and took the attic stairs up. She thought she heard footsteps before she arrived at the top, but she saw no one. The attics sprawled in a maze of interconnected rooms over the main portion of the manor, then led back to small guest and servants' chambers over the wings.

Shouts from the schoolroom drew her on. The boys didn't sound frightened. She heard a female voice and smiled in relief—Dottie?

Knocking briefly, she entered without waiting, assuming she wouldn't be heard over the commotion.

Patience stepped back in startlement at the sight within. Lavender and one of her younger sewing ladies were battling with measuring sticks, while the boys attempted to cut cloth in what appeared to be some form of mathematical competition? Mr. Birdwhistle's head swiveled trying to watch Lavender and the boys at the same time.

Dottie was nowhere in sight.

TWENTY-EIGHT

HUNT: FRIDAY AFTERNOON

HUNT DELIBERATELY STOOD TO ONE SIDE AS HIRED HANDS lowered the coffins into prepared graves in the former priory's ancient cemetery. They'd buried five people here since he'd arrived at the beginning of the year. At this rate, they'd have to rent the chapel's field and turn it into a graveyard. Or start stacking coffins.

The curate said a few words. Monsieur Lavigne stepped up to do the same. Arnaud and Henri held back as Hunt did. The lords had stayed inside with the banker and solicitors. The ladies should be in the parlor. Hunt wanted to be there too.

But there was a killer on the loose, and he was far more likely to be male than female. Hunt hated to suspect the French count who had accompanied Elsa's mother, could see no reason why Avignon would harm a lad he didn't know well, or a secretary he didn't know at all. But Avignon had been here when Barbeau died. He was French. He knew the Lavignes.

And he was easing away from the funeral before it was finished.

Henri had been right—Avignon must have recognized

Lady Reid's former servants and was now trying to escape. Why?

Hunt nudged Arnaud, nodded at the fleeing Avignon, and murmured, "Keep an eye on the rest. I'll steer this one into Walker's hands."

His cousin looked grim but nodded. Crossing the cemetery in long lopes, even with the hitch in his gait, Hunt easily kept up with the shorter, stouter man's scuttle.

Avignon aimed for the stable. Intent on his purpose, he startled when Hunt caught his arm and steered him toward the garden door. "We will be gathering before dinner in the great hall. You do not wish to smell of horses in front of the ladies."

"I have had word of a business difficulty," Avignon protested. "I must arrange to return to the city."

"Not tonight. The roads are dangerous. You might accompany some of my associates back in the morning." Hunt couldn't accuse the man of anything. He couldn't lock him up until he had evidence of wrongdoing. The military had been simpler.

Avignon continued to argue until they were through the door and Walker appeared. "Comte Avignon wishes to speak with Mr. Browning and Lord Spalding. Are they in the library?" Hunt didn't release his prisoner's arm. He needed to give Jack as much time to search as possible.

"No one has moved down here," Walker reported.

Knowing Walker's taciturn ways, Hunt assumed that meant the nobles were in the library and no one had come down from the upper floors. How did he warn Jack and Adam and the others he'd sent searching trunks?

"The mourners will join us shortly." Hoping Walker had a means of sending word upstairs, Hunt continued steering his guest down the corridor, talking of brandy and dinner and pretending he wasn't holding a count prisoner.

He desperately wanted to see Clare and know she was

safe. Women were a distraction. He needed to be leading his men in action. He had an enemy to defeat. But he could not abandon the women and children. Battlefields should not engage women.

If a killer harmed one of them, if he could not maintain safety in his own damned home. . . he'd not wait for Spalding and Villiers to shut the manor down and throw out the family. He'd do it himself. Clare would hate him.

Leaving a resigned Avignon in the hands of the lordlings, banker, and solicitor, Hunt crossed over to the parlor. The instant he opened the door, Clare was there.

She stepped out and shut the door behind her, then fell into his arms and hugged him. "Thank heavens you are here. I have been so worried, I can't think straight. Dottie is missing. Patience hasn't returned, and I don't know where everyone is, and I'm terrified."

He held and rocked her, understanding she'd suffered multiple tragedies in a few short years, and feared the worst at all times. He wanted a peaceful life for her, not constant terror. "It is not your task to worry about the entire world, or even your entire family. You are to care for yourself and Oliver. I would appreciate it if you would look after me from time to time, but I am capable of doing that on my own. I'm not so certain I'd be capable if I lost you, so think of me before you take risks. Losing you would rip the heart from my chest."

She relaxed a little against him. "I can only look after you if you let me. And I don't know if I can *not* look after everyone else. I have done so for so long. . ."

She was afraid of losing more family. He understood.

"Take care of the helpless, if you must. But think of the manor as a small city. We have working classes, merchants, professionals, an occasional influx of lords and ladies, and you cannot possibly care for an entire city, even if some of them are family. Let me be the officer who directs the soldiers

195

to guard the walls, and be grateful this isn't actually war." He leaned down and kissed her until she was fully engaged and no longer tense with fear.

Then he set her back and admired her tear-dampened blue eyes. "I love you. Now go nibble scones and save some for me. I'll be back after I discover what Jack's been up to."

"I love you, too, but I'll love you more if you send someone to tell us how the boys are faring." She sniffed and pulled out a lacy handkerchief. "I will not ask about Dottie and Patience, just Oliver."

He touched her nose and smiled. "Now you understand."

It wouldn't stop her fretting, but she smiled before he walked away. He'd never considered a wife as more than a convenience, someone to warm his bed and prepare his meals. Perhaps it had taken losing an eye and almost losing a leg to knock some sense into his head.

Hearing the loud laughter from the upstairs salon where the aunts reigned, Hunt took the last few steps two at a time. With luck, he'd find Patience and Dottie there. He knocked briefly, then opened the suite's door at what he assumed was a cheery welcome.

A brisk card game was in play, and if he did not mistake, at least half the participants were bosky. He was fairly certain his Great-Aunt Lavinia had just slipped a card beneath her elaborate skirt and winked at him. Elsa's mother appeared wearily amused at their antics. And the Champlains—were falling all over themselves in laughter.

Dottie and Patience were nowhere to be seen.

Assuming the aunts had this lot in hand, Hunt performed a brief bow. "Clare says tea is being served in the parlor, if you are so inclined."

His aunt, Lady Spalding, waved her plump, beringed fingers. "Elsa will send our trays here. If anyone is interested in playing brag, send them our way."

Assuming they were safe enough, Hunt left them

laughing and scanned the dark upper hall for signs of life. Surely Jack had finished his search? He had no desire to stomp through a mile of corridors, testing doors.

He stopped in his chambers and found James puttering about. "Where is everyone?"

"I believe Mr. de Sackville has finished searching trunks and has gone to the kitchen to see if anyone has gone missing. He says Avignon is packed and ready to abscond but his valet isn't upstairs. He may be in the kitchen."

"George, the squinty-eyed one? He wasn't at the funeral. Did you discover anything?" Hunt loosened his neckcloth but quit fiddling at his valet's scowl.

"Villiers' valet, Robert, is a lazy lout. His trunk resembles a rat's nest, and I believe he's been rooting through the late secretary's belongings. I cannot imagine his lordship doing so. Roberts keeps a small pistol, but it is not loaded." James stood to attention as if making a formal report. "He is not anywhere about upstairs."

James had not gone to the kitchen with the kegs of ale. A nosy lout most likely would. "And the Champlains?"

"Her maid was packing trunks until Lady Elsa sent her away. Sir Oswald's trunks are already packed, and Leon, his valet, is not anywhere about either. You will need to check with young Adam about the staff rooms in the attic."

Leon and Nadia had not been sociable, Hunt had been told. They were unlikely to be in the kitchen. He suffered a frisson of alarm. "So our suspicious guests and the French count appear prepared to flee. I wonder if the lawyer's arrival set them off? He reports the viscountess's inheritance may have been stolen."

If the family's generosity in offering accommodation to anyone who asked for it endangered the household. . . How the hell could he tell them they couldn't invite guests? And the Champlains claimed to be *his* family.

"Thieves are not necessarily killers, sir." James looked dubious as he considered their fancified suspects.

"The twine trick does seem unlikely for any of them, agreed. Shoving a man downstairs. . ." Hunt sighed. "I need to check on the boys and see if Adam is done searching the attic."

He needed to be in three places at once. He hoped Adam had followed Jack to the kitchen, but he had promised to check on the boys. And look for Dottie and Patience. They were probably in their rooms but shouting at them from the far end of the sprawling manor would probably be uncouth.

As Hunt stomped up to the attic, he pondered how he could obtain a confession on the basis of nothing. Fleeing the scene of a crime did not constitute guilt. He couldn't arrest a knight and a count for behaving suspiciously.

Adam stood guard outside the schoolroom. He relaxed in apparent relief at Hunt's approach. "Captain, sir, I've not found any documents up here, but I was warned to guard the boys and the ladies until you returned."

Quincy's son was young, eager, and took orders well, but he wasn't quite ready to think for himself. Hunt waited for the footman to open the door. "Who gave you the order?"

"George, the count's valet. He helped me search, but we found nothing unusual. Then we learned Miss Talbott had gone missing and we didn't want to lose anyone else." He held the schoolroom door open.

George? Avignon's squinty-eyed valet had helped search the servants' rooms? Wasn't that like putting the cat among the pigeons? That was one valet accounted for, at least. Could he hope Leon, Norsworthy, and Robert were in the kitchen?

Dottie wasn't in the schoolroom? This could not be good.

The tutor had the sense to look relieved at Hunt's entrance. Lavender and Patience appeared annoyed and anxious, in that order. The boys, however, had apparently solved a complex problem involving cloth scraps which one of Lavender's ladies was sewing for them.

"We are creating your family tree, sir," Oliver said, of his own accord. He seldom spoke without prompting.

"French people." Davy cut a scrap, his tongue thrust between his teeth as he concentrated.

"Shall we frame it when you're done?" Hunt asked, unable to imagine how one created families from scraps.

"Or we quilt it and use it for a dog bed." Lavender crossed the schoolroom in an adolescent temper. "May we go now? I have work to do."

He had no idea if Quincy guarded the gallery below, and he didn't want to upset the schoolroom inhabitants by issuing warnings.

Patience stepped up to solve the problem. Apparently already apprised of possible criminal flight, she suggested that they all go to the gallery and look for new fabric scraps.

Hunt pulled the tutor aside. "Keep them behind closed doors until we let you know it's safe. I've set Quincy as guard."

Mr. Birdwhistle was an extremely sharp-witted, discreet young man. He nodded and helped the boys gather their work while Hunt held back the ladies until they could all leave at once.

"Adam, you take the lead. When everyone is safely installed in the gallery, see if Miss Talbott has joined the ladies in the parlor. Check her room if she has not."

A missing heiress needed to be found. Hunt didn't like the idea of sending a footman to a young lady's chamber, but he didn't want any more lost ladies—or maids. Women had few defenses against desperate criminals.

Once the nursery set were on their way to safety, Hunt contemplated the maze of attic rooms. He could play hide and seek in here for a week and never find the culprit.

Why had Avignon's valet warned Adam to guard the nursery? So he could aid his employer's escape?

Most of the male guests had been given rooms in the bachelor's hall across from the gallery loft. Their personal servants had a choice of the few moldering attic chambers in the old manor with easy access to their employers, or the newer, more private rooms over the wings, more easily accessed from the back towers than through the attic. Avignon's ugly little valet had complained about his room near where Jones had died—in the distant wing.

Hunt hastily threw open servants' doors in this front part of the attic while he was here. He knew little of Dorothea Talbott except that she'd fled Avignon's courtship in London and brought her little brother here to claim their share of the manor. And Clare said she talked to ghosts. One more Reid eccentric, more or less, didn't bother him.

But she was young and female and vulnerable.

He found no one in the servants' rooms over the main manor.

Elsa and Jack's servants lived in their suite, didn't they? They were elderly and the stairs would be treacherous. But all the rest should be up here. . .

He stomped past crowded storage rooms in the old part of the attic, swinging the lantern he'd picked up at the top of the stairs. There were no sconces up here. The place was a tinder keg. He ought to use the discarded furniture for firewood come winter. Clare objected to his using ancient ledgers as kindling.

Hunt had reached the back of the attic when he heard a distant moaning. He was not a superstitious man. He did not believe in ghosts. But the noise raised his hackles.

Alert, he searched carefully. He couldn't avoid squeaking boards and winced when he hit one. The moaner didn't appear to notice. He followed a cleared passage through the final storage area to the locked tower stairs leading down to the manor's bed chambers. Unlocking the door, he could hear the moan more distinctly. The sound was definitely coming up the stairs. This west tower not only led down to the manor family floor, but to the wing where their bridal suite was located. . . A lump of fear rising in his throat, he unlocked the panel and eased down to the hall and peered out.

George, the squinty-eyed valet, leaned against the wall at the far east end of the passage, pistol in hand, frowning in puzzlement. The valet glanced at Hunt and almost seemed relieved, if one could read an expression on a phiz like his. George nodded to the east tower that Hunt couldn't see from this end. He stepped out.

Dottie Talbot, book in hand, slowly spun in circles near the attic stairs, the ones leading to the kitchens and Elsa and Jack's new suite.

TWENTY-NINE

ELSA: FRIDAY TEA

ELSA HAD NEVER BEEN SO GLAD TO SEE ANYONE AS SHE DID JACK, who clattered into the kitchen after the funeral. She flung herself into his welcoming arms and let him cuddle her in front of all her staff, half the servants, and Mrs. Upton.

"That bad, pet, is it?" He stroked her hair and kissed her cheek. "Everyone alive then?"

She snickered and sniffed. "If that's our standard, yes, we're all alive. But it's time for tea. May we take the trays up now?" That wasn't her worst concern, just the immediate one.

He glanced at the room, probably counting heads. "All accounted for down here?"

"Avignon's, Sir Oswald's, and Villiers' valets are missing," she whispered. That had been her main worry—that Jack had run afoul of a mischief maker who might just be a killer. "I believe everyone else is accounted for."

"Spalding's secretary?"

Another of the new servants, she understood, and nodded. "Norsworthy is alternately flirting with my staff and arguing with Lord Spalding's valet. I shall put a pot over both their heads shortly."

He kissed her forehead and released her. "Better places to

whack a cock. Have you seen Dottie? We seem to have misplaced her."

Elsa choked on a laugh about the cock. Alarmed, she stepped back and tried to count heads again. "She's not in her room? She was supposed to be guarding the upper hall to let you know if anyone approached."

"Don't fret yet. She could have joined the aunts or Lavender or Clare or any number of things. It's easy to miss each other in this place, but she should be fine. We have an army prowling the ground floor. Send up tea. I'll search for stray valets in the cellar. No one is leaving until this is all sorted."

Relieved to have him in sight, Elsa set the maids preparing tea trays for more people than they had hands to serve.

While Jack searched the multitude of rooms in the cellar, Elsa sent tea and cakes to the parlor, nourishing fare to Lavender's ladies in the gallery, and heavier fare to the library where the men would be gathering. She'd have to carry a tray up to the aunts herself. She wanted to see if Dottie was there. And check her bedchamber if she wasn't.

Jack returned, frowning. "No sign of our missing valets, but the outside door is unlocked. I'll go out the cellar door. Have Mrs. Upton lock it behind me and hang on to that key! Make Spalding's pair of cocks sit on the service stairs to prevent anyone but staff and us entrance."

It was fine to tell her she shouldn't fret, but his frown sent her straight into the boughs. "Can you not fetch Henri or Hunt or someone to go with you?"

"To go to the stable, where all your loyal grooms reside? I shall be fine. Stay here, and I'll be back after I issue a few orders." He kissed her cheek and sauntered out as if there weren't killers and thieves lurking in every cranny. Killers and thieves who might even now be saddling horses—

Refusing to worry, knowing Jack was right, she gave his orders to the housekeeper, who jangled her keys officiously in understanding. Mrs. Upton would keep the kitchen in line. Dinner might be the soup simmering on the fire, but no one would starve. The marquess's servants were less happy about being assigned seats on the stairs, but she offered them brandy, and the treat mollified them.

Carrying the tray for the elderly aunts past the pair, Elsa hurried up the service stairs. She'd chosen their bridal suite because it was so close to this passage. Jones's death in the dark tower at the far end of this wing gave her cold shivers now. Perhaps she'd ask if the walls of all the service stairs might be painted bright white. Perhaps she could send for some of the art work from her estate. Remove the doors so screams could be heard. . .

Male cursing at the top of the stairs crushed that reverie. She never dropped trays carrying food, but she almost turned and fled until she recognized Hunt's colorful phrases. She edged open the door with her elbow and almost hit Hunt carrying a limp Dottie.

Elsa froze in horror. "Is she—"

"Communing with spirits," Avignon's ugly little valet declared.

That did not sound normal, but then, what did these days? How did one treat spirit communication? At least Dottie was accounted for now. Hunt literally had her in hand. "You had better take her to the infirmary. Meera will have smelling salts. She may still be in the parlor. I'll send her back as soon as I deliver this to the aunts."

"I'll have Walker fetch her." Hunt held the door with his elbow. "You shouldn't be wandering loose. I thought Jack was keeping everyone in the kitchen."

"There is no one but our staff and Spalding's there. It seems our other guests have prevented their servants from enjoying our little party. Jack has gone to check on the stable. If my mother and the aunts are safe up here, then I should be too."

The little valet looked mildly alarmed. "None of the personal servants are in the kitchen?"

Odd question from a valet. Elsa answered anyway. "Norsworthy and Ernest are. You're not. And Jack has blocked the doors, so you shall go hungry with the rest of them." Unconcerned with people who wouldn't stay where they belonged, she carried the tray down the main corridor to the blue salon, where the cackling had apparently halted. Perhaps they'd all passed out. She nudged the door open.

Instead of knitting as usual, Hunt's usually cheerful aunt was making notes on expensive stationery, looking very businesslike. Lady Spalding glanced up as Elsa entered. "There you are! We thought you'd left us here to starve. Where is that little girl who usually carries up the tray?"

"We've don't have enough staff and half of them are tipsy. Where are the Champlains?" Should she be worried that they weren't here? Wasn't the whole point of this separation to keep everyone from fleeing?

Or perhaps it had only been for the length of the funeral. If Hunt was back, then everyone else must have returned. And Jack was in the stable, preventing escape by any means but foot. Elsa tried to relax her fears—but having no motivation for two deaths did leave the imagination to go wild.

"Avignon huffed in and told them the funeral was over, and they must greet the Lavignes." Lady Lavinia effortlessly poured the tea, evidently not having imbibed whatever she'd added to the earlier cups. "He seemed a bit peevish."

Avignon? Shouldn't he be with Hunt and his cousins? Except Hunt had been in the tower. . .

"He's a good man," Elsa's mother warned, narrowing her eyes. "He knows his duty. It was quite a shock discovering so many here he'd thought lost to him."

Like Arnaud, the *real* Comte Lavigne? Who else? Arnaud's uncle?

"Dottie came to the manor to avoid him. Are you certain

he did not follow her considerable fortune?" As an heiress, Elsa had good reason for cynicism.

Elsa's mother glared at the insult. "Charles had no notion Dorothea is a cousin. The Talbots pushed the connection. He seemed rather relieved to be rejected. He is much too sophisticated to be leg-shackled to a child. His interest is in Lady Reid, not flighty children."

Charles. Comte Avignon? A memory eluded her. "Avignon knew the late viscountess? Why would she interest him?" Chastising her mother for using intimate names was hypocritical since everyone in the manor had fallen into Hunt's bad habit of ignoring titles.

"Avignon apparently knows everyone," Lady Spalding said dryly, loading her plate with teacakes. She nodded at the notes she'd been writing. "Take those to my nephew. The Champlains were very informative, once they loosened their tongues. The little maid usually takes some of this wealth of goodness to your servants." She gestured at the teacakes. "The Turbins are French. If we are suspecting the French, you should look in on them."

The Turbins—*whom Avignon had apparently recognized.* She'd left the Comte's ugly valet, George, just around the corner from their room in her suite. Should she be concerned?

George, at least, wasn't French or related to anyone, she didn't think. Did she even know the valet's full name? Still, given that he worked for Avignon, she supposed he might be a hired killer or thief. He certainly appeared as if he'd emerged from the London stews. And he might be wiry and strong enough to push Jones or tie twine in trees. . .

Surely no one would harm an old couple—*who knew Lady Reid and about the pearls.*

Stomach lurching in alarm, Elsa kept a plate of biscuits. Did she run to Jack? The stable was too far. Hunt, in the infirmary. . . But that was down the stairs where the valet lingered.

Holding the plate, she bobbed a curtsy as if she were a maid, took the notes the dowager marchioness waved at her, and taking a deep breath, stalked back down the corridor. The valet was only standing there. Surely he wouldn't harm her. She'd show him that she protected their brilliant valet and maid—the first personal servants she'd been allowed to hire on her own.

Avignon's ugly manservant lingered in the back hall by the service stairs, half-hidden in an alcove that ought to hold a statue or bouquet. Frightened at his behavior, remembering Jones had been pushed to his death on similar stairs, she dithered. But George saw her, held a cautioning finger to his lips, and gestured for her to join him.

She might be able to pound him over the head with the cake plate if he tried to harm her. He wasn't any taller than her. . .

He helped himself to one of the biscuits but continued holding a finger to his scruffy beard to indicate silence. *What the devil. . .*

A muffled voice issued from her bridal suite. Jack's valet? Victor's voice never trembled like that.

A louder voice barked a question. Elsa strained to listen, but she couldn't hear what was said. Annoyed, she handed the plate to the valet and stepped inside the stairwell, which shared a wall with the small chamber the Turbins had taken for their own.

"You will deny knowing me, understand?"

Avignon. *Charles*, Comte Avignon. Elsa frantically searched for the memory scratching at the back of her mind.

"If it comes down to your word over mine, who do you think will be believed—a count or a servant?" he shouted.

THIRTY

CLARE: FRIDAY TEA

THE TEA PARTY IN THE PARLOR AFTER THE FUNERAL WAS A SAD one. Clare sipped and tried to pretend Sophia Lavigne wasn't silently sobbing, while her parents clung to each other as if they'd been separated for a year. They'd seen the funeral party returning. What did they do now? Wait for the solicitor to bring them more bad news?

She wished she knew what had happened to Patience. If the curate's daughter had been here, she'd think of something consoling to say. Clare wished she could retreat to her writing room. Instead, she sat here fretting over the disappearance of Patience and dotty Dottie and wondering if all was well in the nursery, while Meera sat uneasily silent beside her. As an apothecary and physician, Meera was more comfortable with herbs than dealing with grief. Out of respect, she wore a dark blue shawl instead of her usual parrot plumage. Combined with her shiny black hair, the effect was that of a plump crow.

A quick knock on the door startled them. Walker entered, and Meera's eyes lit, which warmed Clare's heart. After years of heartbreak, her friend deserved joy.

But Meera's expression quickly changed when Walker didn't smile back. She rose even before he spoke.

"Miss Dorothea had a fainting spell. Hunt just carried her to the infirmary."

Oh dear. Torn between Dottie and their grieving guests, Clare hesitated.

Monsieur Lavigne waved his hand. "Go. We will return to our rooms. There is much for us to consider."

Like how they would survive. Or even return to France. Clare couldn't help them.

If Hunt was wandering about, it must be safe to leave. She nodded gratefully and followed Meera and Walker to the hall—

Where a troop of lords and. . . what had Hunt called them? *Professionals*? That description should cover a banker and solicitor. In unusual excitement, the lords and professionals poured from the library, waving papers and arguing loudly. Jack's bibliophile father wasn't with them. Did he stand guard over the library?

"A ladder," Bosworth shouted. "We need a ladder!"

The stout banker usually stuttered and never shouted. They were hunting for a killer and possible pearl thief—and he wanted a ladder? Was the killer on the ceiling? The roof?

Clare had to gather all her feeble resources to determine what was expected of her—when she'd rather flee to her small office. Hunt had said she need do nothing. . . But that seemed an impossibility around shouting lords and fainting heiresses. Curiosity could not be denied.

Henri left the mob to turn down the gallery hall, presumably in search of a ladder or Quincy.

She ought to continue on to the infirmary. Poor Dottie. But presumably, she did not need to look after the adults in the household. Besides, Dottie had Meera and Hunt with her.

The Lavignes emerged from the parlor. They stared in amazement at frockcoated gentlemen jostling each other in an attempt to all enter the vestibule at once. Even the haughty

Marquess of Spalding held a paper and waved it in Lord Villiers' face while arguing. What madness was this?

Quincy emerged from his position guarding the carriage exit at the end of the gallery hall. His usual stoic demeanor wore a worried frown. If Henri hadn't been set to fetch him. . . where had Henri gone?

Quincy ignored the shouting men to approach Clare. "The Champlains have called for their carriage, miss. Their servants are carrying down trunks. The lord and lady appear. . ." He hesitated, apparently seeking proper words. "They seem a bit under the influence of strong spirits?"

The Champlains were drunk?

"No one is supposed to leave!" she cried, trying not to panic.

But a butler was in no position to tie up guests determined to flee. Clare thought the Champlains unlikely killers, but departing without farewell was decidedly suspicious behavior. Why on earth was everyone running around with papers when they had a killer in their midst?

"I'll fetch Hunt. See if Arnaud or Henri can stop them." She thought she saw a flicker of relief given permission to do what he wished to do. Quincy had good instincts about rapscallions.

Wearing the formal tailed frockcoat Lavender's ladies had tailored to fit his massive physique, the butler strode ponderously back to the front hall.

Abandoning the Lavignes, Clare ran for the infirmary at the rear. When she arrived, Meera was talking with a conscious Dottie. Hunt and Walker were nowhere in sight.

Dottie wanted to talk. Clare waved her down. "The Champlains are escaping. Where did Hunt go?"

"Ned signaled for him outside." Meera frowned. "Perhaps he was warning about the Champlains?"

A deaf mute adolescent, Ned was usually outside or in the stable. Now what did she do?

"Walker? Did he go with him?"

Meera nodded. "Don't they have stable boys to prevent anyone taking out horses?"

Yes, but this didn't feel right. The Champlains should have said their farewells, not sneaked out during a funeral. And if no one stopped them—

A clatter on the service stairs down the hall caused them to swivel in that direction.

Elsa ran out, holding an empty tray and looking rattled. Elsa was the one with a cool head on her shoulders. . .

"Help! The aunts are attacking Avignon and my mother is in hysterics!"

THIRTY-ONE

PATIENCE: GALLERY

W<small>HEN</small> H<small>ENRI</small> <small>HURRIED INTO THE GALLERY, LOOKING JUBILANT,</small>
Patience thought she might weep in delight. He was safe, so
must they all be.

As content as if they'd been in the schoolroom, the boys
had scattered scraps of cloth across the marble tile floor.
Unfazed by whatever was happening in the rest of the household, the tutor and Lavender argued over a measuring stick.
A maid had just carried in a tray of food for Lavender's
button makers, so Patience thought it ought to be safe to
leave. Adam hadn't been given any instructions other than to
guard them, so she hadn't wanted to disturb the young
footman by demanding she be allowed out. It wasn't as if she
had anywhere to be at this hour. The funeral service had taken
her from her gardening, and it was too late to work now.

Henri's arrival signaled all was back to normal, didn't it?

He grinned, grabbed her waist, and pulled her away from
the others to whisper, "They think they've discovered another
of the earl's letters. We are to take down one of those
monstrous paintings in the vestibule. Arnaud said he left a
ladder in here, and I've come to claim it."

She thought his arm around her waist excited her more than the news of still another foolish letter that led to Bedlam and nothing more. She had a mad urge to kiss his whiskery cheek but that was much too forward. Instead, she properly stepped back and nodded to a far corner. "Behind the draperies."

He was carrying it across the floor when sharp voices rang from the other side of the wall. At the door, the tall, uniformed footman froze, listening. Looking mildly concerned, slender Mr. Birdwhistle ushered his charges—and Lavender—behind the makeshift dressing room Paul had built. The gallery-ballroom was large enough to house a village of workrooms but wasn't a good hiding place.

As the argument escalated, Henri set down the ladder, and grabbed one of Lavender's small pattern knives from her sewing kit. Alarmed, Patience picked up scissors from the dressmaker's table. Unaware of the possibility of escaping killers, the sewing ladies looked puzzled but continued gossiping over their tea.

"We only do as told, monsieur," a male voice cried in protest from the other side of the door. Holding her knife, Patience eased up closer to Henri and Adam. She had only just learned the manor was legally her home. After a lifetime of traveling about the countryside, she would gladly defend this permanent abode as if she were a knight of old.

Not that she had any clue of who the enemy might be.

"I have been told no one is to leave until the master gives word," Quincy intoned in his deep baritone on the other side of the wall. "You may leave the trunk here."

"Isn't it a little late in the day to be leaving?" Patience murmured. These didn't sound like dangerous killers.

"My lady is not herself," a female voice nearly wept. "We must take her away from this dreadful place. You cannot hold us prisoner!"

"Nadia and Leon," Patience whispered in puzzlement, recognizing the whine. "The Champlains' personal servants."

Henri nodded. "Hunt and Jack are preventing the coachmen from taking out the carriages and horses. Poor Quincy is simply the messenger." He leaned one shoulder against the door frame in order to listen better.

Armed with only his fists, young Adam simply awaited orders, planting his large body between the door and the gallery occupants.

Patience didn't know whether to be thrilled or terrified. Surely portly Sir Oswald and tiny Lady Champlain and their servants weren't dangerous? A little odd, perhaps, not terrifying. . . But none of their guests were terrifying and still, two people had died.

She glanced toward the boys, who appeared oblivious to the tension. They'd brought ink and pens to write on the cloth scraps and were engrossed in arranging the patchwork. Lavender appeared to be showing them how to make straight lines.

Patience finally let it sink in that she was no longer the curate's protected young daughter who simply obeyed orders. She was one of the adults in this room, ones who must make decisions and defend the harmless. She was a *Reid*, the descendant of a long line of powerful earls.

The knowledge didn't make her braver.

Sir Oswald's booming voice carried easily through the panel. "Whot's the meaning of thish? Where's our carriage?"

He slurred words as if he might have partaken of a little too much ale. She'd sung for the patrons of Henri's tavern a few nights since he'd opened it and recognized the signs. Henri usually sent her home when men reached this level of inebriation.

"You must ask the captain," Quincy intoned. "There appears to be a problem in the stable."

A problem? Or simply a delay caused by Hunt?

Henri whispered, "I warned Hunt that Avignon had recognized the Turbins. I'd thought the count would be the one to flee."

"Perhaps Avignon warned the Champlains after the funeral?" she whispered back. "Are they all in this together?"

Henri's eyes widened in alarm, but a new voice prevented further discourse.

"I'll carry out the bloody trunks if you won't!" A man's voice, not one Patience recognized. "His lordship has ordered the Champlains to leave."

His lordship? *Villiers*, Elsa's half-brother? *Spalding*, the marquess? Or Comte Avignon?

"The earl and marquess are in the vestibule hunting for jewels," Henri whispered, as if in answer to her thoughts. "I'm wagering that's a bluff."

The vestibule, on the far side of the enormous gallery—so close, but so unreachable. The manor was vast. The original fortress construction had few doors. Patience eyed the ladder and the loft rail above. Someone needed to alert the rest of the household.

Following her gaze, Henri nodded. "Fetch Birdwhistle. Send him up."

If the Champlains or their servants were killers. . . Patience hurried over to speak with the tutor.

He nodded but glanced at Lavender and the boys with concern. "Perhaps we ought to all escape?"

She had thought only to warn the household that the Champlains were running away. Surely they weren't actually a danger?

More angry shouting and a gunshot proved otherwise. A scream that very much sounded like Clare's rang clearly through the thick panel.

Trying not to panic, Patience helped the tutor carry the long ladder to the loft railing and usher the boys up. Being boys, they eagerly scrambled up and over the rail.

Lavender protested, but Patience showed her how to tuck the back of her gown into the waistband at front. It revealed her dainty ankles, but at a word of reassurance from her workers—who were arming themselves with long needles and scissors—she reluctantly agreed. The tutor followed after, dutifully keeping his eyes on the ladder and not the ankles above him.

The gallery door crashed in. The sewing ladies jumped from their chairs and backed toward a corner as Quincy fell onto the floor, holding a hand to his bloodied shoulder.

Henri and Adam dashed out in pursuit of the shooter. This time, Patience screamed.

THIRTY-TWO

ELSA: EAST TOWER

FLEEING THE CHAOS SHE'D LEFT OUTSIDE HER SUITE, ELSA RAN down the tower stairs holding her empty tray. In the back hall, she spotted Clare and Meera, and shouted, "Help! The aunts have gone mad!"

Outside the infirmary, Clare stared at her as if she were the one who had gone mad. Elsa needed Clare's sensible head to tell her what to do. "The Turbins. . ." she tried to explain. "Avignon was threatening the Turbins. I ran for help. . ."

Because Avignon's ugly valet had vanished, but that was too many words. "The aunts. . . I warned them. . ."

She'd never seen the old ladies move so swiftly. Instead of running for Hunt, they'd grabbed their knitting needles and the silver serving tray and marched to war like their Viking ancestors. Crying protest about Avignon's innocence, Elsa's mother had followed after them.

"They're beating him up! They'll have an attack of the heart. . ." Madness was well beyond her upbringing. She didn't know how to explain.

Holding a hand to her bosom, Elsa tried to catch her breath—when a blast of gunfire echoed from the main corridor.

Accustomed to men and guns, Elsa didn't startle at the discharge. If she'd had a weapon, she'd have blasted holes in the walls to send Avignon fleeing. Maybe someone else had done the same.

Only, gunfire had Clare blanching in terror and shrinking back into the infirmary. Not the reaction needed.

Remembering her cousin's justified fear of weapons, Elsa caught Clare's arm, not allowing her to retreat. "I'm sorry. I need you *now*. The men can take care of themselves. The aunts may come to harm if we do not stop them."

Or the Frenchman might be a killer. He'd threatened the innocent Turbins! Any man who threatened hapless, elderly servants had to be a villain—and the aunts and her mother were in danger. She grabbed Clare's arm and tugged her toward the stairs.

Clare resisted. "The boys. The boys are in the gallery!" Breaking free of Elsa's grip, she ran *toward* the gunfire, not away.

What the devil was happening? Had the entire world gone mad?

With a frown, Meera picked up her skirt and followed Clare toward the gunfire. Apparently gunshots caused more injury than old ladies. They didn't know the aunts very well.

Panicking again, Elsa contemplated escaping to her kitchen, but villains needed to be stopped. The humiliation of a bunch of old ladies beating Avignon into submission ought to be sufficient punishment for threatening servants, if no harm came to them. She couldn't count on that if he was a killer.

"It's the ghost." Pale and distraught, dotty Dottie drifted from the infirmary, rubbing her temple. "I've been trying to tell everyone, The Lady is agitated."

While sensible Clare fled toward danger, irrational Dottie headed for the stairs and the aunts.

Elsa didn't think the slender heiress much of a warrior,

and helpless ghosts were most definitely not the problem. Mad old ladies and a villainous Frenchman were. But she'd take any help she could find.

Where the devil had the men gone? Toward the shots, of course. Or were they still in the stable? Surely, with all the stable lads about, they couldn't come to harm? Reassured that Jack was outside, Elsa ran after the ghost-watching heiress.

They found the irate mob in the hall at the top of the stairs.

Avignon's slight valet had vanished at the first sign of trouble. He couldn't lay hands on a marchioness, a countess, and a baroness, and his employer would not care to have his servant observing his humiliation.

The Turbins weren't so reticent. They had emerged from the suite to watch with interest as the haughty, seventy-five year old baroness beat at Avignon with her lorgnette every time the Comte tried to dodge around her. Not to be outdone, plump Lady Spalding wielded a knitting needle and held a tea tray like a shield.

Elsa's mother, on the other hand, had given up hysterics and simply kicked her suitor every time the Frenchman tried to escape. As a former countess, she knew how to wield wrath with a lifted eyebrow. Actual physical confrontation. . . Elsa could never have imagined it in a hundred years, but a threatening worm like Avignon deserved a good kick. Had her mother finally recognized him for the scoundrel he was?

They had no men to run to their rescue. Lorgnettes and knitting needles would not stop a rat for long. The question was, how dangerous was Avignon if he couldn't even stop a knitting needle?

"Avril," Dottie cried, senselessly, distracting the aunts. "The Lady is calling him Avril!"

Who? The ghost? The ghost was talking now? Everyone stared at the beautiful but jingle-brained heiress. Avignon attempted escape again, but Elsa's mother kicked him in the shin.

Elsa closed her eyes and tried to make sense of Bedlam, but the name haunted her. *Avril*? Opening her eyes again, she glanced at the horrified Turbins, and the memory sprang loose.

"*Charles* Avril? Mother, stop that now!" Much larger than her slender mother, Elsa stepped between her and an agitated Avignon.

The shorter Frenchman shrank back. She took another intimidating step in his direction, and his stout, balding figure practically melted into the wall niche. So much for polished sophistication.

In her sweeping petticoats and purple gown, plump Lady Spalding came to stand beside her. "I must say, bringing rascals to task is tedious business. Where are those lazy men?" She pointed her knitting needle at Avignon's midsection, causing him to cringe.

"Apparently, we have more than one villain in the manor, and the other has a pistol." Elsa prayed no one else had come to harm. Jack was in the stable, wasn't he? Perhaps the guests were shooting each other. Since it was silent now, she had to hope the men had the problem under control. She'd seen the captain and his cousins in action. They were formidable.

How the devil did they handle Avignon? Start with ridding the scene of her hysterical mother. "Mother, will you please see if you can find Spalding or Villiers or anyone useful? I have a roast on the fire and don't trust Anne to baste it."

At this order, Avignon attempted to edge past her. Elsa crossed her arms and blocked his feeble effort. Gentleman to the core, he would not touch her.

"Why do we need the men?" Lady Lavinia added her tall frame and silks to the barrier, preventing further attempts at escape. "I've always dispensed of unwelcome guests myself. And what Lady is Dorothea nattering on about?"

Ah, practicality at last, almost. *The Lady*, as in the late viscountess, the Turbins former employer. Elsa turned toward her servants. "Charles Avril is the Comte Avignon?"

They nodded, wide-eyed.

"*He* took Lady Reid's pearls? And threatened you not to tell?" Elsa returned her glare to Avignon, who cringed and sagged against the niche wall. She twisted the threat she'd overheard. "I am inclined to believe honest, hardworking servants over a cowardly fake count."

"You actually threatened servants over *fake pearls*?" Lady Spalding asked in astonishment. "Everyone knows my mother sold the real ones and replaced them with imitations."

"Not all, my lady," Marie Turbin said tremulously. "Once you married and the earl passed away, she retired here, where her expenses were few. She parted with the remaining pearls sparingly. I cannot know how many left were genuine, but she locked them up as if they were."

The Lady's daughter, the stout dowager marchioness, huffed indignantly. "Well, I never. I could have had a proper come-out ball instead of the shabby affair she said was all we could afford?"

Meera snickered. Elsa rolled her eyes.

"The Lady wants me to swat you," Dottie cried. "I have never felt the spirits this strongly. She is quite angry."

"Mother was always angry. She flew into rages over burnt cakes. Do not put yourself into a pother." Lady Spalding twirled her knitting needle dangerously near Avignon's lower parts. "I don't remember this vermin hanging about. How does he know of the pearls?"

"I did not leave France until your grandparents were killed!" Avignon finally spoke, attempting to gather his dignity. "I tried to help others escape as I had."

"If you're wealthy, you could have helped without taking

a poor widow's pearls!" As a widow twice over, Elsa's mother regarded her potential suitor with wrath.

"Lady Reid and her daughters did not need the pearls, so much as the rest of her family did!" Avignon cried. "You have your estates and this beautiful home and they had nothing!"

"*We* are family and you did not help us." With amazing timing, Monsieur Lavigne entered the tower, looking puzzled at the confrontation. "What makes you think Avignon has wealth? His family were courtiers, nothing more. They were reliant on a court that no longer exists. What is happening here?"

"Is he even a count?" Elsa's mother demanded.

The grieving Frenchman shrugged his lanky shoulders. "No one is nobility these days. His great uncle may have been. I am no one to point an accusing finger."

"He took Lady Reid's pearls." Pearls that might rightfully belong to the Lavignes, if Elsa understood rightly. Or perhaps to Lady Reid's daughters?

Lavigne raised his dark eyebrows in a haughty manner that revealed he hadn't always been a broken man. "Then what did he do with them?"

THIRTY-THREE

HUNT: STABLE

ONCE THEY'D ASCERTAINED NO ONE WAS STEALING HORSES OR escaping yet, Hunt sent Walker back to the manor to guard the women. His friend had grown up poor and hated dirtying good clothes.

Uncaring of his fancy coat, Hunt crawled under the Champlains' carriage to dismantle a wheel to prevent anyone from sneaking away in the night.

Performing the same task on the rickety rental the Lavignes had arrived in, Jack cursed. "Look at this! The bastard has nicked the axle so it will break under stress—at high speed or maneuvering a bad curve." Filthy and angry, he shoved out from under the small landau. "I'll hang this villain personally!"

Hunt slid over to examine the axle and whistled. "I was hoping to find secret compartments or something interesting. This is just vile. The Lavignes have nothing! Why would anyone harm them? I cannot imagine any of our guests sinking so low."

Or crawling under carriages or climbing trees. He was missing something.

Before they could explore more, mute Ned raced in,

signaling urgency. Even Jack read the lad's sign and leaped up. "What's he saying?"

"*Problem* is all I can ascertain. He's agitated and wants us to follow." Hunt grabbed a whip and a hay fork, regretting not carrying a more useful weapon on him.

Clare would not approve if he went about with a shotgun.

They raced down the drive toward the manor. Before they reached the carriage portico, a tall young man ran out, wielding a pistol and dragging a struggling woman with him.

Clare!

Hunt choked on a roar of rage and horror. Jack caught his arm, preventing him from charging like a berserker. The delay allowed the film of red wrath to fade into the cold logical need to annihilate the enemy.

When the scoundrel shouted, "Throw down your weapons and bring me my horse!" Hunt broke Jack's hold. Curling his whip, he calculated distance with his one good eye.

"*Villiers'* man?" Jack murmured. "What the devil?"

Not caring who the fool was, Hunt stepped closer, taking his measure, looking for a way around Clare. Villiers new valet wasn't a small man, nor a weak one.

"He shot *Quincy*," Clare shouted in grief and horror.

In retaliation, her captor jerked the arm around her neck, bringing her chin up to silence her. "Lay down your weapons!"

Damn. Hunt halted to prevent causing her more harm.

"Roberts, the earl's new valet." He answered Jack's question while setting down his whip and hayfork and studying the situation. His distance sight in his one working eye was still good. "Single barrel, right?" he asked quietly. The valet's pistol still smoked—from shooting their *butler*? Hunt prayed Quincy's bulk had protected him, but Clare was all he could focus on now.

"Bastard could still break her neck," Jack warned, understanding.

Henri and Patience ran out the side door, and Roberts swung to point the empty weapon at them.

"He's cornered," Hunt muttered. "Trapped rats run. Let's give him a bolt hole. Fetch a horse."

As Jack jogged back to the stable, Hunt shouted, "Let the lady go. You can have your horse."

"The horse first," the valet shouted. "I'll shoot anyone who comes close."

Sir Oswald staggered out behind Henri and Patience. "Boy, don't do thish! You don' like ships!"

Hunt's thought processes were too fixated on Clare's terrified expression to make sense of this.

"I won't need your bloody ships! I'll have the pearls and the land. You lost your courage when you married *her*." Roberts threw a disgusted look at the doorway where presumably. . . his *stepmother* stood? Villiers' valet was Sir Oswald's son? That didn't make sense but Hunt couldn't interpret the exchange any other way.

If it weren't for Clare, he would simply kick the young bastard in the ballocks and throw a facer to lay him flat. But Clare suffered enough night terrors as it was. His task was to shield her from scenes of violence—not easy, since he'd been trained to react with aggression.

Sensing Jack leading an animal from the stable, Hunt eased closer to Clare. She focused her gaze on him, which helped him keep his fury in check.

There hadn't been time to saddle the horse. With luck, Roberts would break his fool neck trying to mount. The scoundrel really hadn't thought this through. An empty gun in one hand, a struggling woman in the other. . . he would need a third hand to grab the horse.

Given sufficient time, brainpower worked better than firepower, Hunt conceded.

He took the reins Jack handed him and studied the valet. Roberts was tall and muscular, well able to push an older man like Jones down the stairs. If he'd been on ships, he knew how to scramble up and tie knots under the worst conditions. The twine in the trees had no doubt been his doing. A lot of other questions remained, but Hunt was fairly confident the handsome young valet was their killer. He wouldn't mind murdering the bastard simply for abusing Clare. Add the deaths of good men. . . Fury and the need for justice over-ruled caution.

Tugging the horse's reins, Hunt approached, exaggerating his limp, trying to look harmless. "Horse for woman," he commanded.

Clare kicked backward at the valet's shin, but he wore boots and she wore slippers.

The valet warily studied the horse. Henri and Patience eased around behind him—wielding scissors?—waiting for an opportunity. Patience, a curate's daughter! Henri was a bad influence.

In the doorway, Sir Oswald shouted and cursed. From around the front corner of the manor, Hunt noted movement in the shrubbery. Someone had left through the front door. Friend or enemy?

Hunt roughly jerked the horse's reins, until it reared up in protest, endangering all in its path with sharp hooves. Abruptly releasing the agitated animal, Hunt grabbed Clare and yanked her to him.

Roberts had to drop Clare and the weapon to seize the leather with both hands to prevent the horse from escaping.

With a cry, Clare collapsed in Hunt's arms. He hugged her close, pulling her away from the prancing animal and the scoundrel attempting to mount it.

Shouting, causing the animal to dance away, Henri slashed at the valet's arm with a small knife, while Patience rammed scissors into Roberts' shoulder. The valet screamed but still managed to haul himself onto the horse's back. Sir Oswald stumbled onto the drive, shouting incoherently.

Calmly, Jack released the whip he'd rolled up at his side. With one wicked shot, he brought the muscled valet to the ground. Sailors seldom made good riders.

Hunt held Clare, allowing her to bury her face in his shoulder while Jack caught the horse and Henri dropped to his knees to hold a small blade to the villain's jugular. A drunken Sir Oswald wept.

From out of the shrubbery emerged Arnaud and Walker, carrying shotguns to prevent any further attempts at escape.

"What the devil is happening?" Clare whispered from Hunt's embrace, lifting her puzzled face for answers he didn't have.

The manor had finally driven his genteel, bookish fiancée to cursing. Hunt tried not to laugh in relief as he hugged her tighter. He loved this woman so much, he might burst from the strength of it.

THIRTY-FOUR

CLARE: FORMAL DINING ROOM

CLARE PICKED AT HER BURNT ROAST, THEN SIPPED THE FINE WINE Elsa had brought from their declining stores. Even should Napoleon be defeated, they could not afford to replenish their cellar, provided the vineyards of France recovered.

She was trying hard not to relive the last trying hours, but she'd been attacked, held *hostage*, by a killer! And their beloved Quincy was in Meera's infirmary, recovering from a gunshot to the shoulder—received while protecting their household. On top of all else, his wounds were enough to make one weep.

Only Hunt's courageous, swift action and soothing embrace had prevented her from grabbing Oliver and fleeing, screaming, into the night.

Or maybe she'd grown up a little. The world was full of horrible events. Running away wouldn't solve anything. If she thought about it instead of panicking, she understood horrible events were better handled in the company of people she trusted to come to her aid. She had lived in despair for so long at losing her meager family. . . But now she had more family to lose. She'd ponder the significance later, perhaps work it into the next novel. Should she ever finish copying this one.

At the other end of the table, Spalding and Villiers argued with Arnaud over an old painting, as if they hadn't buried two men today and locked their killer in the crypt. Someone would have to take Roberts to the assize court for sentencing. Understanding his actions might not happen if the men didn't start asking questions.

They'd wanted food first. She understood the need for normalcy. She just didn't think normalcy was. . . normal. Unless people dying regularly was normal. She supposed it might be.

"What have you done with the Champlains?" she finally forced herself to ask.

With their banker and lawyer dining with them, conversation was difficult. The two *professionals* did their best to look unassuming, but human nature was what it was. They listened.

"We locked them in their chambers with their servants. Interrogating the inebriated isn't fair. The aunts have given me a wild tale, but I'd rather wait until the culprits dry out before questioning." Hunt's American circumspection had returned—after he'd attacked a killer with a horse. Or perhaps after consulting Browning, the solicitor.

Or he'd remembered he acted as magistrate, not a soldier punishing disobedient troops. Hunt's many facets fascinated her. His steadiness was the reason she wasn't in hysterics right now. She pondered fainting and being carried off to her chambers with smelling salts—but then she'd miss all the interesting bits.

"What I want to know is how Avignon escaped the library to torment the servants." Hunt glared at his noble guests and cousins. "He probably warned the Champlains to flee."

This time, Bosworth winced and admitted, "We were

trying to provide you with the funds necessary to improve this hulking fortress. Avignon told us the earl prized the portrait of the lady hanging in the vestibule, and we should look to it."

After all the excitement, the aunts had not deigned to dine with them this evening. It was up to Clare or Elsa to point out the fallacy of their excuse for this dereliction of duty.

Instead, usually shy Patience frowned and asked, "I thought Avignon did not arrive in England until *after* the revolution? And the earl died before that? How would he know what the earl prized?"

Next to Patience, in their seats at the middle of the table, Henri chuckled. "It seems Avignon paid the valets to search the library until they found one of the earl's letters simply by opening and closing books. The letter mentions the painting, but he was quite convincing about the earl. Arnaud hasn't had time to clean the vestibule paintings, which set off his curiosity."

"No one argued with me." Arnaud continued eating. He'd added a little more meat to his bones since he'd come out of hiding, but Clare thought he might never eat enough after years of starvation. "Now that we've retrieved the actual letter, I'll have to study it, but it does mention the portrait in the vestibule."

"And where is Avignon now?" Elsa asked.

"We are uncertain of his many stories. Considering the one about taking pearls, I suggested he dine in his room for his own protection," Hunt said dryly. "Perhaps we should put him to searching the library."

Before the conversation could devolve into another treasure hunt, Jack spoke up. "Are we interrogating the lot this evening then? I'd like to know we won't be stabbed in our beds before the wedding."

"You will take Elsa to Newchurch and honeymoon there, away from this Bedlam," Villiers ordered, predictably.

"You are currently eating Anne's cooking," Clare pointed

out. "If you make Elsa leave, we will tie you to a chair and serve you what we'll be eating while she's gone."

Elsa grinned at her plate. Clare wasn't as appalled as she should be for speaking to an earl in such a manner. Villiers was human and Elsa's brother. Brothers needed to be set in their place.

"We are isolated." Hunt sipped his wine. "The late earl was wealthier than kings, and he left the riches mostly to women. There will always be those who believe ladies are vulnerable. As long as we stand united, we are strong. Stand with us, and let Elsa and Jack have their happiness. Isolate her in her estate, and she will become a victim as she has before."

"Being united did not save Jones," Villiers countered bitterly.

"*You* brought Roberts into the manor. Did you give Jones time to investigate him before you hired him, or were you more interested in looking pretty?" Jack asked cynically. He and Villiers had a history of disagreement.

"Roberts came with impeccable references. We had no way of knowing he was Champlain's son. It seems he is a good forger." Villiers emptied his wine glass and looked for more.

"It appears Barbeau's inquiries set off a chain of events no one could have predicted." Elsa waved her fork impatiently. "All this blathering won't help. Let us interrogate the participants, send the wicked off to hang, and let me prepare our wedding feast as planned."

"You shouldn't have to prepare your own wedding breakfast," Villiers complained. "You'll have enough wealth to hire the best chef in France."

"I'll make inquiries about chefs," Spalding, the slender marquess, suggested. "I am finding this isolation in the manor beneficial. I can discuss news from the latest diplomatic pouches and London will not hear of it until the newssheets do. I just received word that Napoleon is marching on Brussels."

The men exploded in excited chatter, diverted from argument by this news from the continent.

Clare caught the impatience in the eyes of her female cousins and directed Adam to take their puddings and tea into the family parlor. *Someone* had to deal with domestic affairs.

The Lavignes were already there. As was Dottie, who normally dined with the aunts. As always, their French guests looked anxious, but a little less so now that the killer had been caught.

"We believe we know what happened," Dottie declared as the tray of cakes and fruit was set out. She held out the notes the aunts had taken and given Elsa earlier. "I don't think Lady Reid's spirit will rest until her family is safe."

"That's a rather large order." Clare took the paper to study it. "We will have to hope Napoleon loses and war ends and there are enough young men alive to restore fields and. . . I am a city girl and even I understand the difficulty."

"If vineyards are like orchards, it might take years," Patience added sympathetically.

"With enough labor, we can have grapes by next spring," Monsieur Lavigne claimed, looking less gloomy when talking of his fields.

"But that takes money. According to the documents the lawyer sent, the Champlain trust leaves the pearls to the *descendants* of Jeannette and Gabrielle Champlain. That includes the Lavignes since it does not specify the eldest or sons," Dottie rashly declared. As an heiress, she had no notion of the changes a single pearl might make in lives. "Over the years, Sir Oswald has been claiming that inheritance and has stolen most of them. He should be made to pay."

Clare studied Lady Spalding's neat, spiky handwritten notes. "Sir Oswald confessed to forgery?"

"Lady Lavinia persuaded him to admit that he did so at Avignon's behest," Dottie clarified. "Avignon was convinced Arnaud was dead. He had been told the rest of the family was lost, including the Lavignes. Lady Reid died in 1801," Dottie reminded them. "How much communication could there have been then? How would anyone know who had died?"

"Sofia was an infant," Monsieur Lavigne explained. "These were the war years, when I was coerced into the army. Adele took Sofia into hiding with the peasants. Our homes had already been destroyed."

"You are saying that Avignon had reason to believe the entire Lavigne family was gone?" Clare asked.

Adele Lavigne nodded and spoke softly. "As aristocrats, we did not wish to be found. I had friends. We worked together to keep food on the table. Even I did not know Jules was alive. This was many years ago, you must understand, after his parents died. We were young. We knew nothing."

Clare glanced at the notes. "Sir Oswald employed his ships to rescue aristocrats. Even if he thought you dead, he did not think to search for Arnaud or Henri?"

Lavigne shrugged. "All we knew was that our nephews had been sent to Lady Reid and England to school. I suppose, to protect them from spies, she did not mention her great-nephews to her visitors. It is not as if Sir Oswald ever met the younger generations. He may not have even known of us. His family departed France decades ago. They were sailors, as he says."

Clare had spent all her life never having met her extended family, and they lived in the same country. She understood. Only the manor had brought some of the Reids together again. Without elders to gather around, families needed a place to connect.

"But forgery is illegal," Patience objected. "Are you saying

Sir Oswald forged death certificates so he might claim the Champlain trust?"

"He did not need to forge Lady Reid's, and hers was the one that mattered. Her pearls were not part of the family trust, but she left them to her sister's family—the Champlains. The only Champlain the solicitors could find—thanks to Avignon—was Sir Oswald." Dottie picked up her tea.

"And of course, the English solicitors could not search all of France," Jules Lavigne said in resignation. "We should be honored that Avignon did not simply walk away with the necklace."

"That wasn't honor. He knew there were more pearls in the solicitor's vault, and he wanted a share of them for his efforts," Elsa added cynically. "If they fraudulently proved Sir Oswald was the last of the family, then the solicitors could disburse the family trust over the years, as specified."

Jules Lavigne bowed his head. "There is much blame to be placed, but that will not restore Barbeau or our lands. All we wish to ask is that what remains of the estate be distributed properly."

Clare sat back with her teacup. "Extremely wise. That avoids paying lawyers and tying the proceeds up in court for years. It also means you must share with Arnaud and Henri, if I understand rightly, as descendants of Lady Reid's sister."

"Oh, jolly fun," Patience declared, reaching for a biscuit. "Captain Huntley cannot rule on a case involving his family, can he?"

Clare gave up adjudicating and settled into the sofa to enjoy her tea. Someday, if she ever had time to write again, she'd find a way to work this into a novel.

No one could possibly believe this story was anything but fiction.

THIRTY-FIVE

HUNT: SATURDAY

HUNT WONDERED IF ANY OTHER MAGISTRATE'S COURTROOM WAS
as grand as Wycliffe's two-story, oak-paneled great hall. Or
their juries as diverse. Having a marquess and earl with their
legal knowledge to guide him was a boon. Unlike in most
courtrooms, however, he would not exclude the women and
servants who had been terrorized by an avaricious young
killer who lacked anything resembling a conscience.

"I'm the great-grandson of French aristocracy, the son of
an English knight," Roberts declared, brushing his thick black
locks off his forehead. "There was no reason the pearls
shouldn't come to a good Englishman like me instead of the
enemy."

"I told you, I would buy land," Sir Oswald cried. "You
needed only to wait!"

"And slave away at a desk until then?" His son sneered.
"Or until your whore presented you with a more well-born
heir? I only did as you did before you married *her* and turned
proper." He didn't even look at his stony-faced stepmother.

Sir Oswald had been a privateer in his youth. He had no
doubt killed in the heat of combat. And he had forged death
certificates to claim riches that did not belong to him.

Hunt did not sympathize. "We are here to judge you, not your father. When your father told you Barbeau had introduced himself and declared the Lavignes alive, what did you do?"

"My father paid my allowance with those pearls, and the frogs would take them away and probably sue us for everything we owned! Once Barbeau told us more heirs lived in England, and he meant to meet them, it was simple enough to ask about Wycliffe Manor and learn of the weddings."

"How did you manage to be hired into an earl's household?" Hunt asked, not concealing his incredulity.

Despite his night in the crypt, Roberts—now known as Robert Champlain—had managed to stay well-groomed. He'd insisted on washing and shaving before appearing in their makeshift courtroom. "I chatted up the earl's valet and learned Villiers only kept a small staff in town. I had references drawn up, and once I disposed of the doddering old fool, I presented myself in his place, knowing there'd not be time to find another manservant."

"What did you do to my valet?" Villiers demanded in an ominous tone.

"Got him drunk. Put him on a ship." Roberts shrugged. "He was naught more than a ponce anyway."

Hunt winced. Jones, Villiers' valued secretary, had probably hired a man of his own predilection. Such men no doubt looked after each other. No wonder Jones had disliked the other valet's replacement.

Hunt allowed the earl to question the prisoner about which ship and hoped the one the poor valet was on had only crossed the Channel and back. Once satisfied with his information, Villiers growled, "Hang him."

Robert looked a little rattled at that condemnation. He was too caught up in himself to understand the damage he had done.

"So you kidnapped the earl's valet and presented yourself to Jones with forged references?" Hunt prompted.

"Traveled here in proper style," Roberts said smugly. "Arrived before the frog-eaters, just as I planned."

Frog-eaters. The Lavignes. Bigotry blinded men to humanity. Hunt's temper escalated. "How did you learn about the hidden path? How did you know Barbeau meant to take it?"

"Avignon and my father talked about it, laughed over the old days." Roberts glanced at his father. "They thought it amusing that they smuggled brandy to an English earl's estate. They even told the Frenchie of the shorter path so he might arrive before nightfall instead of plotting how to stop him. They've grown old and staid in their ways."

A bloody opportunist. Had Roberts a conscience at all, he might have gone far. Or perhaps not. It took intelligence to craft *legal* opportunities.

Sir Oswald sank in his seat and covered his face. Looking ill, his wife fled.

"And how did you intend to divert Barbeau?" Hunt worded this question carefully.

"Thought I'd tie him up and put him on a ship like the other fellow. Offered a guinea, had one of the old soldiers ready to take him to the coast, see if I didn't. Not my fault the frog was such a poor horseman."

A broken neck had killed the lad. Barbeau died because of this monster. "So what did you do when you discovered the lad suffering in the lane?"

"I'm no sawbones, now, am I? No ship was going to take him like that. I just relieved him of the documents."

He'd left the poor lad there to die.

Hunt had already verified privately with Avignon that he'd been with Mrs. Turner that night and had no knowledge of Barbeau's missing documents. The lady had confirmed it. "And where are the papers now?"

"In my trunk. I hoped to use them to prove I was heir, but they were all in French." The handsome, privileged young man lounged in the chair as if he truly were heir to fortunes and titles.

There were many things that Hunt could say about that, but he wasn't a captain chastising a private anymore. He had to be impartial and not choke the scoundrel with his bare hands.

"And Jones? Did he merely step in your way in your eagerness to run down the stairs?" All right, he hadn't contained his temper.

Hunt's noble audience didn't object. He glanced at the ladies. Even his aunt was nodding her graying curls.

"Nah, he threatened me. The ponce threatened *me*. I caught him sneaking out in the middle of the night, and he said he was going to see me hang. Had to defend myself, didn't I?"

It was all downhill from there. Walker wrote up the notes. Spalding agreed to have the prisoner hauled to the courts on Monday in his carriage. Hunt hated sending a man to his death, but Roberts was a bare shell of a human being.

He felt a little sorry for Sir Oswald, who had been a man of his times and not exactly the kind of father to raise a civilized gentleman. But a heedless killer— And it wasn't as if Oswald was entirely innocent. After learning the heirs were alive, he'd hastened here to see if he could cover up his unintentional theft.

The great hall courtroom remained silent as Hunt sent a protesting Roberts to the crypt in the company of a couple of rough ex-soldiers. The once homeless troops were gradually finding a place for themselves around the manor.

Hunt knew everyone was waiting on his final verdict— one which affected the living.

"I cannot act as judge on the matter of forgery and theft from my own family," Hunt declared. "I cannot be impartial. Villiers, Spalding, will you preside in my place?"

He'd asked them earlier. This was a formality for Walker to record.

Hunt took a seat beside Clare on a sofa turned to face their makeshift dais. She cuddled closer, reassuring him that he had not outraged her delicate sensibilities.

Feeling her warm curves pressed against him, he regretted their decision to postpone the wedding. He'd hoped to finally have her in his bed tomorrow night. He could rationalize that life was short and the future unpredictable, as these last months had proved. He didn't wish to die never knowing the delights of her embrace.

But if the future was unpredictable, he wouldn't risk her happiness for a night's pleasure. He'd give her the protection of his name first.

He squeezed her hand and listened as the two nobles questioned Avignon and Sir Oswald, and Walker recorded it all. He didn't think these notes would be forwarded elsewhere. It was enough that they were recorded here in the presence of aristocrats with the power to wield authority.

Browning, the family lawyer, would file any formal paperwork later. The solicitor would protect his grandfather in doing so. The old man really should have looked for the heirs himself.

They took the testimony of Avignon and Sir Oswald that they had truly thought the family dead and simply followed the solicitor's orders to provide a witnessed statement of those deaths. Champlain's sailors had willingly signed the fraudulent statement, as had Avignon.

Sir Oswald was a direct descendant of a collateral branch and had a right to the family trust. A man couldn't be blamed for supporting his family and attempting to help his fellow emigres, however illegally. That he and Avignon had actually attempted to carry out Lady Reid's wishes in aiding emigres gave their testimony credence.

The theft of Lady Reid's pearls and the fact that her

daughters should have shared in their grandparents' trust was a different matter. The daughters had been very much alive. Hunt understood where Robert Champlain had learned his notion of justice. The English daughters had wealth and didn't need the trust as much as the emigres did, in Avignon and Oswald's minds.

"I will sign over my rights to the remainder of the pearls in the vault," Sir Oswald promised. "I've invested some in hopes of buying land. I'll let the court decide how much of the investment belongs to others. I have no heir to pass on land to now. I am the last of the Champlains. Our name must continue under the Lavigne titles."

Clare buried her face in Hunt's shoulder to hide her tears at that declaration. Sir Oswald had just admitted that his only son must hang.

The marquess was more cynical in his response. "You think to avoid hanging along with your son through your generosity? What about the pearls belonging to Lady Reid that you presumably gave to your son so he might live like a lord?"

Sir Oswald squirmed. With a sigh, Avignon shoved from his chair. "The lady wished her pearls to go to her French relations. Perhaps it was not written down. Perhaps English law might say they belong to her daughters, but she desired them to aid her sister's family upon her demise. There should be a letter to that effect among the solicitor's papers."

The solicitor frowned and started sifting through his folder of yellowed documents.

Hunt stood. "I will speak for my mother in asking that my grandmother's pearls be treated as part of the larger trust." He turned to his aunt. "Lady Spalding?"

His aunt pondered the request half a moment, then waved her beringed hands. "I detest pearls and my daughters don't need them. I agree."

Most likely to spite Spalding's family, who wished to take

her home away, but Hunt returned to his seat, hoping this would smooth the rocky path of inheritance.

"Would the parties want their own solicitors present or will Mr. Browning and Mr. Bosworth suffice to decide a fair and impartial division of the trust?" Villiers asked when the testimony was recorded.

Arnaud stood. "Henri and I have discussed this. As long as we are able to maintain residence in Wycliffe Manor, we have a home. Our uncle and his family live in uncertainty, with no home unless Bonaparte is defeated. And even then, the expense of rebuilding our joint lands is great. We would like to suggest that we use what remains of the inheritance to form a family partnership."

Hunt heard Henri's fine business mind behind that. As expected, his younger cousin stood to explain.

"If we invest all the family funds in rebuilding the Champlain and Lavigne lands, Arnaud and I will happily take annual payments in the form of any wine, brandy, or other saleable product produced. We will allow the court to decide on a fair percentage."

Sofia was weeping. Her parents looked stunned. Typically, Hunt's independent cousins had not discussed this with anyone else.

Villiers and Spalding were stepping away from the dais when George, Avignon's pockmarked valet stood up.

"If you ain't locking up the count for theft and forgery, then my time here is done. You might wanta look to the paintings he and your thievin' knight were on about. The count didn't come here outta the goodness of his black heart. Lord Spalding, if you'll be so kind as to send me back where I belong, I'll be going where I can earn my way."

THIRTY-SIX

PATIENCE: SATURDAY

"WHAT IS A BOW STREET RUNNER?" PATIENCE ASKED AS HENRI escorted her to the orchard where she meant to gather a few blossoming branches to decorate the chapel.

The uproar after the ugly valet's announcement that he had been *spying* on Avignon had been too chaotic to take in, and then the gentlemen had departed for Hunt's study, leaving everyone else in the dark.

"They are paid to catch criminals," Henri explained. "They normally do not work outside of London, but apparently Spalding has been hiring this one for his own purposes. I hadn't thought Runners tracked spies."

"But Avignon isn't a spy, is he? He's a count! He courted Dottie. Mrs. Turner is his friend and she was a *countess*." Patience knew she was naïve in the ways of the larger world, but how could London society allow a spy in their midst?

"There are all sorts of spies. Avignon worked for the Bourbons, but it isn't as if deposed royalty pays well. Spalding was simply aware of suspicious correspondence between Avignon and France. When he heard Avignon was headed to the manor, he didn't want a possibly dangerous man associated with his stepmother. He is fond of the old lady. She raised him after all." Henri held the small stepladder so she might climb up and prune a few branches.

"The Marquess of Spalding felt guilty for suggesting his stepmother move out of her home and into the dower house," Patience concluded. "I may be ignorant of many things but not human nature."

"Possibly. But now we know why all the valets were in the library and following each other about. And if the paintings Avignon and Sir Oswald mentioned are worth anything, Arnaud can determine their value." Henri took the branches she clipped. "I don't believe Avignon actually meant to steal paintings or books although he may have offered a fractional amount of their worth. When one believes a cause is justified, it's easy to be less than honest."

"And he cannot be arrested for taking advantage of greed and stupidity." Patience snipped a branch a little too sharply. "Although Lord de Sackville would have thrown him out on his ear if he'd offered too little for the books. Will Hunt actually hire a Runner? Does he fear we'll have more crimes to be investigated?"

She was feeling uncommonly bold these days. She'd sung in a tavern and helped capture a killer. It was a very large leap for someone who had spent her years as charwoman for her father. She wasn't, however, feeling bold enough to wish for more deaths.

Henri took her hand as she climbed down. "I believe Hunt has decided we need a bailiff to oversee the grounds and a steward to direct your laborers more than we need a detective. And George is not very fond of the country. He has agreed to return if called upon but otherwise prefers London."

Patience was relieved at that news. Hiring a spying valet and thief catcher meant no one could be trusted. She would hate to live with that level of distrust.

With Henri holding her hand, she was losing track of her thoughts.

"Uncle Jules has decided to linger while the paperwork is being filed on the trust. He knows about overseeing workers, so he'll help you for a while." Henri swept her into his arms once she stepped off the last rung.

Breathless at his embrace, Patience tilted her head back in surprise.

Mistake. Henri lowered his head and kissed her.

She had never been kissed before. She was a tall, gawky spinster with no prospects. But she had longed for Henri's caress for so long, she didn't care. The heat of his lips spun her senses, rendering her incapable of more than noticing the strength of his chest and urges she didn't understand. Even the tickle of branches at her back meant nothing.

She gasped breathlessly when he set her down. She ought to say something. He was supposed to be guarding her against unwanted attentions. But, oh dear Lord, she *wanted* his attentions so very awfully much.

"I have been longing to do that for weeks," he murmured into her hair. "I will not apologize. You are too amazing to continue thinking you are no more than a gardener."

"I like gardening. And orchards. And flowers," she added defensively, before understanding that she needn't defend herself to this man. Henri was the grandson of French nobility, left penniless by war. Unlike the prisoner in the crypt, he knew what it was like to work for a living. . . just like her.

He wasn't degrading her dreams. He was. . . Patience stared at him in astonishment. "Are you courting me?"

Henri's infamous, beautiful grin spread across his face. "I have been this past week or more, *ma chérie*. Do you object?"

"Oh." She thought about it for half a second. And the newly-awakened woman in her answered, "Not if it means you will kiss me again."

THIRTY-SEVEN

ELSA: SUNDAY

JUNE 18TH, 1815, WAS A MOMENTOUS DAY IN HISTORY, BUT THE inhabitants of Gravesyde Priory were a far distance from the winds of war and cries of battle and blissfully unaware of anything but happiness and a sunny day.

Elsa laughed in delight as Lavender entered her bedchamber carrying a hair comb lavished in ribbons and attached to a gauzy veil. Too excited at marrying the dashing man she'd adored since childhood, Elsa had given little thought to accessories for her wedding day. She'd always considered herself too plump and plain to be more than dowdy and frumpy, but her young cousin had proved her wrong. The image in the mirror showed a beautiful, blushing bride, svelte in silver-blue sarcenet. The comb perched like a crown on top of her fair hair, wrestled into pins for a change.

"Jack will not be able to speak a word when he sees you," Lavender declared in satisfaction, stepping back to admire her handiwork. "You should wear this shade of blue more often. It compliments your eyes."

"Your eyes are so large," Clare declared. "With those long dark lashes, you are more beautiful than any of us. Why can't I have dark lashes? It's a good thing I am not marrying today.

The comparison between your beauty and my scrawny bespectacled looks would be too humiliating."

Elsa laughed. "Beauty is surely in the eye of the beholder. I only see plain old me decorated like a birthday cake, but you are a vision of delicate fairness, like a fairy princess. Look at Lavender, though. She is the one with the even features of a true beauty, if she'd quit hiding behind all those ruffles."

Lavender's lush lips formed a moue of disapproval at their flattery. She stepped back to admire the handiwork she could rightfully take pride in. "I do not wish to be seen for my looks, which is all men notice. I intend to wait until I am at least five and twenty before considering married life. By then, I hope to be as smart at choosing a husband as the two of you. And Meera."

"And Patience?" Clare whispered. Their tallest cousin wasn't here but decorating the chapel—with Henri at her side.

Lavender grinned. "I saw them kissing in the courtyard. I am already designing her gown. Do you think she will wait until autumn? She is a bit slow at romance."

"A harvest wedding, perfect." Satisfied that all was harmonious in her world and that she'd never be more beautiful than she was at this moment, Elsa turned toward the door of her old bedchamber for the last time. Tonight, she would join Jack in their new suite.

Or perhaps a little sooner. Jack was frothing at the bit. She loved that he wanted *her* so much.

"How is Quincy faring?" Clare asked when they met Meera at the foot of the marble stairs.

"Even with a bullet hole in him, the man refuses to rest. He has already gone into the village to direct the setting up of tables. Poor Adam is to be left guarding the manor on his own." Wearing her own wedding dress—the fanciest gown she owned—Meera waited with the rest of the party for the earl's coach to return.

All but Jack and Elsa—and the aunts—would walk the path into the village. The older ladies had already taken the carriage down to tyrannize Patience and the servants over church décor and set up of the wedding breakfast.

"We must make Quincy sit down," Clare fretted. "What about the Champlains? Have they been persuaded to stay? Even if Mrs. Huntley doesn't know them, she might like to meet them once she arrives."

Elsa understood that her friend and cousin was having difficulty separating her duties as hostess from expectations of a bride and her own feelings—one of the many reasons Elsa preferred the kitchen. Chopping onions was much simpler than dealing with social complications.

"I think the men must stay to set up the trust," Elsa said, unclear of the details.

Jack trotted down the stairs, and Elsa quit thinking entirely. He looked incredible in his fitted buff trousers and dark blue long-tailed coat. His new valet had starched his neckcloth into a perfect fall over his gold embroidered, white satin waistcoat and trimmed his unruly hair to perfection. He would grace any palace with his—athletic— elegance. She knew his coat's shoulders weren't padded.

But it was his smile of delight and his look of love that had her nearly swooning. She readily grasped the gloved hand he offered, if only to prevent stumbling over her own tongue. She was quite certain it hung out as she gaped. She was marrying a man far above all others. She, plain Elspeth Villiers, the heiress who hid in kitchens, had won the heart of the bravest, kindest man in the world.

"Let's not leave the horses waiting," he whispered, donning his tall hat and tugging her gloved hand through the crook of his arm as the carriage pulled up.

Well, he was also the best horseman in the world.

~

LISTENING TO HER FINAL BANNS CALLED, KNOWING THIS WAS TO have been her wedding day, Clare sniffed behind her handkerchief. Hunt hugged her in sympathy. Having someone who understood helped. She wasn't alone anymore. The days of living in lonely terror, with no one to lean on, were well over.

Having just one ceremony was better, Clare told herself. Elsa deserved a day all her own. One didn't get married every day. Perhaps it was just a piece of paper in the eyes of church and law, but for a woman. . . Marriage was an immense step from the security of home and parents into the unknown, tied for a lifetime to a man one usually did not know at all well.

Elsa was fortunate to be marrying a man she'd known all her life. So when the two stood before the altar while Mr. Upton, the new curate, spoke the words of the ceremony, Clare could smile again with happiness, knowing her cousin and friend's future was the best it could be.

Patience had filled the small altar with roses and blossoms from every tree and shrub available. The small chapel smelled heavenly. It had no pews, only benches, which was why the aunts did not often attend. Today, they were sniffling into their lace hankies as the elegant Earl Villiers gave away his half-sister, and the tall, stoop-shouldered Baron de Sackville stood at his son's side. Elsa's mother appeared stylish in her magnificent hat covered in bits and pieces of everything, but Mrs. Turner could not outshine Elsa's smile as Jack slid his ring on her finger—a real ring and not the impromptu one he'd first given her, one made with the gemstones he'd brought back from India.

"They make a handsome couple," Clare whispered to Hunt once the vows were said and Patience sang a hymn to accompany them down the aisle.

"Don't expect me to look so fashionable," Hunt warned as he rose to follow the couple out, taking her arm in his.

Feeling lighter than air now that the burden of this last

week was past, Clare laughed. "You are handsome in anything you choose to wear. I am looking forward to seeing you in your night shirt."

He shot her a look of surprise, coughed at her boldness, and countered, "Night shirt? I'll have to ask Lavender to make one."

Clare blushed, laughed, and trying not to imagine him in nothing, followed him down the lane to the village square and Henri's tavern where the breakfast had been set out for all to enjoy.

Wycliffe Manor wasn't just for the earl's descendants anymore. The entire village of Gravesyde Priory had some part to play in the household. The staff and the few village merchants and neighbors joined the family in sharing the feast meant for kings that Elsa had prepared. As promised, Henri sent the local lads on a mad chase up to the manor to fetch a gold sovereign from the stable.

Everyone raced up the walking path and drive—not the hidden lane that apparently only smugglers, and now the manor occupants, knew.

Once the ale barrels were opened and the pipers played a happy tune, Lavender danced with Quincy, and Elsa's assistant cook swung arms with the tutor.

And by the time the coach carrying the newlyweds rolled away, no one really noticed. The festivities had just begun.

"THUS A NEW GENERATION BEGINS," LADY SPALDING SAID fondly, her plump, beringed fingers clapping time to a jolly reel.

Lady Lavinia watched the carriage disappear around the bend. "Shall we wager on the date of the first child?"

"That is tempting fate, my ladies." Henri strolled up. "A wager on whether any of the earl's paintings or books are worth enough to buy our own carriage might be preferable."

"And trust that you don't already know?" Lady Lavinia looked down her lorgnette at him. "Besides, haven't the invitations to the book auction already gone out? I'm certain the baron knows their worth. In any account, I can buy my own carriage."

As if waiting for this moment, the new curate stepped up. "That would be a boon to the parish as well as yourself, my lady. We might enjoy your company in the chapel more often. The newlyweds have promised the funds to build several fine pews. We would be honored to have you enjoy them."

"You need a wife of your own, young man." Lady Lavinia tapped him with her lorgnette. "And no looking at my granddaughter. She can do better than a country curate."

Mr. Upton sent a wistful glance to Lavender, who'd left Quincy dancing with her other grandmother, while she swung about with Mr. Birdwhistle. "She does not know I exist. I need to find ways of encouraging more of the families hereabouts to return to church. I am sure there are fine young women among them. If it is known that ladies like yourselves attend, that might attract them."

Henri coughed. Lady Spalding narrowed her eyes. But her stepson, the marquess, strolled over before she could accuse conspiracy.

"I must leave in the morning, my lady. The dispatches from London are urgent. Shall I return you to your estate on the way?" he asked the dowager. "I will not insist that you take the dower house. Your father left you the property for life, and I respect that."

Lady Spalding made an inelegant noise. "No, you do not. Like any man, you see only the advantage of removing your daughter and her husband and their noisy friends from your own estate. I do not wish to hear them either. Your youngsters are idle and monstrously frisky. I shall take the dower house, when I choose to visit. For now, Wycliffe Manor entertains me more."

"There will be babies," Lady Lavinia warned. "And possibly more murders. And marriages," she added in satisfaction. "They need our advice."

Apparently drawn by the company, Hunt and Clare arrived to hear this last. Clare enthusiastically hugged the slender baroness. "Oh, yes, please. We are only just learning to deal with each other and this enormous task. Your advice is most welcome!"

Hunt's plump aunt nodded complacent agreement. "We know it is, dear. And Lady Lavinia will be here to guide her granddaughter and keep me company." She hesitated a moment and added, "Especially if young Elspeth will continue cooking."

Behind them, laughter arose as their stiff and proper housekeeper, Patience's mother, was persuaded to take a turn in the reel with Quincy, the butler.

The scent of jasmine wafted through the sunbeams, and Dottie stopped dancing with Ned to glance around in anticipation, causing the whole reel to collide and tumble with hilarity.

"Let us hope my sister arrives soon," Lady Spalding said as Hunt swung Clare off to join the dancers. "That young couple has earned a little happiness."

"And what about me, my lady?" Henri asked, smiling as he held out his hand to the dowager. "Do I not deserve happiness? Dance with me and let us discuss jewels and treasures and how we will spend our fortunes."

Lady Spalding swatted him with her fan for his impertinence but allowed him to lead her in a proper promenade. His tall, broad-shouldered form set off her short, round one as the dowager performed a bouncing curtsy and kicked up her heels to the delight of the other dancers.

The curate bowed before Lady Lavinia. "Would you do

me the honor, my lady? We should see that the gathering remains respectful."

The late earl's daughter snorted haughtily. "Stuff and nonsense, boy. Life is for living. Find yourself a lively bride and practice enjoying yourself for a change."

She danced with him anyway.

GRAVESYDE PRIORY MYSTERIES

The Secrets of Wycliffe Manor
Book #1

Be wary of what you wish for. . .

In Regency England:

The descendant of adventuring—dead—aristocrats, Clarissa Knightley supplements a modest inheritance by penning gothic novels that cost more than they earn. Upon learning that she has mysteriously inherited a share of an earl's estate, she rashly packs up her household. In remote Gravesyde Priory, she hopes to find a safe haven and family who will welcome her and her young nephew.

Instead, she discovers a drunken American army captain, his African servant, and ancient, surly caretakers. Terrified, prepared to flee, Clare is lured to linger by the prospect of secret diaries, hidden jewels, and an increasingly intriguing man. Then a killer strikes.

The crumbling manor's ominous and baffling history offers fascinating fodder for Clare's horror novels—if only she can survive real-life madmen and a spectral murderer who may seek the jewels at any price.

To Buy, Please Visit
https://patriciarice.com/series/gravesyde-priory/

The Mystery of the Missing Heiress
Book #2

Wycliffe Manor, a magnet for murder...

On a long-delayed errand to remote Wycliffe Manor, ex-Lieutenant Jack de Sackville stumbles across the murdered body of London dandy, Basil Culpepper, in the hedgerow, a long way from his usual haunts. To Jack's dismay, he discovers the earl's daughter Culpepper ruined hiding in Wycliffe's kitchen.

Disguised as a lowly cook, Lady Elspeth Villiers may have liked to shoot Culpepper for ruining her life, but she dropped out of sight for more immediate reasons than an old scandal —her wealth has become the focus of greedy men. The arrival of Jack, the man she's adored since childhood, along with Culpepper's corpse, mean her hiding place is no longer safe.

But once Lady Elsa reveals herself to the unconventional inhabitants of Wycliffe Manor, they become the protective family she has never known. Outraged to learn the beautiful woman he once loved and lost has become a target of greed, Jack joins the investigation into Culpepper's death.

With a murderer on the loose, the amateur sleuths must

unravel a deadly tangle of kidnappers and counterfeiters or the Manor's eccentric inhabitants will be in as much danger as their cook.

To Buy, Please Visit
https://patriciarice.com/series/gravesyde-priory/

❧

The Bones in the Orchard
Book #3

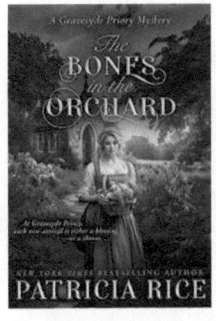

At Gravesyde Priory, each new arrival is either a blessing—or a threat. . .

Wycliffe Manor has been neglected for decades. Its new heirs are determined to create a welcoming home. Yet soon after the latest family moves into the nearby parsonage, bones are uncovered in the orchard. . . and odd strangers arrive.

When her curate father returns his family to Gravesyde for the marriages of the manor's heirs, gawky spinster Patience Upton has high expectations—until her father is murdered. Shock at learning her father had a mysterious past, leads to alarm that the killer may have been after his notebook, which she now possesses.

After the chapel is ransacked and a witness killed, it's clear the murderer isn't done. Desperate to find the truth, Patience accepts the aid of Henri Lavigne, Wycliffe Manor's smooth-talking rake. Intent on saving his new home and family from danger, Henri is drawn to the clergyman's guileless daughter but wonders if she hasn't reason to conceal the killer's identity.

Before there will be any courting, much less marrying, the inhabitants of the manor realize if they want a chance at a future, they must hunt the killer themselves. But are they hunting one murderer. . . or more?

To Buy, Please Visit
https://patriciarice.com/series/gravesyde-priory/

ABOUT THE AUTHOR

With several million books in print and *New York Times* and *USA Today's* bestseller lists under her belt, former CPA Patricia Rice is one of romance's hottest authors. Her emotionally-charged contemporary and historical romances have won numerous awards, including the *RT Book Reviews* Reviewers Choice and Career Achievement Awards. Her books have been honored as Romance Writers of America RITA® finalists in the historical, regency and contemporary categories.

A firm believer in happily-ever-after, Patricia Rice is married to her high school sweetheart and has two children. A native of Kentucky and New York, a past resident of North Carolina and Missouri, she currently resides in Southern California, and now does accounting only for herself.

ALSO BY PATRICIA RICE

The World of Magic:

The Unexpected Magic Series

MAGIC IN THE STARS

WHISPER OF MAGIC

THEORY OF MAGIC

AURA OF MAGIC

CHEMISTRY OF MAGIC

NO PERFECT MAGIC

The Magical Malcolms Series

MERELY MAGIC

MUST BE MAGIC

THE TROUBLE WITH MAGIC

THIS MAGIC MOMENT

MUCH ADO ABOUT MAGIC

MAGIC MAN

The California Malcolms Series

THE LURE OF SONG AND MAGIC

TROUBLE WITH AIR AND MAGIC

THE RISK OF LOVE AND MAGIC

Crystal Magic

SAPPHIRE NIGHTS

TOPAZ DREAMS

CRYSTAL VISION

WEDDING GEMS

AZURE SECRETS

THE GENUINE ARTICLE

THE MARQUESS

ENGLISH HEIRESS

IRISH DUCHESS

Regency Love and Laughter Series

CROSSED IN LOVE

MAD MARIA'S DAUGHTER

ARTFUL DECEPTIONS

ALL A WOMAN WANTS

Rogues & Desperadoes Series

LORD ROGUE

MOONLIGHT AND MEMORIES

SHELTER FROM THE STORM

WAYWARD ANGEL

DENIM AND LACE

CHEYENNES LADY

Dark Lords and Dangerous Ladies Series

LOVE FOREVER AFTER

SILVER ENCHANTRESS

DEVIL'S LADY

DASH OF ENCHANTMENT

INDIGO MOON

Too Hard to Handle

TEXAS LILY

TEXAS ROSE

TEXAS TIGER

TEXAS MOON

Mystic Isle Series

MYSTIC ISLE

ABOUT BOOK VIEW CAFÉ

 *Book View Café* LLC (BVC) is an author-owned cooperative of professional writers, publishing in a variety of genres including fantasy, romance, mystery, and science fiction — with 90% of the proceeds going to the authors. Since its debut in 2008, BVC has gained a reputation for producing high-quality ebooks. BVC's ebooks are DRM-free and are distributed around the world. The cooperative is now bringing that same quality to its print editions.

BVC authors include New York Times and USA Today bestsellers as well as winners and nominees of many prestigious awards.